THE CURE

THE CURE

Rachel Genn

corsair

Constable & Robinson Ltd
3 The Lanchesters
162 Fulham Palace Road
London W6 9ER
www.constablerobinson.com

First published in the UK by Corsair,
an imprint of Constable & Robinson Ltd., 2011

Excerpt from 'A Teamster's Farewell' from *Chicago Poems* by
Carl Sandburg © 1916 by Holt, Rinehart and Winston and renewed
1944 by Carl Sandburg, reprinted by permission of
Houghton Mifflin Harcourt Publishing Company

Excerpts from *The Waste Land* by T. S. Eliot and 'Twice Shy',
Death of a Naturalist, by Seamus Heaney, reprinted by
permission of Faber & Faber Ltd.

A copy of the British Library Cataloguing in
Publication data is available from the British Library

ISBN 978-1-84901-583-7

Printed and bound in the EU

1 3 5 7 9 10 8 6 4 2

PEFC
PEFC/16-33-111
CATG-PEFC-052
www.pefc.org

In memory of Rita and John, for everything

1

Eugene hadn't needed a drink, not for weeks. She was all he'd needed, and he was thinking just this when the pain pumped up through his foot. Looking down he saw a short plank stuck to his boot and he sat on the dusty ground of the site and pulled at it steadily. Two nails inched out of the sole, angling from a common origin into a V: a rusty fuck-you. Waiting for the blood to come out of his boot, Eugene made up his mind.

A hangover held the heat around him. Ireland rarely got this hot, and even when it did, a place like Galway could usually keep its cool because of the sea. They were hardly out of May but the heat and noise of the building site were fierce.

Glimpsing movement, Eugene looked up and shielded his eyes from a crawling JCB; the noon sunlight was making too much of the yellow. The blood didn't appear on the ground.

Vincent, his brother, jumped down from the rig to crouch beside him. Their faces were almost always threatened by a blue beard. The younger, Vincent, was a quicker, more casual version of his brother, taller than Eugene and slicker in his movements. No one ever mistook them for one another and Vincent felt sorry when people took it for granted that Eugene was the younger.

He prodded Eugene's boot. 'What's up?'

'I'm going.'

'Home?'

'London.'

"Cos of a fecking nail?'

Vincent began to laugh but Eugene kept his head down and his brother's laughter stopped soon enough.

Eugene was still at work at four in the afternoon. The site felt scorched, and at five the sun had only just given up bullying the ground in front of the cabin. He sat in the shade and waited for the site manager, who finally emerged and began fitting a padlock to the door. Eugene didn't get up. 'I'll be working my notice, Al, from tomorrow.'

'Is that right?' Al didn't turn.

'I'm away to London.'

'There's work enough here.' Al stared at him for a moment. 'If I'd quit every time . . .'

'It's still cheap at the Beacon.'

'The pub your father was at?'

'Aye, and Jack's still there.'

Al pulled at the padlock. 'Thought that'd be the last place you'd go.' He checked the padlock again. 'You told your mother yet?'

'Not yet.'

Al put the keys in his pocket. 'Good luck.'

He chose to tell them on Sunday, but then Sunday came up

on him too suddenly and Eugene ended up in his mother's living room in Salthill, shaking the words out of his mouth. His mother blanched, while Theresa mocked him with a smile thrown towards the floor and an elbow into Vincent's ribs. A couple of neighbours talked right the way through it.

Eugene left the lot of them downstairs and stood on the landing, holding his decision like a busted umbrella.

Moving to the bathroom, he stared at his own eyes in the cabinet mirror. He needed something for hard times, a sharp certainty that he could use against them, but his reflection gave him nothing new.

As he looked around him, familiar items now seemed to glow with a pathetic novelty as if his mind had already made souvenirs of them. The towels, which had never smelt clean, were stuffed lazily behind a painted rail, loosely attached to the wall. The cigarette scars on the plastic bath were a brown memorial to Seamus, his father. He grabbed the blind, which didn't roll properly, and pulled it over his head, then leaned on the peeling sill. The window was open, useless in the early-summer lull. He looked out to the sea as if to ask it whether he had made the right choice. The waves teased him – you have, you haven't – until he pulled himself back in and returned to the mottled mirror on the cabinet. They'd be saying he was leaving home for the wrong reasons, childish reasons, and it was this suggestion that had worried him in circles, like a wasp, stinging his resolve.

Eugene slid into the memory of Seamus and the first of his father's many accidents that he had witnessed. As always when he began to look back at his father, Eugene had to shut his eyes. On the day of this particular accident, he had been standing outside the bathroom when he realized his father's voice was different; in fact, its tone had made Eugene stand on one foot. Seamus usually let words fall as heavy as chain but today his voice reeled out fast and high, like fishing line.

Eugene could hear Jack in the bathroom too, upbeat, reassuring Seamus from his position behind the door. His father's voice came from somewhere closer to the floor.

'A compound fracture. That's what they call that. Seen a rake of them now, with falls from the scaffold.'

'Aye?'

'Looks sore, right enough, but you'll be back on site for Christmas, surely to God.'

'Who knows I was in the pub?' said Seamus.

'Not a crater – and, anyway, sir, don't be minding them . . . The days are long enough! A working man cannot be made ashamed of a couple of drinks for his dinner.'

'Oh, aye . . .'

'Sure, a scabby awld sandwich, Seamus. That's not enough of a dinnertime. Don't be thinking about that now.'

Jack smoked away. His chest was narrower than his waist and his jowls were already sagging in his late thirties. Seamus had a hard, shadowy jaw and his own cigarette was clenched between his teeth, untouched since Jack had lit it for him.

On site and off, Jack made excuses for Seamus to use whenever he needed one. He carried on with a pretty litany of all the injuries that had come and gone before this one, and it was at this point that the little Eugene went into the bathroom carefully: shoulder first, his chin just reaching above the door handle. He stood still beside his younger brother Vincent and they watched, their backs to the wall, bare, bony shoulder-blades against the tiles. Their father knelt beside the bath, his mangled hand hanging heavy off his wrist and dripping. Jack was close, stooping at Seamus's back, ready for instruction.

Eugene replayed this scene many times, squinting, looking hard for where the shame comes from. He knew what it was, right enough; he was a very small boy, but shame came easily and early to all the Mahons. Certainly not Jack's puffed-up praise of Seamus. It wasn't in any of the words, so far as Eugene could tell. Neither was it in the dark blood detonating in the bottom of the plastic bath or the terrible white of the bone against the grey fray of Seamus's shirt cuff. No. It was definitely a smell: the cloy of booze made obscene by summer and midday. Jack swayed and Seamus told his boys in his new keen voice not to be afraid. Still kneeling, he held out his good arm to his sons in a stiff appeal for them to come to him, and they looked on in tentative silence.

Eugene did not go to his father and it was this decision that he remembered most clearly because it had the snap of a switch. Instead, little Eugene looked away and started to move, crabbing around the wall-tiles, pushing his spine on to the cold of them until his fingers could no longer feel the rough grout and he was out on the landing again. Through the open bathroom door, he saw Vincent move in and slip his hand over Seamus's shoulder before Seamus looked quickly from Eugene to Vincent and closed the door with his foot.

There had been many minor accidents for Seamus, but the Big One came in 1980. London had looked powerless under the snow in December of that year, but beneath the white, the capital needed to stretch and the City finally began to let a little wealth trickle out and over to the East End. Work on this side of London had started to power up in the years before the Bishopsgate bomb, and around here, Irish men were still welcomed. The cold weather and the magnet of Christmas had already started to pull cheap labourers back to their home towns, meaning that Seamus had moved up to drive a crane in the Mile End Road for a man named Buck O'Halloran. More money. The kids were older now; he visited home rarely.

Eugene grew stealthy in Salthill and, with his father mostly absent, he convinced himself that he could live with the disgraces that Seamus had left behind, discovering that if he kept mobile, the shame wouldn't cling and he could whip out of it, leaving it hanging in mid-air, confused as a pall of smoke on a still day. Without his father, Eugene grew odd and dark and strangely beautiful, and began to gain a very quiet confidence. He started to see a future without a past so, more than anything, he was angry to hear of the Big One: he had sincerely hoped that his father might have learned to keep his accidents to himself over in London.

A neighbour told of the injuries, standing at the door to the kitchen. His mother stood at first with hands on hips, daring the news to be terrible. Then she crouched with her hands over her ears. This time, Seamus hadn't injured himself, she could have stood up to that, but had let the crane block cripple a ground worker. His boss, Buck, had lost the job and Seamus might be looking at a prison sentence. Again, it came at Eugene like a smell; invisible but taking away the space to breathe.

It was a year after it had happened that Seamus came home for good, but on his return it seemed, to the rest of the family at least, that the house had grown. Although he was only in his late forties, Seamus was smaller and softer in ways that made him upsetting to his family. He took his meals on his own and drank in the house because the pub was changed and uncomfortable, and the unpredictability of it exhausted him. There was a jukebox now, up on one wall. He didn't know the regulars and no longer had the agility to spar with unknown drinkers. He did not know how to defend this new self.

At home, there was no sanctuary because, though they never let on, his family couldn't hide their disappointment at the change; none of them wanted the terrible weight of a penitent. In the end, his lack of selfishness frightened them – so much that Eugene's sister, Gloria, could barely speak to him and their mother stayed over at her sister's in Leenane for a week at a time. Eugene, still a boy, remained close, but threw the paper at his father in the morning without looking at him, on one occasion spilling his tea. At the sound of the unsteadied cup, Eugene winced – but he made sure he didn't do it again.

Not five years later, they came together on the day of Seamus's death; a perfect spring morning with the crocuses just opening, like shy hoorays from the grass, knowing that their silent but relentless demand for the return of Seamus's mean vigour was the thing he had been unable to live up to. With him having left as he had, quickly and without a fuss, they felt robbed, and without anything to rage against, their mother became sharp and whirring. Though less frantic, Eugene and Vincent and Gloria began to grind against each other almost as soon as Seamus was buried.

His funeral was an angry affair, rumbling with unfinished business. Jack came from London and wobbled through every room at the wake, swearing to anyone who'd listen that he had been there and, as God was his witness, Seamus had never 'done anything a working man should be ashamed of'. Eugene's mother wanted to get Jack out or at least persuade him to eat something, so they fetched bread and marmalade – but Jack didn't even look at the plate. Instead, he rammed a tall bottle of whiskey tight into his handkerchief pocket so that, from his low seat in the corner, Eugene could see one side of Jack's face melting through glass and amber. Jack's presence was excruciating, bearing as he was this proud emblem of his friend, their father. All anyone else saw was a flag full of bullet holes. Gloria turned on her mother before the breakfast was over. After two days' solid drinking, no one was sorry to see Jack leave for London and the Beacon, the pub near Bethnal Green where he and Seamus lodged.

Seamus had been dead for more than a decade and Eugene should have been looking forward. He wanted London to pull him. What he needed was the promise of progress: something to pound into the ground, to rip down or push against for ten hours a day, so that his mind didn't slip backwards and his soul didn't look for nourishment to things that could never sustain him.

He looked in the mirror a last time to show himself how strong he was. His eyes clearly said he didn't have to leave, for God's sake, and Theresa, smiling at the fucking floor like that, no longer had a hand on him. Closing the cabinet door, he leaned to suck warm water directly from the scaly seaside mouth of the tap. He splashed his face with a single cupped hand and, without using a towel, went back down to face them.

2

Della was sweating already and it was just morning, just June.
From her bedroom window beside the Beacon, she watched
the greenish light frame the point of the spire of Christ
Church in Spitalfields. The morning carried sounds of
stragglers from last night, hooting up the alley from Grey
Eagle Street and down the way from Club Row. A raucous
caw, then a momentous silence. She didn't like to deal with
noises like this before she started serving. A woman screamed
and Della held her breath until laughter erupted. Exhaling,
she felt her heart slow effortfully as the voices receded.

She put on a floor-length viscose wrap printed with large
purple and orange orchids, the belt trailing. She left the
bedroom and walked along the corridor that joined the house
to the pub. At the bottom of the stairs to the rooms she rented
out, a Miller Lite mirror showed her once again that the skin
of her face served her better now, in her fifties, than it had in
her twenties. More under it, she thought. It had been stolid
in her youth but had weathered well. Her hair was burgundy

this month, and even when it was unkempt, she reminded herself that it was luxuriant enough to have survived decades of dyeing. She pinched the bridge of her broad nose as she arched her eyebrows to feel a stretch in her eyelids. It had not been her plan to run a pub and boarding-house but the early death of her mother had pushed her into it; she certainly hadn't planned on doing it alone.

The Beacon had been hers outright for thirty years, and each morning as she entered the bar she faced a fact: this was not a pub that should be seen in daytime. Breathing deeply, she acquainted herself with her bar and rubbed her wide, rough palm in a circle over each cheek as if to encourage herself that she was still doing the right thing.

Crossing the snug, she stooped to pick up the Saturday mail at the foot of the front door, which opened on to Bethnal Green Road. She sifted the white bills, and her attention was hooked by a buff envelope with a handwritten sender's address. It was an address that struck her because she had worked hard to plane it from her memory. Ireland. Salthill. His other home. She swung a stool from the table-top and sat down. As she read, the old badness swelled, the wide hump of grief that had taken her so long to get up and over and even longer to scramble down. She looked back at the name: Eugene Mahon. It must be one of his. Della left the note on the bar.

When her daughter, Julia, reluctantly pulled the towels off the pumps at lunchtime she glanced at the back of the envelope and placed her finger on the address. 'Who's this? Do you know them?'

Julia stared hard into her mother. Her looks as always were battles. To Della, her daughter's hair seemed liquid, camouflaged by the dark of the bar. Julia held it away from her face, but as she moved forward to look at the envelope the weight of it took over and she gave up, letting it separate heavily to make a narrow frame for her mulberry-coloured lips and her black lashes, the tip of a very fine nose. Looking on, Della yearned for herself at nineteen but more keenly still for the days when she could have reached over to touch her daughter's hair.

'I think I do, darling. He needs some lodgings.' Her tone was bright and she polished the bar with vigour. Julia became suspicious and stated baldly, 'We don't have the room.'

'I'll open up the End.' Della balled the duster tighter.

'The End? It's full of crap. I'm not moving it and neither is Rhodri.'

'Hold on a minute, Little Miss May Balls. There'd be no Oxford without this pub. Remember that before you start telling me what you will and won't be doing.'

'Can you do your dressing-gown up?'

'Get out if you don't like it.'

'Not even you would put someone in that room and charge them money for it.'

Julia was very like her mother. Della saw she would not bend and pushed on, 'His father used to lodge here with Jack. They were pals,' but she lost faith in the sentence and it trailed. Looking up from the bar, she saw that Julia's mouth had been pulled down and open. She clamped her own lips together, then snapped, 'What do you care? You're only here for holidays.'

Julia slunk into the back for the drip trays and returned to the bar. Without looking at Della, she said, 'Brilliant. Let's get more people like Jack in here.'

'I think it'd be nice to give the lad his dad's old room.'

'Nice?'

'Think of the symbolism! The significance!' Della threw up one hand as she'd seen Rhodri do, but Julia didn't look at her and Della congratulated herself that she had hit the mark with her imitation of Julia's boyfriend. She closed matters with a thin and churchly hum.

Julia shrugged, and said to the glasses above the bar, 'Don't – don't – call me "darling".'

Della went upstairs, exhausted by acting. The letter had disturbed potent memories, and the first thing that came back to her was the smell. For Della, the stink was guilt and it smelt like the bite of the disinfectant blocks that too quickly sizzled to nothing in the urinals. Had anyone asked her before that night, twenty years ago, if she would open her legs for someone in a public toilet, she would have considered the question, because she liked to give the impression that she was balanced, and she would have denied it. Yet when he had steadily sucked her neck, she had felt that with his mouth he could beckon bits of her bones to rise to the surface, leaving them scalloped and brittle. She pressed her feet against the wall and tried to equal the pressure with her back. Between the sink and the toilet there wasn't much room for the V of her thighs – 'Weightlifter's thighs,' Seamus had kidded, his fingers digging into the underside of them for a second. He had held her face in front of his mouth but their lips hadn't touched. They had concentrated instead on the elegant dynamics of easing into and lowering on to. Finally, they had kissed. Perfectly hard. Even then, at the moment when wanting becomes having, she had known that she would wake with the barbs of who and where carelessly jagging over her.

The memories were out, lifted high on disinfectant fumes. Thinking about him, Della had put her hand to her throat, and when she realized, she pulled it sharply away. She had to get up, move, do something. The key to the End was in the toby jug with the leprechaun's face beside the till. Scrabbling for it, she got dirt under her nails.

The End was a tiny box room at the north end of an unlit corridor that lay above the pub. It mirrored the one downstairs that ran from the back of the bar to where Della lived. There were six rooms for rent upstairs, inconsistently decorated and maintained such that entering any of them gave you a flavour not just of the period when Della had felt forced into decorating but also her mood at the time. In room six, Jack's room, she had become so angry with the watery paint she had bought from an Iranian over the bar that she had moved on to fitting the light. In her easy fury, she had yanked the pendant off the ceiling but had put a bulb in it anyway. Undressed, the bulb was slung, slanting under the fitting's wiry guts.

The Iranian had given her a bunch of ragged peacock feathers when she had collared him over the paint. There weren't enough to make a satisfactory arrangement on the wall of room six but, with coloured drawing pins, she made a sparse fan. The painting had never been finished but Jack hadn't complained and she wondered if he had even noticed. It was difficult to complain when you didn't pay rent and Jack had not paid a penny since Seamus had left. Della tried very hard not to think about this.

She hadn't opened the End for years and mounted the stairs to the rooms slowly. As she reached the top, she could hear someone clanking around in the communal kitchen and hoped to God it wasn't Jack. She stood still to listen, thinking that if she was quick at the top of the flight he might not see her sidle down the corridor. Then came sounds of swifter movements from table to microwave. Still, she listened; a whisking noise, a glass bowl, a clinking fork, and she started up the stairs again, certain now that it could not be him.

The key to the End turned grittily and she started to push the door open carefully – she knew it was possible that something might topple out of the room. She felt the resistance of the weight of the not-really-wanted. It smelt funereal; mouldy.

The End had been Seamus's room and had been decorated with what Della in her early thirties had believed to be quiet panache. One wall was plum, the rest grey, but as the demand for care increased, Della's impatience had taken over: by the time she was installing a sink, she was applying the mastic with her fingers, pushing it up to the wall in careless globs. A gilt mirror sat above her handiwork. The frame had survived a hurried hanging but the glass had succumbed to a too-long nail and had cracked into a Y that had disintegrated every onlooker since Seamus.

She peered between the stacks of magazines and records that had, at some point, become part of each other. A meagre blanket hung at the window. She flicked her eyes to the mirror and, even in the gloom, felt burned as she remembered his carnal grin spreading, so sure, so satisfied, as he caught her in the mirror, half in, half out of the door.

3

Eugene hobbled on his sore foot to O'Malley's Stroll Inn for a leaving party to which he had only invited his brother. He looked around him as he walked. With two days left before his departure, he was paralysed by curiosity about whether he'd see Theresa.

They had been at the lough when he had found her out. He felt foolish when he thought of his mood on that day because he had been suffused with contentment, stuffed with it. Now it made him grimace. The memory would be for ever a dirty film over his pure, deep feelings for her.

He remembered being able to smell the shade of the cemetery a way off; the half-life of mulch under the yews. The pungency of wild garlic and the tang of the pewter lake crowded out the cloudiness and the slight chill of the day. He remembered reflecting that he could almost smell the time of year, and felt that he had learned at least something in his small, circular life, and with the clarity of satisfaction he felt wise, that he could trust his senses.

He had been lying beside Theresa on a faded thin quilt. She was turned towards him and he was watching the clouds nearly move. He looked at her, shielding his eyes from the weak sun and he noticed that although she was speaking to him she was looking at Vincent. He followed her gaze to where it was fixed. Vincent, his Vincent, was at the water's edge, jumping, intermittently escaping the bitter lip of the lough, and skimming stones, counting the bounces then paddling again, watching the minuscule bubbles lace around his foot. He'd lie about the number of bounces if I asked him, thought Eugene, as he stared at his brother.

Eugene's body was taut and wiry but stiffened under observation, giving rise to clumsiness. He even felt his face to be clumsy and he rubbed his hand over a sandpaper jaw, pulling at his lips. Vincent's physique had its limits but when he moved he showed that he knew these limits intimately. He worked well within them, and although he could clown, he had an aura of stark modesty that everyone leaned towards eventually. He had been poured into himself without spilling a drop, and in manhood he had settled into himself uncommonly well. Like Eugene and his father, Vincent sometimes could be crippled by a quiet awkwardness but was definitely the most beautiful of the three, with his long limbs, his black hair and the odd delicacy of his mouth: a blare of mauve, a sweet additive in his sallow face.

Eugene looked back to Theresa but she was studying Vincent so thoroughly that she didn't notice that beside her, over herself and Eugene, over the sheet and the sprung stones, leaned a question. Fear turned in Eugene's belly and, not knowing what to do, he pulled the quilt from under her, startling her. He wrapped it round himself and covered his face.

'What's wrong?' she shouted through the quilt, but he couldn't show her his face because she had already answered the huge, heavy question. He had no hope that he was wrong. Without his usual responses, her voice rose and he was sad to hear panic creep into it.

'Have you gone deaf?' Her guilt made the words shrill and he wished she'd give up. It was his lack of an answer that finally forced her to.

When he brought his face from under the quilt the sun had nearly set. Vincent had gone but she was there, kneeling, vigilant with fear.

'Why are you still here?' he said, his voice alien through disuse.

'I'm waiting for you to tell me what's wrong,' she replied, with what seemed to him now a practised hurt. He'd never heard this tone before, and for the first time in their weeks together, Eugene felt the unnatural wedge of dishonesty that can slow the progress of new relationships.

He walked home to his mother's, looking at the pavement and his stupid feet. When he got upstairs he locked himself into the bathroom and vomited. She had followed him all the way to the front of the house, but after he had closed the front door on her that night, she had never tried to contact him again.

The sun outside O'Malley's was bright enough to turn the gloom of the snug into a grey gleam where the smoke hung in hammocks at head height around the bar. Eugene wished his brother would hurry up. Being alone was no good for him. He practised how he would look at Vincent, and lit another cigarette.

Vincent popped his head round the pub door. 'Nobody here yet?'

'Yourself and that's it.'

Vincent went to the bar. 'You all right for now?' he asked, pointing at his brother's glass.

Eugene looked away. 'For now,' he said.

4

There's a clanking from the kitchen, like metal on glass. It nearly pulls Jack out of the sticky net of his dream, but then the noise stops and Jack sinks back into sleep.

In his dreams Jack is very good at walking. He is so good at it that he rolls seamlessly into dancing mid-stroll. He wears tap-dancing shoes, and as he turns corners he takes flight for a couple of steps. He can steer with his guts somehow. On touch-down he realizes he can leap balletically across roads with a lift of his heel. He can be tall just by wanting to be, and when he's out of town, he finds himself scissoring and curving through trees like a pair of compasses. When he's asleep, Jack can finish sentences and make decisions without panicking. He goes into shops and orders whole lists of things from memory, and when it comes to paying for them, he knows why he's standing there, and he can get the change out of his pocket and place it on a counter or in a waiting hand without creating a fuss of showering pennies. When he's not awake, Jack can keep his clothes clean and can answer any question you want to fire at him. Floating around the city, he sits in pubs all over town where the drinks are on the landlord and he has a seat at every bar, where the young are in thrall to his years of experience as a labourer and the old pay homage to him with meaningful pats to the back. His hair is still tough and fights back when he pushes his hand through it; it's not grey-yellow but a honey colour. There's still force in his arm, he can trust his grip and has no reason to think that his legs will ever give way.

His dreams make sure that Seamus is still here in his old room, where Jack can speak to him with easy confidence. Jack grabs him and holds him and tries to squeeze him into hearing his silent 'Don't go,' but Seamus is always stiff in his arms, playing dead with embarrassment, and when he is released he punches the big knot of Jack's shoulder. They share jokes that don't seem to have words and it's almost the same as it was when Seamus was here. But sometimes Jack gets the old anxiety because Seamus is always just about to leave him, and when he does, it's still always three in the morning. Seamus has left the big brown envelope many times, stuffed with money and the letter, on Jack's table. The conversation plays again.

'You'll have to give it to her. I can't do it.'

'Who?'

'Cilla fucking Black.' A pause, then he whispers, 'Della. Now don't forget, you gob-shite, and I'll see you at home!'

'Get to fuck.'

But Seamus isn't joking any more, and even though he's supposed to be asleep, Jack can tell that the bluff courage that supports Seamus's voice is watery.

Seamus always leaves with the same face, with the smile of someone who is already ashamed of their weakness even though the cowardly act is not yet behind them.

5

Della had to jerk the door to the End to close it, and as she did, she backed into somebody in the corridor. There was no money in the meter so it was almost dark, although it was still only early afternoon. From the bony frame and the stifled little scream, Della could tell it was Rhodri.

'Oh, Della, it's you,' he said. 'I thought it was Jack.'

The whiteness of his face made it float in the bleak light. His high cheekbones and pale skin above the greatcoat gave him a look of the undead. He smelt of booze.

'You just getting up.'

Rhodri flipped it into a question: 'No, no, no,' he said, the quick succession designed to deflect any remaining accusation. 'I've been doing some reading for a tutorial I'm giving this afternoon. It's Wittgenstein. He's a German. I get thirty quid an hour for them. Means I can treat Julia.'

Della had already started walking down the corridor. 'Somebody's moving into the End,' she said, over her shoulder.

With his papers under his arm, Rhodri mouthed, 'Poor fucker,' and felt his way down to the kitchen. He'd rambled, conscious that Della might be able to smell the cheap sherry. He'd run out of Lemsip and needed something to open his mind. He sat at the table and put his papers face down. Sugar crunched under them and he cursed Jack. Jack's hands shook horribly in the mornings but he still insisted on trying to shovel three spoonfuls into his tea. Rhodri found it difficult to work once he'd witnessed Jack fighting with the drawers and spoons and sugar and was relieved he wasn't there now.

Sometimes, if Rhodri had to do some reading or marking, he might not get out of his room until perhaps two or three, the afternoon annoyingly bitten into. That was when he might go into the kitchen, expecting space to think or prepare a meal and would find Jack, sitting stonily, holding his hands together or cawing at a joke he was telling himself. It depended on how much he'd had to drink. Jack worked, as did many of the blokes who came into the Beacon, on Buck O'Halloran's site, but you would find him in the kitchen, in the middle of the day, at least twice a week. Rhodri wondered how he kept a job.

He shivered in the kitchen, lit only by its scruffy skylight, and wondered what had to happen to a woman to make her like Della. Yesterday Julia had asked Della for a rent cut for him and, frankly, he'd rather not be there – then again, for the notice Della took of him, he wasn't really.

'He's a student,' said Julia. 'Why are you charging him the same as the others?'

'I thought he'd been a student already, same college as you, you said,' Della had barked.

'Yes,' said Julia, 'and now he's a post-graduate at UCL.' She drew out the phrase. Rhodri stifled a lop-sided smile.

'So when's he getting paid for this book, then?'

'He's working on it. He's had a hell of a lot of teaching this term.'

'I thought you said he'd been to see somebody about it.'

'There has been some interest in it. Writing a book needs a particular stillness.'

'Oh, I see,' said Della. 'Stillness . . .' She smiled a dog's smile. 'That's why he stays in bed until dinnertime.' She had included Rhodri in a stare.

He had been wise to let Julia handle that battle, he thought, as he opened the fridge. It smelt depressingly like something he had bought from the corner shop last week. Shutting the door, he put on the kettle and consoled himself that when he'd finished his book he'd be out of there like a shot. He poured hot water on to the coffee grains he'd chipped from the coffee rock in the middle of the jar; it had Jack's name all over it. He sat down and looked at the article he'd brought with him. There were only four words on the first page that he hadn't highlighted. There were numerous asterisks and notes in pencil – he believed that writing in pencil let more of the self out. He even marked exam papers in pencil and had been pulled up on it at the examiners' meeting.

'Would you rather a machine marked them?'

No one had spoken up. Stitch that.

He decided he'd absorb the coffee before he started thinking about the limits of empathic understanding in psychopathology. It was all about delusion. He pushed the article away and pulled last week's *Hackney Gazette* towards him, sighing and assuring himself that he was staying here for the cheap rent. And, of course, to be near Julia.

6

On the Friday before he left, Eugene had come silently through the back door and seen his mother with her full face in his shirt before she pushed it into the washer. The Saturday was long and fraught so Sunday was a blessing. His mother gave him a hundred euros and, though she couldn't afford it, Eugene knew better than to press it back upon her. He had stood and said, 'Right so,' and his mother had allowed herself to be kissed. Only Vincent and their older sister Gloria came to wave him off. Gloria's face, as always, was an instruction to Eugene to be brave, her gaze stoical for the sake of her emotional little brothers. For Eugene especially, she had always tried to represent reason and in doing so had been no help to him at all.

When Eugene waved back through the bus window he was smiling crazily, trying to make his face sure of what he was about to do. There was something bad at the bottom of this decision and Seamus's pill bottle flashed into his head.

The neck was stuffed with cotton wool but you could smell the bitterness through it.

He didn't smile any more on his way to the boat and he got to Dun Laoghaire with an hour to spare. He checked in with his ticket and felt that it'd do him good to have a walk round the ferry terminal. Within ten minutes he was back where he'd started, sitting down beside a phone, thinking how it would be if he called Theresa. What a magical possibility it remained if he just thought about it the right way because somewhere still he harboured a notion that she was pining for him, that she thought of him as soon as she woke up, that she was scared because she knew how proud he was. He had to give it up: fantasy made a mess of you. She wanted Vincent. She had always wanted Vincent.

He opened the newspaper he'd bought and looked at the words while he remembered the beginning. He burned for the chance to go back there and stop it happening, burned for the chance for it to happen all over again.

Theresa had been in Vincent's class, two years below him, and so, through the rule of school, was of negative interest to Eugene. Eugene was always on the move, never wanted to be frozen by anyone's attention. Still, she had noticed him and, uniquely, told no one but him. And so, secretly, he would watch her with her friends, some who hung on precariously, visibly happy to be relieved of their free will when she told them what to do. She saw nothing wrong in pursuing attention at the expense of others. If you were her only audience it was wonderful, but add another and you'd be invisible – even as her lover. She would do anything to make people like her and Eugene wasn't the only one who loved her for it.

Her ideas would come at him like meteorites.

'There's a place in Cork where Mary cries onion water. They've tested it and said that it can only come from onions. Have you ever heard such shite?'

Another blasted out of nowhere into the pebbles beside them at the lough: 'You know a loach?'

'What?'

'The fish, a loach.'

'What about it?'

'It fidgets when thunder's coming.'

'Who says?'

'Daddy.'

Eugene looked on. He knew she hadn't finished.

'And the French. Loach comes from *locher*. To fidget.' She squirmed over the smooth, ash-coloured stones to get closer to him.

It added a layer to his love when he tried to trace these thoughts to their origins. At first, he imagined that she was fascinated by his stillness, but eventually he saw that it frustrated her. He became even stiller, and began to enjoy the quiet power. Because of it, she sometimes pushed and thumped him in anger and he'd bait her with his discipline until she became sorry. With these sudden actions, she disappointed him but somehow, when she kissed his neck with her beautiful mouth, she managed to redeem herself.

'Being around you's like being in handcuffs,' she said to him, no joke. He smiled because she had been compelled to voice it, and when he remembered her at the end of that spring, he saw her like a swan: magnificent yet suddenly startling. He could deal with that back then.

The smell of her hair was red. He couldn't explain it but when the smell of her came over him it ripped the flesh off his ribs and he'd stay stock still, waiting for her to bring all of it closer to him. He wanted to get her down beside the lough and hold her hands to the ground while he rubbed his face over her skin. She had no qualms about staying near him, smoothing her cheeks across his head, his closed eyes, down each side of his neck as if she were blind and that was the way she would get to know him.

The relationship had lumbered, secret and mellow, into summer. She wore tops to show off her bird-like collarbones.

'I could snap these in a second,' he said, with his finger and thumb around them. He didn't want to hurt her, only to break her down and manage her better. Her eyes had been flinty in winter, but summer freckled her face and this coaxed out a green centre to the grey. It was the fingers he wanted. They were slender but strong, like saplings, and in his mind he'd gnaw them to their green centres. She brought him cold mackerel and asparagus. He'd never had asparagus before. With one stem, he teased her. Its limp bend meant he could control her, force her mouth into making a rash decision. He could open her up like a putty-hearted clam. Aha! It drove her crazy.

With her beside him he couldn't eat much and was struck through with a ridiculous dismay that she had eaten so heartily. She picked up the mackerel skin and began some commentary. She saw things just as they were but could explain them to him in ways that swung him closer to them, bit by bit, like a feather falling. She was talking about how the colour of the mackerel skin was perfect for the half-shadow of where the fish lived.

'Look at this little fella's hide.' She stretched the skin, tented over the points of her fingers; a gently sagging middle that had been filled with a plump salty litheness. 'He's got the wrought iron on his back. Looks like he's been leaning on a gate for too long, the lazy feck.'

Eugene allowed a huff of a laugh, afraid that she'd see his joy in her description of the remnants; afraid that she was perfect for him.

Now, on the boat, he tried to sit down and look out to sea but there was nothing to hold his gaze, and soon he hummed with a need to be moving again. He went to the bar and asked for lemonade, but the voices around him were raucous, views already skewed by daytime drinks, and he didn't wait to be served.

Instead, he moved to where the kids were being entertained by a magician, a grown man who couldn't muster enough enthusiasm to keep the children's attention. Eugene hated him for not being funnier.

Before today, the idea that he was running away had bobbed through to his consciousness so jauntily that, when it did pop up, he was able to get himself right above it, like when he held himself over the limbless beast of the buoy in the lough: his superior position stopped it upsetting the surface.

The sea swelled and retreated and Eugene felt unstable as he realized that love hadn't made him strong or courageous. It had made him still, prepared to stay where he was for ever. There had been something wonderful about no longer having to try. He looked again at the kids' faces. They were sagging, underwhelmed.

The magician tapped a box full of something, pulled at the innards of it and tapped again. At that moment, Eugene felt the force of the things he'd worked so hard to keep down as they ripped through the depths to meet him, like the leviathan from Job, moving through the waters so swiftly that it bubbled a white trail 'as if the deep itself was hoary'.

7

Out of the spattered ferry window, Eugene saw the smoky grey slivers of a new country reaching out into the sea. His future was approaching and, still, he chose to pick over his last night in Ireland.

They'd been locked by duty into his mother's front room and Vincent had watched him and their mother as if he knew that this was their final argument. She'd tried for a while to hide that she was spoiling for something by half cleaning things. Violent swipes at a lamp base, dragging wildly at the curtains, she was subtle as a suit of armour.

It was obvious to her that her children had been trying to get one over on her since the day they were born so she countered this with apocalyptic predictions. 'Every week'll be the same. You'll get paid and you'll piss it up the wall like he did.'

'Why would I want to do that?'

Eugene had avoided her for a few days. It was better if he and his mother kept apart – they were too similar. Like magnetic poles, they repelled: when they reached out to each other, they found themselves pushing in on the magic of rubbery air. Eugene was getting ready to serve her up a good slab of silence and sat swallowing, his head yawing, as if his answers were already balancing in his throat. He knew she was most angry at his silence because she had taught him how to use it. It wasn't her natural approach: screaming came to her first and smothering it had taken practice. Often as a child Eugene had found himself trying to stop his mother when Seamus's excuses made her incandescent with fury. He would crawl on to her and comfy his knees up into her belly, then clamp her mouth shut with a gravel-nicked hand, making faces to please her. She'd let him keep his hand there while she narrowed her eyes to track Seamus's lies, scoring the air between herself and her husband. Eugene would try to block her view but she looked past him, and his hand still remembered her hot breath quickening as she readied herself to fire retribution.

'And what's Theresa done wrong?'

'Nothing!' Eugene did not want to look as if he was trying.

'That's no way to treat someone.' She was shouting now, and Eugene stifled a laugh at her sudden protection of Theresa.

'It's not me she wants.' Eugene stood up and walked over to the wall as if it had become capable of offering succour.

'Bollocks! You're a coward. No gumption.'

'I just don't want to be here any more.'

'Excuses. You've never been so far as Dublin on your own!' spat his mother.

Eugene could see her folding and watched as she doubled over.

'Ah, well, that's just grand. Payment! I stayed with that

bastard for twenty years to hear you say that.' Injured, but not fatally, she sharked around to bite into something more manageable. 'You've never finished anything, Eugene.'

'Rubbish.'

'Even the biggest eejit can start something, and Jesus and his twelve know that your father started more than most.'

'I am not my father.'

'The hard part is finishing.'

'Tell me one thing I didn't finish.'

'You're not your dad? In a pig's eye you're not!'

Eugene watched Vincent wince as she threshed in the wake of another silence and was disgusted at the pride he felt.

'Why would you finish a job when you can just run off, no strings?'

'That's not what I'm doing.'

'Go on run away, you yeller little bastard.'

'I'm not running away.'

'Ah! But your father was a brilliant teacher.'

She turned in on herself now. 'You and Vincent! My sons! Fucking useless.'

'Don't start on me!' Vincent said.

Eugene stood up and left the room, but stayed holding the door handle gently. Through the open door he let his gaze linger on his brother and wondered if that indeed had been a smile.

8

Della had her face right in front of his. What was she saying now? She made Jack worry about the holes in his hearing.

'Jack!'

He sat up straighter at the kitchen table, wondering if this was what she wanted.

'Jack. Seamus's son is moving into the End. You can help to tidy it up. He's coming tonight, from Holyhead.'

Seamus's name had not been mentioned for so long. 'Seamus?' whispered Jack.

'Not Seamus, his son! Eugene. He's coming to work for Buck and you need to help me clear the heavy stuff out of the End.'

'You what?' said Jack, but Della had left the room.

Della shouted similar instructions through Rhodri's door.

'I'm working!' he said from the bed, trying to sound vertical.

'What?' she bellowed through the keyhole.

32

He jerked to sitting. 'I'm working on it,' he sing-songed. 'Put it in the yard. Jack'll help.'

When he heard Della safely distant in the kitchen, he cried out that he might as well have had a chimp to help him and that he had more in common with chimps than he had with Jack. It was his intention that Jack should hear him.

He got up and kicked his clothes and papers around the floor, then waded through them to open the door. 'Julia is going to be furious,' he said indignantly, as he paced with a kimono under his greatcoat into the kitchen. Jack was there making tea. As Rhodri entered, Jack turned to look, burned his hand on the kettle, called it a cunt and elbowed the side of the shower cubicle that stood beside the sink. It boomed ominously. Rhodri no longer found it preposterous that there was a shower cubicle between the fridge and the sink and that there should be a bath and lavatory annexed awkwardly off a communal kitchen.

'The sugar fairy!' Rhodri sniped.

'You what?' said Jack, turning, sugar trilling to the floor.

'We've got to clear out the End. You're used to lifting, aren't you? That's your job, isn't it? I've had a disc removed.'

Jack remained confused.

'We may as well get on with it. I'm not spending my fucking Sunday evening in that dungeon.'

'What disc?' Jack asked.

Rhodri opened his mouth, closed it again, and went under the sink to look for the rubber gloves.

Rhodri felt he had every right to be pissed off. He had finally tightened up one of his aphorisms, to be included in his non-fiction classic *100 Instant Arguments* (although by now he hoped that everyone downstairs knew it a

The Hundred). He was in the middle of this project but was being ordered to clear out a room that had been filled with someone else's shit for twenty years. He had tacked down the logic of this most recent truism a couple of weeks ago but now had the hard work of playing around with the actual semantics.

He thought a lot about how fortunate he had been to hit on an idea that was accessible yet high-minded enough to thumb his nose at the academy, and felt blessed that he had escaped the years of futile peer review. Because his unorthodox approach stood out, his opus, in the form of two brief communications to *Metaphor and Symbol*, had been jealously criticized. He hadn't responded to the criticisms, although Julia, bless her, had kindly taken up the lines of attack and woven sensible and plainly clever answers between them. He kept this under his bed.

Instead, against his mentor's advice, Rhodri continued with his hobby-horses and on the back of these he billed himself as 'The Crumpet Man's Thinker'. He'd let this slip to those in the bar who listened and were with him on it, though there were sometimes looks that led him to wonder if it made him sound homosexual. An editor who had seen *The Hundred* was 'eager' to see examples. That had been two years ago but, as Rhodri repeatedly told Della, the brevity of a popular little gem such as *The Hundred* did not reflect the amount of real work that went into it. He was always forced to look away first.

Rhodri took a pile of clothes down the back stairs and thought he should open a second-hand shop called Somebody Else's Shit. He found this amusing enough to nominate it for inclusion in his foetal idea for a column: 'Grey Matters – where Psychology meets Philosophy meets the Popular'.

The better Sunday supplements were crying out for it. Perhaps even the *TLS* if he shaved off the expletives.

Jack was still where he'd started, just inside the End, rolling cigarettes and drinking cups of something clear. Since Rhodri had uncovered patches of space on the single bed, Jack had made himself more comfortable there. Later, when Della turned on the light to check the room, Jack didn't flinch: he just looked at her and she turned her head this way and that, over-inspecting, until she said, 'Come on 'ere, up off that bed.'

Jack didn't move.

'Jack.'

Jack slapped the mattress and it protested with dust.

'Jack, I want to lock up.'

'I seen you two in this bed right here.'

'Come on.' Della was impatient.

'He had a wife and kids.'

Della folded her arms.

'He didn't need another one.'

Jack's eyes were scarcely open but Della found that she avoided them anyway.

9

As Eugene got off the ferry at noon, he blinked through the rain at Holyhead and saw nothing but a few scattered houses, individual only in their expression of misery. He wondered at the residents' tenacity as, closer to the terminal, he scanned paint-peeling pub façades and all-weather banners promising home-cooked food and quizzes that, even with his small-town understanding of things, Eugene knew to be false promises. In the near distance, a shallow ramp hauled heavy goods vehicles up and out of the place. He'd hoped for something less like home. His neck was open to the weather so he pulled up his denim-jacket collar and looked at his ticket. The rain slowed and fatter drops splotched it with dark circles.

The coach pulled in, the word 'Victoria' on the front making him smile stupidly for a second. As he made his way up the aisle, the stench of a toilet became stronger and, a few seats from the back, he found he had to slide past a couple who smelt like cigarettes smoked in the rain. The woman was twice the size of the man and spilled under and over the arm of her seat. She was feeding a jar of cockles from a plastic spoon to a colourless baby on the man's knee. As Eugene settled himself behind them, he realized they were telling a woman across the aisle about themselves and he began to feel asphyxiated.

'And when we get married in two years, he's going to buy me a limited edition.'

'Two and a half grand,' the man piped up.

'You send a photo and some material from your wedding dress and they make it specially.'

'Ah,' said the woman across the aisle. The angle of her head said she wished she had never spoken.

'You can even have the makeup done, the same colours, everything.' He had done his research.

'And I'm not keeping it in a box, no way. I have my dolls out. In my living room.'

'Over five grand's worth,' the husband said proudly.

Eugene looked out of the window and wished he could pass through it. This was how life was to some people: a promise of dolls and cockles. He didn't want to live off promises and he made up his mind that he could live very well without other people.

When the engine started, a toxic blast of air-freshener from above the toilet made Eugene wish for the old odour of piss. At Milton Keynes a man got on, whose aftershave stank like melted peardrops. He slammed himself into the seat beside Eugene and shouted into a mobile phone for the best part of the ride into the outskirts of London. The man was foreign so Eugene didn't have to suffer his opinions. He couldn't bear listening to others' conversations and the way they always got things so wrong. Eugene excused himself to go to the toilet, and as the bus navigated roundabouts, he added to the yellow sluice on the floor and tried not to bang against the stained metal walls.

Back in his seat, he found that what he could see of the streets was too new to stick in his mind, so he let his head drop back and found it restful to let the strings of images wash over him as the man beside him, still on the phone, jerked open his legs to help him laugh at a joke.

Apart from a couple of cigarette breaks, the hours had dragged up to nine o'clock when they arrived in the last bit of silvery daylight at Victoria. The air was a diesel-haze that seemed to bother no one but Eugene. Everyone around him looked like a murderer, and he knew he was making an oaf of himself by staring. A pigeon almost flew into his face and he flinched dramatically. When he saw its feet he nearly cried out as it landed doggedly, rocking on two balls of sore pink wax, and he looked around him to see if anyone else cared.

A huge black woman passed him, pushing out a massive power as she ploughed through the crowds. Eugene held his breath as she swayed by, as if her wake would shatter his outline. The slow swing of her behind and her heavy tread proved to him that she belonged on this patch, at this very point. He tried to imagine himself as her, knowing where to buy the foods she'd enjoyed growing up and where to get the bus to her doctor's, but thinking about it made him feel as if he were falling down a steep incline.

He rolled another cigarette to prove he was useful. He used Vincent's lighter and placed the warm lump of it back in his pocket next to his tobacco and the pub's address. He pulled in the smoke and his throat protested, but he ignored it and swallowed another tube of smoke. He felt adrift and remembered Seamus in front of the fire, just before he died, looking as if someone else were holding up his hands. His limbs were doomed: intent and action never to speak civilly again. In the last months, his movements had drawn attention where he didn't want it, stammering hands shouting, 'Look at me!'

'They just won't listen.' It was an apology as he reached for his tobacco, his other hand flailing towards his glass on the mantelpiece.

Eugene took another drag and, looking down, saw that he didn't even recognize the rubbish around his feet. The smoke was not treating him properly so he threw the exhausted cigarette end into the gutter and spat a dirty mouthful after it. Still, he had no desire to move. He had to get used to the idea that familiarity was not something you could rush.

A man sat heavily on the low rail beside Eugene, and a girl of about ten moved in close to try to light the man's bent cigarette. Eugene got up and went to lean on the wall but found that the pillar across from him was taken up by a couple kissing fervently without a care in the world for who might notice them. He lowered his eyes and drew himself in because he had to rely on his insides, what he knew; believe that the slow alchemy he had set to work by leaving home was going to yield. He looked again, straight at them this time, to show the world and himself that he was glad it was over, that he'd already used up what heart he'd been given.

10

Eugene stared at the tube map on the wall at Victoria station concentrating on looking as if he knew what he was doing. His eyes tried to make sense of the complexity and were drawn to a colourful thickening just above the middle of the map where three lines had ganged up, a candied trio turning a corner, then separating after Liverpool Street. He picked out the flask shape of the Circle Line in yellow and almost put a finger up to follow it east from Victoria, but at the last minute he folded it back into his fist. Theresa would be able to sort this out in a second, but he was confused by the asymmetry of the network. It wasn't natural. The wiry chaos of the lines kept throwing him off. His eyes went east, to where he wanted to go, but the names of the stations seemed ugly and functional: Mudchute, Shadwell, Mile End, No Hope, No Vincent To Help You Now. He gave up on the map.

A taxi pulled in for him but left him fumbling with the door until he realized he had to tell the driver where he wanted to go before he'd let him in. He hadn't even got the address out of his pocket when the driver pulled off. He flagged another. Again, with the doors still locked, the driver asked him where he wanted to go.

'The Beacon.'

'You'll have to say it slowly.'

'Between Bethnal Green and Shoreditch?' tried Eugene, looking at his piece of paper.

'You got it written down, son?'

'It's a pub.'

'What about a map?'

Eugene looked blankly at the driver. 'I think it's a pub in Bethnal Green.'

The driver sighed and looked straight ahead, then turned and waved at him to get in.

Eugene had no idea how much it would cost and held the roll of money in his pocket as if to force it into being enough. The back of the taxi was huge and, sitting in the newness, he allowed himself a flash of excitement.

Although it was after ten, Eugene was wide awake, wired now with nicotine and anticipation. The taxi driver didn't speak, and after a few moments Eugene stopped expecting him to. This was a quiet lesson on how quickly loneliness could be learned and he took it. The embankment buildings loomed eerily up to his left, and he wondered if the Beacon would be as old and tall as these serious hulks that were guarding the inky water.

Further east, the buildings became more modest and he craned and stared as they sped straight on into more lights and streets lined with people, relaxing a little as the buildings became lower still, feeling he could almost live up to them. Side roads flitted by bathed in pinks, hard neon letters floating above doorways down deserted alleys, and his eyes flicked from these back to the crowds. He cramped with jealousy, thinking of the connection that they had to each other and to these streets.

A left turn, and a little way down Bethnal Green Road, he noticed that promotions and writing on vans were no longer only in English. His eyes darted to keep up with the illuminated strips of shop fronts and eating houses as they drove eastward. He felt sad that he was not going to know these shops and doorways quicker: wanted to know them now, now, now, his eyes making tiny saccades as each place was succeeded by another.

He handed over half of his new pounds to the taxi driver and looked up at the sign for the Beacon. A badly painted picture of a lighthouse represented the pub. The taxi turned in the road and left Eugene standing on the dark front step, listening to the echo of his knock.

It was Della who opened the door and shook his hand, saying, 'You must be Eugene, come in, come in.'

'Aye, the very same,' he said softly.

She stood still for a good while, then moved aside, saying, 'I'm sorry – I knew your dad, that's what it is. I'm knackered, long day, I'm sorry.' She was scarlet.

'Don't worry yourself.'

She motioned for him to sit at the bar, didn't dare look. The weak bar lights were having their after-hours' glory; the rest of the pub was black.

'You've just missed Jack.'

Eugene heard a humph from under the bar.

'Your dad's friend.'

Another humph, and he leaned slightly to see a girl stacking glasses under the pumps, knees bent, not looking over. She had bare arms, peachy, long, strong. Her near black hair looked thick enough to resist if he fitted his two hands around it, and it hung in a molten-looking mass over the shoulder closest to him. Eugene found himself hoping she didn't dye it.

'Aye, I know Jack right enough.' Eugene remembered Jack at the wake, crying, his mother trying to force food into him, explain him away.

Della pulled a Guinness. 'This one down here is my daughter Julia. She helps in the holidays.'

'How're you doing?' he said. Something was muttered. Della poured more Guinness into the settled half.

'If you don't mind, Mrs . . .'

She finally looked at him and, after a long pause, said, 'You can call me Della.'

'I'd rather just have a Coke,' he lied. 'It's late and it's my first day on the site and all tomorrow.'

Della brought him a Coke, looked away again because her thoughts were now shuttling. The eyes were Julia's but not quite. Her heart was hammering and she gripped the glass to stop her hand shaking the flat Coke all over the bar and into his lap. She needed another look. Seamus again in front of her, odd and twitching. Seamus! I nearly called him Seamus! The nearness of the mistake threatened her and she tried to flatten it down, make nothing of it, but she knew that her face had flooded with the secret and her stomach had stiffened at the sight of the impossible black hair, thick, doing what it wanted. The eyes were Seamus's . . . and Julia's. Violet. Same waver in them as the father, full of fear so that they seemed to be taking the piss; the eyes were their own defence. Julia's? Public schooling had stamped out the waver: they were steady, just outside deep blue and permanently set to no surrender.

He was rolling a cigarette. Oh, my God, she thought, his hands! He's wearing his dad's hands – Seamus gloves.

She smiled at him. 'Is that all you want? Anything to eat?'

His Coke was gone and he was stubbing out his roll-up with the end of his finger, his Seamus glove, tan at two tips.

'No, thanks, that'll do me now. Had a good feed on the ferry.'

Julia had gone to bed without saying good night. Della knew it was because she couldn't stand to see her mother acting. She turned off the lights in the bar and led Eugene up the back stairs to the End.

When Della called his room the End, Eugene tried to remember if he'd seen a tube station called that. Going up the stairs, she talked about the benefits of still having an electricity meter, and Eugene knew enough to grasp that the benefits weren't for him. At the top of the stairs where the pub finally became his new home, the place stank and not fleetingly either. Further into the corridor the damp smell lingered and Eugene realized that the bad air was definitely a trait of the house and not just a symptom of its uneasy marriage to the pub.

Della opened the door to his room, made a few gestures and left. It seemed she couldn't wait to get out. No curtains, just a blanket hanging at the window, so the day's stale heat was still held prisoner in the room. He pulled back the blanket and looked down on to a yard. He knew that his father must have done the same thing. It was no comfort. He undressed and got into bed but he couldn't sleep for thoughts of home. He missed Vincent's breathing and he needed the toilet. The practicalities of the bath and toilet being in the same room began to dawn on him.

He opened his door a crack and saw Jack in his pants and socks, bumping and lurching from one wall to the other. Eugene tried to pretend to himself that Jack was just half asleep but he knew the code: he was blind drunk.

Eugene pulled his head back in but not before Jack had seen that someone was there and let out a greeting scrambled by a laugh. Pity started to poison Eugene and he tried to close the door, but its cheap rough bottom stubbornly scraped the sticky carpet. He was suddenly angry with Jack for making him feel like this. He jerked the door open again and willed Jack to do his worst, show him how bad things really were, get it over with.

Jack was walking slowly but too fast for himself, his flat feet contacting the ground as if he were crossing a greased pole, giving him a roll, showing his life was a cycle, either getting up or falling down. He stopped and held the wall, and the shadow cut him up like a butcher's diagram. The chest had never been broad or open; there was no confidence in it. The skin drooped from his arms, which were now resting on the door jamb, and as he tried to navigate the narrow doorway, his biceps, two poor eggs, balled at the tense end of a sway. Eugene felt a flash of hate for Jack because Jack's arms were exactly like his father's had been just before he'd died.

In his last stint in the hospital, they'd strapped Seamus's arms to his sides with taut blankets, his head above the white of them, burning amber against the pillow. But when his mind had pushed itself above the cloud of his sedatives, Seamus had pulled out his wasted arms and examined them as if they didn't belong to him, sometimes asking Eugene or Vincent, 'Have you seen these?'

They never answered. They wanted him to shout, protest, not to rely on his children. Instead, they sat wishing hard that he hadn't asked them the question, and ringing with the knowledge that they'd never be rid of it.

Not really knowing what else to do, they'd make Seamus sit up for a bit. Eugene would slowly swivel him on to the edge of the bed until his skinny yellow feet reached the floor. Then Seamus would rub over the top of Eugene's shoes with his stockinged feet: a thank-you. He'd sit there obediently until he felt sick or started seeing things and had to be laid down again.

Eugene closed the door on Jack as he heard the heavy piss miss the bowl. Jack shouted something in a feisty tone, something for the beginning of a night, but Eugene was already in bed. The toilet would have to wait.

11

As Jack falls back into bed, something picks him up and forces him backwards, guiding him. He is lifted upwards then carried along, the air sucking through his belly until he can steer for himself. Looking down, he sees that it's the ruins of his own history he's after picking over. Jack's recent recall is drowned by booze, but points of his pissed past are preserved, and on certain nights they break the surface.

Jack glides down Cambridge Heath Road, and just before Roman Road he's allowed to hover, taking in the mercantile grandeur of York Hall, a red barrel-bellied Georgian building that has been home to fighters from all over the capital and beyond. Jack is taking notice now, warming up. This is where he and Seamus saw the young bantam-weight, McCullogh, beat the bejesus out of a Bow boy.

Encouraged, Jack swoops up and over to Whitechapel, and looks down on the roof of the Royal Hospital. He slows and then slickly slants down to the front entrance, which is crowded by amputees with nothing left to do but smoke, their drip bags hovering, some flaccid, some firm, just above their heads. Jack's been there: laughs, remembering Seamus's face, come to collect him. Seamus, disgusted by their lack of legs, their true love for the fags, his own love of the fags hidden from him by his still rude health.

Then up and over to the weird, wide Mile End Road and before Jack even gets there he knows where he's going. It's the car park off Globe Road, the last job they worked on together. The air rushes through his belly as he begins to steer more certainly for himself.

Jack comes at the old site from the west and notices that it's snowing. Immediately he's scanning the site for Seamus. It's December, that's right, but he's not cold at all when he's flying. He's there in control, still drives the JCB. Happy about that, feels for the keys in his pocket and looks down on the machine as if it's an old friend. Apart from patches of yellow that the snow has let through, most of the heavy plant is secret under the snow.

The crane is lit with Christmas lights, the jib twinkling, and the window to the cab seems full of colour. But it's daylight – Seamus should have turned them off. He must have forgotten. Jack flies over to the window of the cab and slows smoothly; his brakes are in his gut as well. It's amazing what you can do with guts, thinks Jack. But as Jack gets closer he can hear the crane alarm and it frightens him. He's only heard it once before.

In bed Jack gathers the covers in his fists and makes a *ma* sound with his dry old lips. He hovers next to the window and sees Seamus, the cab swaying wildly, the block danger-ously whistling through the air down near the ground. Seamus is sweating, pulling and pushing the levers, and Buck is screaming up at him from the ground telling him, 'Stop, for fuck's sake, Mahon! Stop, will you!'

Then the snow thickens and Jack falls. His guts are no use at all.

12

The city-centre dawn was weak, its breaking and entering foiled by streetlights. Eugene woke in the End with his feelings wrapped around Theresa, and now his mood would be low for the whole day. Sleep was the only chance to rid himself of her: if she was there when he woke up, she'd be there when he closed his eyes.

He wondered what they'd be doing at this hour back home. There'd be shouting probably if his mother was about. Growing up, Eugene had been taught by his father that you could use the mornings to wade into the smooth pool of the day: that it was possible to warm to the cold a little before bare-facing it on the street. His mother did it all wrong. She was always alarmed, knowing she was already too late. She would start attacking the day five minutes before she was due out of the door, and that attack wouldn't end until the evening. But his father would wake at five and thaw the bitter out of the cold with too-sweet tea so that when Eugene, trailed by Vincent, padded into the front room, blue-white in his pants, Seamus would hand them both syrupy beakers.

Nobody spoke. They gravitated to the small fire, sitting and lying, Vincent's arms blindly seeking heat in Eugene's legs. Eugene didn't push his brother off even if he met with a patch of skin that was colder than his. They sat too close to the two-bar fire, its ropy lead fraying, yielding the bare wires to the cold. They'd hook elbows under knees and mottle the backs of their thighs, getting as close to cooking as was possible. Eugene wondered how the other side of his body could be so cold and why it was that his back couldn't speak to his front.

Eugene and Vincent were the fire's little audience and would scuffle around the rug breathing each other's air. This was a time when Eugene could shut his worries up with a drink of tea and his brother's back against his. Even as a kid, Eugene knew there was never an absence of anxiety, just times when it could be more easily hushed. It was at night when it wouldn't shut up. A sharp memory poked through.

He was in his sister's bed, crying, hot and quiet. In his mother's house, each bed had multiple mattresses; mildewed strata with their own secrets, shushed by the next and stuffed with newspaper when they wouldn't keep quiet. Just shut them up, she must have thought, as she'd heaved a fifth on to Gloria's bed. He'd climb the five rubbery steps of the mattresses to lie beside Gloria and refused to let go of his hopes. 'I'll be good. Please.'

'Don't be stupid. How can I take you to work?'

'I can hide.'

'Eugene!'

'I'll take a comic.'

She turned her back and he heard her sigh but he didn't stop.

'I love me comics.'

School made him sick and Gloria knew it, but she wouldn't bend backwards to him – she said it would do him no good – but his words trotted out steadily like prayers. He'd chosen Gloria as his personal saviour, and she'd listen night after night to his snotty pleadings until he'd fall whimpering into a thin sleep.

He'd start again in the morning but in the light he couldn't keep up the pressure and she knew it, so she'd just put a finger on his lips. She'd have him warm her tights in front of the fire. Dressed, she'd light a fag, ready to go.

'Good luck,' she'd say, ruffling his hair, and, gently, she'd escape him, her pencil skirt letting her half run to her bus. He watched as she trotted to the end of the road, her cigarette making smiles in the dim grey morning, and as her heels clicked out of his day, he pushed his face against the steamy window, trying not to spill his sorrow.

He blinked his way back to the present. He mustn't be late for work. The blanket-curtain hung heavily above his head as he lay under the window. From this position, he pulled it forward and let the light pour in. He had a gift: he weighed the light in his head and its quality gave him the time. He had no use for a city's fungal spread of clocks. The calculation had steps: first like puffs of ink in water, indistinct possibilities billowing, then like precocious ferns unfurling to finite points giving him his answer, the exact time.

The dread of being late had also been stamped into him early on. His mother was always late to pick him up. After school trips, he would count off his disappearing classmates until he'd be left with a couple of teachers and Gabriel Hannan. Gabriel was a handicapped boy, a 'Child of God', who got a special lift at a special time. As the children dwindled, the teachers spoke to each other in strange personal ways, and Eugene became desperate for the other kids who could shade him from the glaring existence of Gabriel, shining and hopeful in his wheelchair.

He got out of bed and smelt himself. How was it that Vincent could smell like a new loaf for a week and the stink of Eugene'd be the same if he had three baths a day? He threw a deft but awkward hand behind him, pulling upward at the back of the sweatshirt neck to remove his top layers. This act never looked slick: rather, it enhanced his angular oddity. Then he went to get washed, make a cup of tea, have a fag. He had barely slept and his eyes felt gritty but he was glad he didn't have the radiation of a hangover to cope with. He was looking forward to his first cigarette and suddenly thought that this clear-headedness might be the start of a good pattern. Just as quickly, he was ashamed of his optimism, thought it naïve, and dipped into a wish for home that made him hate himself. The fag would level him out.

He heard Della rouse Jack with instructions to show Eugene where the site was. He waited for Jack in the kitchen, and when he came in, Eugene stood up and offered his hand. Jack moved doggedly past him, over to the sink. Eugene sat back down and put his hand into his pocket.

Jack put together some bread and meat. As always, his hands shook, but the meat eventually shivered its way between the bread and he stuffed it into a bag. He had a long glug of something Eugene couldn't see. He sat down at the other end of the table and kept his eyes on his cup.

'You ready for work, boy?'

'I am indeed.'

'Right so.'

Jack drained the cup and set off down the back stairs, making it very clear that he didn't want to talk. They walked the half-mile to the site between Old Street and City Road, Jack in a thin leather jacket and boots too big, trousers flapping halfway up them. Eugene followed a couple of steps behind.

They walked through the gates and the security guard was taking off his visi-vest, ready to sign out. He shouted to Jack, his English changing gear in the wrong place, 'Whoo-oo! You have shit in your bed, Princess?'

'Where's Buck?' Jack replied.

The guard pointed to the makeshift office, still laughing, and Eugene prickled for Jack but was relieved when Jack left him alone. Two Portakabins stood beside each other. To the left was the cabin, where the men gathered between jobs, ate, played cards. To the right was the office, where you'd go to find Buck, the boss, having subbies meetings, arguing with money men or keeping contractors to their promises.

Jack went round the back of both cabins to sit in the prefab toilets. All the locks to the stalls had been kicked off so he lowered himself breathlessly to the floor, with his back towards the door of the cubicle, trying not to listen to his guilt. The boy was the spitting image of Seamus. Jack took out a quarter-bottle and had a bigger swig than he normally would at this hour and breathed heavily after his first whack of the day.

Buck was looking through a sheaf of drawings and, on seeing Eugene, gave him the same look as Della had. Eugene felt cheated: he wanted to rub himself out, start again as his own story, not be a part of someone else's. Thinking this, he tripped up the step on going in. Buck didn't register the clownish start and, on seeing Eugene, was up and open, arms out, a fifty-something bull with a thick neck, love in his face and strawberry-blond hair. He had huge shoulders and short legs that seemed under-equipped to deal with the muscular mass of his upper body.

'Ah, I've been expecting you. How are ye doing?' asked Buck, as he pumped the smaller, smoother hand in a way that Eugene felt was not just automatic. 'Hope you're not missing the awld country too much, eh?'

Eugene nearly choked on the hope. Buck smiled and kept hold of Eugene's hand, which told Eugene that Buck had been there, knew that puck in the throat, had licked up his own tears in the dark and survived. Knowing this made the simple response 'Grand' difficult for Eugene to say. Buck smoothed over it, asked him quickly about his mother, his journey and then, knowing he had to get to the dirty past that connected them if they were to make a good start, he searched out the sores of his history and sluiced them. 'I was sorry to hear about your father passing away.'

It stung. At the mention of Seamus, Eugene lowered his head and Buck offered, 'Aye, he did good service here.'

Eugene immediately saw that Buck was used to handling the truth. Nevertheless he smiled, and as they left the office, he felt as if Buck was like Moses leading him out of the desert; no need to return to the country of shame. He followed him out of Egypt and on to the site.

13

The site was beginning to crawl with men now. This was a much bigger job than anything he'd worked on in Ireland. The crane was slinging steel for the fixers and the scaffolders were up on the back of an old stone façade next to the street entrance to the site, making sure nothing had been tampered with overnight. On the ground, Eugene saw joiners quickly loading out materials so they could have an early break. Buck was describing the job to Eugene as they walked round, a hotel, French chain, mostly concrete underground and a steel frame above ground. Eugene had seen enough of the area to ask, 'A hotel?'

Buck barked a laugh and slapped him on the shoulder. 'How long you going to be around for?'

'As long as it takes.' Eugene smiled. 'When did you start up on your own?'

Buck resisted a good-natured urge to say, *When your father lost me my job.* Instead he said, '1981. The interest has been killing me ever since. This is the first decent-sized job I've had in ten years.'

'Things finally picking up?'

'I'm behind on this job already.' Buck pointed up to the large façade retained with an intricate scaffold at the back. 'That old façade is a mighty ball-ache.'

'Looks grand from the front, though.'

'The concrete works are already late because of it.'

'And you want me in the concrete shed?'

'The dunkey that's in there now turns up when he feels like it.'

Eugene nodded silently. In the cube shed he would be striking moulds of concrete that were used on site and sending them off for testing; hot, invisible work, which was dull and thankless. He'd also be responsible for the initial slump tests, making sure the mix was consistent so that it would reach its intended strength.

Buck pointed down into the foundations. 'We're out of the ground now. The car park's nearly done.' He let his arm sweep from one side of the site to the other. 'From here on in, the only concrete is in the floors, seven storeys. Here, have a look.'

On the opposite side of the site to the façade, a tower crane swung the tapered concrete skip over shuttered reinforcement bars, the wheel underneath letting out rich elephant-grey sludge, and the banksman motioned, acting as the crane driver's eyes on the ground. It had once been Seamus in the crane with Jack on the ground as banksman but Buck thought once again that it was best to leave the past out of today.

The cube shed was a low-level prefab next to the cement mixers' wash-off area; drums were cleaned here before they returned to the yard for another load. Inside the shed, the casts from last night's concrete pour had been stripped and were ready for testing. Buck dusted off the bench where the moulds stood.

'With the concrete we've got coming in we need to be steady in here.'

'I can do steady.' Eugene grinned down into his shirt-front, then twitched in his collar, raising one shoulder, worried suddenly that he sounded sickening.

They wound their way around the rest of the site and ended up back at the cabin. Eugene stood just inside the door, while Buck went to look for someone to go through the health and safety with him. Early workers trickled past him, swapping trainers for rigger boots. Two sat heavily in front of him and began playing cards, the like of which Eugene had never seen. Luxurious colours and exotic poses made him lean over a little to glimpse a card picturing a fine-boned man, with a flopping chestnut Mohican and a ferocious moustache, who brandished a mace; the whole figure was garlanded with what looked like sheaves of wheat and cherries. The threat of violence in such a beautiful picture made Eugene wonder at the deck's origin. From another peered a beautiful pink-cheeked woman, head wrapped in a scarlet scarf fringed with tiny bells. She deftly carried a lamb and, her fingers wrapped round its bony shins, was still able to keep a hold of a vodka bottle. Eugene longed to rifle through the pack.

The card-player on the left was a giant of a man, his cards dwarfed by his shovel-like hand; on his shaved head there was the blue bleed of a very old tattoo. The arms and hands were indigo with prints and the background was skin that must have been burned by all weathers. There was no rounding of the back, no stoop in the shoulders, though from the look of the stories his skin told, Eugene imagined there'd been plenty to bear.

As he slid the cards down, the giant slung low lamentations in a foreign language out of the corner of his mouth to a pointed, rattish man with hair the colour of dried blood, who, Eugene reckoned, was in his early fifties and so looked a little older than his friend. Eugene leaned over to see more of the cards and heard puffs of resignation from the shorter man's mouth. He spoke softly, the mouth opening just enough to slip out another *ach*. Eugene was close enough to smell them and, parsing the air with tiny turns of his head, he believed it was the smaller man who gave off a sweet fustiness that both intrigued and satisfied him. He wondered if his hair was the source of the fumes or whether the faint mesh of grey freckles that contained him had a smell of their own.

The giant glanced over his shoulder at Eugene, startling him, but quickly looked back to his cards. As if in apology for his friend, the smaller man smiled briefly, and Eugene felt a glow from him; a warmth. He bet himself there wasn't a bad word in or out of this man and, buoyed by a brief swell of optimism, felt that the little man was going to be good to work beside. Like the seaside. Eugene was happy to be invisible and to watch these fellows quietly clinging to the falling minutes before their share of work had to start.

Buck was beside him again. 'Looks like it'll have to be me.' He introduced the card-players as Uri – the giant swivelled but did not smile – and Babe.

'These are my masters of all trades!' said Buck. Babe turned to Eugene and Buck, rubbing his high brown forehead. His intelligent eyes seemed desperate to explain

that his hairline had once been low but he had been relieved
of it some time ago. 'This,' Buck explained, 'is Eugene.'

Eugene felt a tinge of pride and gave a half-smile.

'Come on to hell,' quipped Buck. 'Safety first.' He brandished a couple of thick folders. 'Another ball-ache.'

With Eugene and Buck away on to the site, the card game
was sharply interrupted as Buck's son, Noble, burst into the
cabin looking for his father. He pulled off a baseball cap and,
with his fingers, brushed dust out of his white-blond hair on
to the floor of the cabin.

· 'Uri, where's my dad?' Noble shouted, shattering the peace.

Uri didn't look up from his card hand. A long pause. 'Has
taken new boy back on site. Health and safety.'

Noble cursed and said, 'Babe. A word with you later.'

Babe tracked Noble across the cabin to where he opened
the fridge and poked around noisily. Babe was the only
person, other than the subbies, who spoke to Noble of his
own accord.

'Who is this new boy with Buck, Noble?'

'Ask my old man. Another foreign chimp he's dying to
help out.'

'Fuck you!' shouted Uri.

'Not like you, Uri, you nonce. You've been processed.'

'What is it - nonce?' Uri asked, standing up, hand on the
dictionary attached to his tool belt. Noble came at him, all
smiles, but at the last second spun out of Uri's way.

'You see?' Uri said to Babe, pointing to the words tattooed
on his thick forearm. Babe read them dutifully: '*Oderint dum
metuant.*'

'What's that Russian for?' a joiner chipped in from the
sink.

'No, *durak*. Are you a sheep's head? It is Latin! It means I do not care if he hates me if he knows I can kill him easily.'

Babe saw the joiner struggle to make meaning out of Uri's sentence and sighed. He spoke Russian and Arabic as well as Turkish, Albanian, French and English, and had the solid knowledge that Buck relied on him greatly. He turned to the joiner. 'It means, "Let them hate, as long as they are afraid."'

'That is what I am saying already,' said Uri, hands in the air.

When Noble was clear of the cabin, Uri asked, 'So who is this new nonce?'

'Are you deaf? Is Eugene. Evgenie.'

'That means nothing. Where has he come from?'

'You think I am withholding information?' laughed Babe.

Uri sucked his teeth. Whenever there was a new man, Uri closed up and was glad that there'd be some things the newcomer couldn't see immediately, like his love of cocaine (though he was proud of the full crescent of his nose, a sickle clawing out of his face, his own bit of the east, which had led him west ten years ago).

He didn't want new men seeing the lies he told, even to his closest workmates, so that he could visit Soho on payday, shiftily rounding the corner of Peter Street and Wardour Street, walking close into the wall until he slipped into the Las Vegas Amusements. There he'd wait patiently to take up his position on the DanceMaster, hips thrust forward, potent with the change in his pockets, holding himself easily, as the talented do, until it was his turn to smudge his feet over the game's flashing arrows. This was his very own piece of the west, memories of which he would take home with him if ever, God forbid, he had to return to Irkutsk.

'New men make my teeth hurt.' He groaned, rubbing a wide finger over them.

'I will make your teeth hurt,' said Babe. 'Now play the game.'

14

As Eugene and Buck rounded the cabin, Noble jogged around the pallets of blocks and stopped just short of bumping into them. The lad looked expectantly at Buck. His thick, fair, almost white hair gave him a blameless air and he had a kid's complexion marred by only two things: a tent of self-pity at the eyebrows and a bubbling scar that slanted through both of his full lips, making them ugly and unequal.

'I need some money.'

Eugene stood to one side and Buck introduced his son. After an awkward moment, Buck backed around the corner and Noble followed.

Eugene's gaze followed Noble's back and noticed that the muscles above his shoulders made his collar stand away from his body. He was about a foot taller than his father but had the same bullish shape. Buck came back shaking his head as he put his wallet away. Eugene didn't ask for an explanation but could see from Buck's face that the relationship, whatever it was, had a dangerous crack in it.

Buck sighed as they walked to the office but said nothing and left Eugene to decipher what it meant and to read the site rules at his desk. Eugene was already yearning to be someone whom Buck would confide in. Half an hour later, Noble silently sidled in and, without looking at Eugene, said, 'Health and safety, number one round here,' then left quickly before Eugene could respond.

Eugene went into the toilets behind the office and sat down to roll a fag to try to cure his ill-feeling. He looked around the walls and squinted: along with graffiti, the chipboard seemed to be covered with tiny grey bouquets. He went up closer and saw they were not flowers but bunches of pencilled numbers. Individual records of how much had been earned, written here in the bog in private. Day-rate posies. It made him smile as he finished his fag. Nobody liked to look like a grabber.

Close to noon, Eugene found himself crushed with awkwardness, crossing the yard in front of the cabin, joining a stream of workers who made up the first sitting of lunchtime eaters. Reluctantly, he headed into the cabin.

The air was steamy and held the mild spice of sausage but, further in, was sharpened by a pickled tang. There was a ragged bunch of men, in the main white but between them some darker faces, bad teeth, flatter noses, scarred hands. A man playing chess was sitting in the steam wearing what seemed to Eugene to be a woman's fur coat. They played backgammon and dominoes, ate huge discs of cerise sausage and smaller, thicker slices like dark brown poker chips. Some men had tubs, lids stiffly opening on to lumps of intense-smelling grey pork and whole small cucumbers. One man, with a wide black face, ate a dried flat fish like a biscuit. The snap of the bite, the nerves and the smell of everything at once turned Eugene's stomach.

He saw Buck and instinctively walked up to him. Buck was talking to one of the men and, without looking away from him, put his arm around Eugene. Buck squeezed, let go and started the rounds. Eugene followed, swallowing hard, flooded with feeling. On introduction, some of the men stood, some bowed, some hailed Buck as 'Very great boss!' Buck ran through the names quickly, as if threading beads: Ali-Aristotle-Sokol-Fernando-Agi-Illian-Vitus-Roland-Uris-Mario-Haji-Beni. Eugene wanted his own name to sit snugly on the string and tried to push the part of his brain that looked forward into feeling part of this easy flow. For now, others' comfort was teasing: all around him and yet out of his reach. He just wanted to be known, to sit and laugh at their jokes, have a smoke and play cards. Buck left him to eat; he didn't know that Eugene never ate in front of strangers.

If only he could fit into a game, a structure, stop sticking out. He stared at the card-players and tried to decipher what the game was from their movements but became mesmerized by a goat this time, slung round the neck of a fresh-faced lad on a card; the festoons around the edge were acorns. The players were still the same: Uri and Babe? Eugene wondered again if he had heard right.

Jack was also at the card table, trying to eat the sandwiches he'd made that morning. Eugene went up to the table and sat down. Immediately, Babe offered his hand and smiled, showing teeth the colour of toffee. Eugene smiled back and his lips clamped closed as if he felt the wind whistle through the brown-ringed holes between each of Babe's teeth.

'Hello again,' Babe said. 'You may call me Babe.' He winked and continued with the game.

'And you-may-call-me-Babe is fucked because Noble is looking for him,' chuckled Uri.

'I was watching your game. Earlier.'

'Uri is always early. He has the rhythms of prison. But I am early because I am wise with my time.'

Uri narrowed his eyes at Eugene, then guffawed and soon enough they were acting as if Eugene had always been there. It made him feel better, so he asked Uri, 'Why d'you call him Babe?'

'It's Fidil, really,' began Uri, and Babe tried to explain but Uri put his hand over Babe's mouth and whispered that little Fidil had undergone massive changes. Babe pulled the big paw away and, between them, they explained that Fidil had once sensibly led to Fiddler (he played) but had taken a wrong turn into Kiddy Fiddler (he didn't), expanding wildly into 'Kiddy Fiddler on the Roof' for a couple of days before leaping to Babe.

'And now, finally, I like it!'

'And Noble, is that his real name?'

'Buck and Deirdre very pissed when he was born, eh, Jack?' said Babe.

'Aye, Noble's the boss all right,' Jack piped up, his mouth full.

'I thought Buck ran this job.'

'Buck backs down to his wonderful son.'

'He doesn't seem like that kind of a fella.' Eugene was disappointed. He already loved Buck.

'He isn't, but Noble is his own law.'

'Is he that bad?'

Babe lowered his voice: 'Let me say it like this. If you English had a single word for total and utter cunt, I would be using it now.'

Uri had tuned in to the lowered voice. 'Huttercunt?' He was already flicking to H in the fat, fanned book hanging from his tool belt. He was paranoid: prison had given him this gift too, and he nurtured it with high-class stimulants. He thumbed the dictionary constantly as if it contained his old reason.

'Forget it, Uri. Come on, shuffle.'

Uri shuffled the cards and Eugene noticed that half a finger was missing on his right hand. The nub that remained above the big knuckle danced, trying to keep up with the others. On it there was a rough tattoo, not like the others, a shakily filled-in diamond. He offered the cards to Eugene to cut and when he did they all laughed at him.

'*Shapku s duraka ne snimayut*,' shouted Uri.

Babe saw Eugene's bewildered face and, with his better English, translated: 'One should not take the hat away from a fool. *Durak* means fool, this is name of game. If you split the pack you are the fool.'

Uri tried to draw him back in, clapped his back, but Eugene wouldn't deal now so Uri pulled open his shirt. On his chest he pointed to a woman sitting astride a missile-shaped penis. 'You know Furtseva? She was my minister of culture. She was like Russia herself, needed a fuck in the ass!'

Eugene looked away from the symbol as the men laughed and Uri pulled his shirt tight round his arms and bent forwards. The cabbage-sized shoulders were covered with perfect pictures of thick, fringed military epaulettes, and he bent down to show a grinning cat on top of each. 'I am laughing off my face at Soviet Union.'

Eugene tried to smile.

Lunchtime ended, and men were streaming in and out of the cabin: ground workers, shutterers, scaffolders. Between them pushed Noble. 'Oy, Babe!'

Babe stood up as if to attention. Without taking his eyes off his cards Uri pulled him back down to sitting.

'Outside.'

Babe got up again and meekly followed Noble out front. The door closed and nearly every bloke in the cabin gave Buck's son the worst signal found in their home towns. Some slapped forearms: fingers up, side, down, and after the jolt of bad-will, they laughed at each other, at the similarity of their differences. Same hate, different fingers. Eugene was hypnotized by the consensus and tried not to think about what it would mean for the future. He looked back to the game but felt confused by the odd division of the cards and stopped trying to understand. Uri was looking out of the window for Babe, but even so, he had noted the drift in Eugene.

'Look at this, my round stone.' It was a circle with a central dot that sat like a flat ring on his finger. 'It means you are really orphan. You have no friend, only you.'

'And this one?' Eugene pointed to the shaky diamond on Uri's stump.

'This I only tell a very, very true friend.'

'So no one knows,' said Eugene. Uri's face betrayed nothing and Eugene found himself holding his breath for a good while. When Uri offered Eugene a pink cigarette with a gold tip from a black packet, he finally let out his breath and smiled. 'No, thanks.'

He looked back through the window, drawn by Noble's mobile mouth, which seemed to be shouting down into Babe's face. He wouldn't let the smaller man explain. Noble flicked Babe hard on the tip of the nose and Babe bent forward, automatically bringing up his hand. Noble beckoned violently and Babe brought out some notes that Noble snatched away as he pushed a fan of small plastic bags up in front of Babe's face, then roughly down the neck of his knitted jumper.

Eugene found himself with his hand to his own nose. He quickly brought it down. Uri leaned to look through the window. 'Buck goes on his fishing trip soon. I think I will go on sick.'

Jack looked up from his sandwich and, for a second, smiled as if he knew what was happening.

Babe came back in and sat down with his mouth closed tight. Uri spoke to him quick and low in Russian but kept his eyes on his cards.

Eugene didn't go on site that afternoon. Noble told him to read through more of the thick folders of safety regulations and as, moment to moment, he drifted away from the dull grey tangle of rules he wondered how men like Uri had convinced Noble that they understood them. It's the newness, that's all, he told himself, as he tried to shrug off the already aching jealousy he felt for Noble's privileged position, and tried to staunch the feelings he'd brought from home that threatened to overwhelm him before he'd even started here.

At half past five, Buck came back and they met up with the men in the cabin. A labour agency they often used was taking everyone out and Uri asked Eugene if he wanted to come.

'Better not,' he mumbled, and Uri shrugged.

Eugene thought he heard Noble say, 'Pussy,' and the uncertainty of this weighed on him on his walk back to the Beacon. Even Jack had joined the gang and gone out.

Eugene told himself he'd feel better after something to eat. Didn't need to be drinking anyway. It made him worse. He began the walk home. It was still light and warm, and this contrasted sharply with his loneliness. He saw a shop that said 'Halal' and thought that was its name. It was a butcher's so he asked for rashers but the man shook his head and Eugene asked for chops. They were closing and one sickly light hung above the counter. Most of the meat had been taken off display and the square, swarthy butcher was scrubbing his block with a wire brush and soapy water. The shop smelt of blood and bleach. The man chirped something to a child and he brought out some lumps wrapped in thick paper. Eugene wasn't about to open it so he laid his hand over the counter for the butcher to take as much as he wanted. He didn't look at Eugene and as he took the money he dripped brownish suds into his palm.

In the kitchen, Eugene slapped the meat on to the gritty grill pan. The pieces looked like chops but were smaller, denser and darker; black commas of meat. The smell they gave off while cooking wasn't familiar but he ate all six anyway. He was glad he was alone in the kitchen because as he chewed he cried. He could never understand why eating made him feel so melancholy. He wondered if his heart would always be where his stomach should be.

15

'What you 'avin', Princess?'

Not here, thought Jack. Not in the pub. He looked up wearily and stared, the nickname hanging in the air between them.

'Well?' asked the kid. It was one of Noble's lackeys.

Jack couldn't escape 'Princess'. People came and went, the name stayed. Since Buck had set up his own business, O'Halloran's had moved from site to site, but wherever they settled for work, there it was, like a flypaper; newcomers and old-timers, they all stuck to it eventually. It didn't matter if they knew Jack or not, the name was enough to pull them in. Jack grunted.

'A drink, do you want a drink?'

'Who says to call me "Princess"?' asked Jack. He looked over the youngster's shoulder at Noble, who was ringed by his usual lads. And this was where it always had to stop because the truth was Jack had earned the name, fair and square: he had been Princess for nearly twenty years. If you told anyone now they would laugh in your face but it was he, Jack, who had provided the money for Buck to secure a loan to start O'Halloran's. After Seamus had got Buck fired he'd had no work for a good while.

Jack had emptied fifteen grand out of a bin bag on a suffocatingly hot day in 1981. Buck had asked no questions, quickly put it down as a deposit on a loan and paid Jack back in instalments as his business built up. The interest on the loan in those early years had crippled him but he never missed a payment to Jack, who dutifully gambled them away and was relieved that, because of the favour, on Buck's sites he was a freed man, an untouchable who could do what he wanted. Privileged; a princess. He deserved the name but didn't want it and so he sat on it unsteadily, taking the name when he should've taken offence and flaring up at it when it was most endearingly thrown at him. It helped the new lads to fit in; a common currency used at Jack's expense.

Over fry-ups, the theories about Jack and Buck would wax and wane alongside the differing phases of refurbs and new build, but the Princess had threaded in and out of every one of the jobs, late and often shirking; of course, there were benders and bedridden times through the drink but he still left his mark, a blunt needle stitching a raggedy hem around the bottom of the O'Halloran business.

It was Buck's turn now to look over at Jack slumped by the bar. He could never relax if Jack was around, and as he thought this, he heard Noble swearing loudly and wondered how he'd got to be quite so far from what Buck had expected. He looked at the baseball cap and knew that Noble wanted his roots chopped through and earthed-over. He wanted nothing to do with Buck's family back home, and Buck wondered whether it might have been different if he'd stayed in Ireland. With the brutal climate of the eighties and early nineties he'd learned well that having his own building business in London was not the blessing he had imagined it would be. Work in Ireland was cracking on while he was still only just getting on his feet.

Buck listened in as Noble turned to Dermot, an old head of the electricians. 'Remember Seamus Mahon, drove a crane on Cosgrove's Mile End job?'

The touchpaper lit, Dermot exploded, describing the accident in lurid flashes, how many pints Seamus could down at dinner, what the maimed man had screamed on the trolley in the hospital and finally how Buck couldn't stand to see Seamus's drunken face any more after he'd lost them both a job.

'Eugene? That's his son.'

'Keep him away from the fucking heavy machinery!' boomed Dermot, and Buck held his empty glass very tightly before he put it on the bar.

The noise of the pub was too much for Jack, and his wish that Eugene hadn't come to work for Buck was taking him over. The hair on Eugene could've been Seamus's, the hands, the walk. Jack ordered another drink because he couldn't get it together to make the move from the bar. Decisions, and getting to them, used to be fluid but now his machinery felt rusted and the scales that used to weigh out bad and better were sprained.

It was painful for him to think about things these days so he no longer bothered trying to read the paper. He didn't even study form any more, just picked out horses with his stiff finger, sticking with those whose names had R as the third letter. Races were chosen by the proximity of their starts to his entry into the stinking bookie's. A jockey's surname and place of birth used to squeeze his decisions more than any of the odds but not now. His gambler's desire had been lost because all his little itches had been gathered into the big itch for the booze.

Resting his head on his hands at the bar, he remembered the day again, proud in his own way that he hadn't begged Seamus to stay. Jack knew why Seamus was really going and it sickened him. Della's belly was beginning to swell, and with Seamus gone, Jack avoided all sight of her. Fat heifer, so she was. Seamus left her a letter along with the money for the babby. Jack didn't want to know anything about Seamus's feelings for Della so he never read it, just ripped it up and put it in his coat pocket. The money, of course, he kept, and and it pulled him with the promise of regret to the Perspex cage in the bookie's on Essex Road.

The bloke behind the counter recognized Jack as he made bad progress through the beaded fringe hanging in the doorway. Up against the Perspex, Jack slowly flattened out the whorl of twenties and pointed shakily to Barlinnie Jimmy, 2.15, Doncaster. Carnival Queen, a double-carpet, a ridiculous bet for a grown man. Morte Della Musica was a rank outsider running its last ever race at Newbury.

They'd had to give Jack a black bag for the winnings. They'd had to call the manager of the bookie's in from home. The money Jack had put down that day had been five hundred pounds: a token of guilt and a sum that Seamus had hoped would keep Della sweet. The magic of long odds meant it had burgeoned and now it was Jack's and it hung heavy as the Sunday papers in a thin black bag from his clawed hand. Out on the street, upset by the sun, Jack headed for Casey's off Hackney Road, and when he finally got there, the gloom of the pub after the sun plunged him into his sort of reality. He ordered a pint and left the bag beside him on the floor, open. There was more Guinness, then a barley wine. Touching the bag with his boot, he looked at it sideways, daring it not to exist. This was Jack now on his own and Jack was taking care of his future.

'Another barley wine,' he creaked.

16

A week crawled over Eugene as he shuttled between the site and the Beacon. It kept him going to believe that there was a certain freedom you were allowed when you kept yourself to yourself. Today he woke early, as usual. First light was seeping in and Eugene felt the thick blood that fuels sleep thin out. His eyes were closed but in the clammy air around his face there were traces of last night: the steam let off by the drinkers, their dinners and their dancing. Slowly, Eugene's undefined feelings fixed on his centre and he thought of his fag, and his first solid thought of the morning was optimistic. I could get used to the End. Then he thought peripherally about his brother and Theresa, and allowed himself an impossible wish: that Vincent would come over here and defuse his overblown jealousies, leaving Theresa to some hee-haw who deserved her.

He had deserved her and that was the problem exactly. There'd been girls who had been far better looking than her, gentler girls whom Eugene could have had. Girls who might have opened him up a little, given him the time he needed to dare to be himself, but she had ruined him early on.

The first time he had gone to meet her, Eugene had walked to the pub as if he'd hung a wind chime in the cage of his ribs and didn't want anyone to hear it. He'd agreed to a drink with her but by the time he'd found the loud and garish pub she had chosen in Galway, called Reapy's, he was on the verge of panic. It had only been a week since he'd seen her but suddenly he felt he would collapse to the ground if she appeared. He went to the toilets to hide, asking himself urgent questions in the mirror. Swearing at himself. He was serious. Did he know that? He peered out into the bar and slid into a seat beside the toilets in case he needed its sanctuary. Then he saw her slim legs chop through the bar with lithe purpose, into the lounge. All his answers.

Over in the lounge he could just hear her voice among others and slid to the very end of the bar so that he could see through to the other side. She was sitting with a group and he felt instantly ridiculous. He almost laughed out loud but found himself immobile, examining his response in imbecilic wonderment – as if he had been shot in the belly and was staring at the blood on his hand. She hadn't meant a date alone, you fucking dolt, and he felt a grim satisfaction at how wrong he had been about the whole arrangement. He gave himself a series of bleak nods to show that, without a doubt, his feelings for her had been fixed.

His relationship with Theresa had taught him that resolve set in store for the future was useless; that the stuff of it could only be tested in the present. He told himself he was grateful to learn such a grand lesson. He had been naïve and had paid for it, and he filled hollow hours telling himself why he should be glad it hadn't worked out.

No one was more surprised than him when the following Sunday he found himself pressed against her, in the shade behind the presbytery, and had stopped shaking just enough to slip his palm down the front of the damp cotton of her pants. She halted the progression of his shaking hand by crossing her legs and he hoped for a moment that it was just the shaking she wanted to put an end to. At the same time, she pushed her tongue further into his mouth and soon enough they were beside the lough again, her chest sticking to his in the shade of the birches that were tilting away from them, slim and uninterested, great confidants that they were.

Back in the End, he screwed up his eyes, feeling keenly the need for someone to soak up the space he found around himself. He'd had a couple more drinks than he ought last night and sighed, because these fantasies, and the costs he incurred with each memory he allowed of her, left him drained and unwilling to move.

He had only washed his clothes once since he'd started work. The woman at the launderette had grabbed the trousers from him and opened them like the flag of a disgraced country. He hadn't been back since. Noble had already warned him that he'd get septicaemia from wearing the same scruffy kit day after day and delighted in drawing out sore and poisoned histories of other thick foreigners he'd worked with. Eugene did a good job of ignoring him.

The End had felt cold last night and he'd worn two tracksuits. Now he had to strip them off and, removing his trousers with his feet, he squandered the warmth from his leggings. He had been so eager to get shot of the sodden weight of his work trousers that he'd flung them, wet with mortar and cement, a stiff sandwich, into the corner. He groaned as he put them on, knowing that the wet clay clinging to his thighs was his own fault.

On the walk down the dark stairs at the back of the Beacon, he was grateful for the stickiness of the ancient linoleum under his socks. He fought with the back door from the second step, with his tobacco and his tea in his hand. He was happy at the prospect of the fag but anger stirred in his chest as he pushed the bony key in and out of a misshapen hole in the dark. The old lock seemed to be hanging in mid-air. The cold seeped under the door, and he tightened his grip on the mug until the tea spilled. He swore softly until finally, bloated with damp, the door smudged open in fits.

There was an early mist: a summer imposter. Happy again, he put down his tea and ran back up to the kitchen to get his book, excitement making him leap the stairs two and three at a time. This type of morning gave him a lunging in his stomach. He came back down and placed his tea on the uneven step. The mist encouraged the steam to billow in clouds. He took a sip and scanned the roughly concreted yard, strewn with the waste of a very public house; obsolete pumps and bottles of brands he didn't recognize. To his right, the damp had put a sheen on a pile of worn railway sleepers; oblong eels, he thought. Against the wall at the edge of the yard leaned an old-fashioned gilt-framed mirror, cracked three ways. Eugene walked up to it and examined the sludge on his boots in its ruined reflection, but his feet reminded him of his father's so he went back to the doorway and his tea.

He sat down and the stone-cold step felt as if it had been saving itself for him. He bent over, opening his tobacco pouch, digging around to distribute the moisture from a potato peeling. In his last few years, Seamus had labelled roll-ups 'a bad dose' but still coughed his way through a fair few of his own. The ground in front of Eugene was a mosaic of cigarette ends, and he felt sorry at the waste of some of the longer ones. Through its one bad washing, his woollen jumper rode up, spitefully recruiting other layers, so he pulled it down and settled his tobacco and papers on the unsteady tray of his knees, letting the anticipation of this first roll-up fill him evenly. Out of the many cigarettes in a day, the first suffered at the hands of opposing pressures: one that urged him to craft a flawless object, the second, the blunt shunt of want. Whatever the result, Eugene loved it like a pride-blind parent.

He sparked up the fag and thought of Theresa again when he clearly heard, 'I'm not your mother!' and a door slammed. Suddenly someone was bounding down the stairs behind him. Before he could stand, Julia had sidled past him into the yard and, hopping deftly between the ruins, was presently pulling the latch at the gate into the alley. A towel was tucked under her arm.

'Off swimming?' he found himself asking.

'Yup.' She seemed relieved that he had caught her before she'd escaped. 'You should try it.'

'I only go to baths where I can smoke.'

She looked at him over her shoulder and, with a tight smile, skipped out of his sight.

'Feck that. Swimming,' he said aloud.

He took the smile she had given him and preserved it for himself and could still feel where her leg had pressed against his shoulder as she had pushed by him.

He pulled at the roll-up and breathed in, and in his mind, the smoke lit up the corridors of what might be possible for the rest of the day, the week, the month.

17

A couple of men hailed him as *Galway!* when he walked
through the site gate, and Eugene tried to hide his delight,
reminding himself swiftly that he was there to work, not to
make love to these fuckers. As soon as he was changed, Buck
asked if he could help unload some scaffold and he was happy
to be involved in something different that was mindless and
difficult.

The subbies from Singh's had been waiting all morning
for concrete and they were milling, impatient for the pour to
begin and to finish off the underground car park. The
concreters were Sikhs to a man and, seeing his surprise last
week, Babe had explained to Eugene that many of them had
fled from the pogroms against Sikhs in India in the mid-
eighties. Eugene was entranced by them and the stories
reaching back behind them. He'd only ever seen a turban on
the television.

He watched the process, admiring their precision. The skip
held the concrete to be poured and the mix left it through a

hatch opened with a wheel. It was lifted around by the crane. Once the skip had let go of its load, the Singhs would poke it with a vibrating metal poker to get the air out of it, then use screed rails, rollers and floats for smoothing and compressing it. More often, Babe told Eugene, this firm used their own painted 6x2s to shift the stuff. These were wooden tamps, used to give the concrete a smooth surface. They painted them to seal them, in Sikhs' colours: purple and orange and pink. These old-fashioned tools were only used by skilled finishers, those who could really visualize how a tamp would move. Babe took pleasure in teaching, saying that the Singhs were high artists: they knew that several passes with the tamp, moving a little concrete each time, were better than one pass that moved a lot.

Ravi and his twin Jasdave now ran the concreting business that their father Randeep had started. Jasdave was austere and he ran the business with Ravi as his ears, because although Ravi had a stutter, he still spoke and understood English better than Jasdave. Most of the men who worked for O'Halloran's would mistake Ravi for Jasdave, ask him questions and then, realizing their mistake, turn to Jasdave to make up for it, even before the stammering had stopped. Within a couple of days of meeting the twins, Eugene knew them apart by sight. In the cabin, the blokes complained that Jasdave was 'hard work' but Eugene could see more to him.

Ravi was confident, even with his stutter, and his exuberance made it easier for him to connect with the blokes from O'Halloran's. They loved his impression of Noble even more when it was stippled with the stutter. Uri was fascinated by him, calling him 'the Indian who talks like his tongue moves heavy weights'. Like his brother, Ravi was almost two metres tall with a back like a billboard, and Eugene loved their house-side size.

On his break from the cube shed, Eugene had climbed on to the scaffold above the pour, listening to the jungle cries of the scaffolders mix with the curls of Punjabi from below. The scaffolders would throw a song down to the concreters and in turn the Sikhs would let go of songs that seemed to hold years of melancholy. The range of tones was new to Eugene and all the more enchanting because of that. Eugene watched, still fascinated by these men with their embroidered slippers, the tulips of their turbans floating across the grey concrete as they rolled the roughness out of the mix. The Sikhs were exempt from wearing hard-hats and this infuriated Noble. It made Eugene like them even more.

Eugene waved down to Ravi and Ravi waved back. He put up two fingers – Eugene had taught him this yesterday.

'I'm g-g-giving you the rods!' he shouted, delighted.

Eugene gave him two thumbs up, and smiled to let his pupil know he was doing well. In exchange for this lesson, Ravi had explained to Eugene about the meanings of Sikh names, which he described as something to live up to, not just to stick on. Eugene liked this idea and had wondered if 'Eugene Seamus Mahon' had anything to live up to.

Tuesday night was a late pour and Eugene stayed at work, avoiding the End. He found that they would sing forceful, stirring, military-sounding songs, fuelled with litres of clear spirit. He stayed mesmerized until they left and found his way home somehow changed by what he'd seen. He returned early in the morning to clear the empty vodka and gin bottles that were strewn over the shuttered concrete so that Noble didn't see them. They drank during the day too, but were more vigilant when Noble was around. When Eugene passed

Ravi he'd *pssst* and tuck a flat, curved quarter-bottle against his chest, then say, 'Eugene, Eugene, two f-f-f-fingers?' offering him the bottle, the measure to be drunk making up the distance between his little and index fingers: 'Singh's tot!' Eugene would decline, laughing.

The more he tried to keep himself in, the more these men dragged him out, and he could feel himself letting go, as if being tickled, giving himself up to joy and reluctance both.

18

Uri's voice grabbed Noble's attention because it was trying to be someone else's. Noble pulled himself around the back of the office Portakabin and, unseen, watched the men across the yard, this new little group, Eugene laughing in the middle of them, and he became incensed thinking of how Buck even talked about this mumbling fuck at home. How long had he been there? A couple of weeks was all, and how hard was it to take samples of concrete? You'd think he shat gold bars. Noble strained to hear what was so fucking funny to all of them.

'And you?' Uri was wagging his finger in Eugene's face. 'Are you ready for safety man's visit? No!' He put his hands on his hips and tipped his shoulders forward. 'Because you, mister, are a shower of shite!'

'Not just me!' Eugene laughed.

'No, no, more like this,' said Babe, and also hunched his shoulders but made a move of the chin that was unmistakable. A kind of searching with the jaw, an uncomfortable yawn with nowhere to go that came upon Buck when he was losing patience.

Noble looked at the Mahon fellow, laughing obligingly, and clenched his own jaw until his teeth hurt.

The door swung open. Buck filled the entrance of the office. He was red-faced and agitated.

'Uri, get over here. Babe, you too.' Noble began a satisfied smile as Babe set off at a trot, distancing himself from the other two. Eugene turned to walk the other way.

'Eugene.' Buck motioned for him to join them in the cabin.

Out of sight, Noble moved across the yard and watched greedily through the side window, but could only see Buck offering each of the men a seat with his open hand.

A moment later, Noble pushed his head inside the door and three pairs of eyes fixed on him. Buck was saying, 'So, you see the problem.' He stopped to stare hard at his son. Noble slowly backed out. With the door closed, Buck began again: 'He's ordered concrete for first thing.'

'Your son is still learning.' The relief that Buck hadn't caught their impression of him almost made Babe sing it.

'Learning, my arse. He forgot I was going away! One holiday a year I take.'

'So many pains in your balls.' Babe nodded.

'We'll have to adapt the scaffold on the Old Street façade. Tonight. Or there'll be nowhere for this concrete to go.'

Babe tutted. Eugene stared at him wide-eyed. He didn't know that this gesture could mean 'of course'. Babe had picked it up from a Neapolitan who'd worked at the docks with him in Durres before the war.

'You can't cancel it?' Eugene offered.

Buck was on the phone, his face creased in irritation.

Noble put his head back through the door. 'You get them yet?'

Eugene had never seen Noble tentative and was mad to know how Buck would treat him.

'No, and I'm not likely to on a Friday night, am I?' Buck squeezed his eyebrows. 'Eugene, you'll be on the street. Shouldn't be many about. You do that?'

'Not a bother.'

Noble tried again. 'Shall I call the scaffolders in for the morning?'

'Too late. What am I going to do with ten fucking loads?'

'Sixty cubes, you said!' Noble's sheepishness flipped into aggression.

'But not before we get rid of this fucking scaffold! I'm away first thing!'

'Don't have a stroke! I can sort it out.'

Buck was red up the neck now and turned away from his son to the other men. 'Babe, Uri, you'll have to help Horace but get it down. Safely, OK? I'll try to get a few of the other scaffolders, see if they can't come in tonight. Babe, do the list.' Buck was punching in the phone number for the concrete yard again. Everyone was silent.

'Go round there. To the yard,' Noble suggested matter-of-factly.

Buck began breathing heavily now and stared at his son as if he'd just dropped through the ceiling.

'To the concrete yard. Have a word in person.'

Buck looked away from him in disbelief. To the rest of them, he said, 'Away you go. And tell Horace to take his time, yes?'

'I'll make sure of that,' Noble added, but no one heard as Buck barked, 'Answer the fucking phone!'

'Get Red Bulls – a scaffolder loves Red Bulls,' said Uri, wisely, 'and pasties. Write it.'

'I'm writing it.'

'What's that?' Eugene looked over Babe's shoulder at a list.

'If we work at night, you order, Buck pays.'

'Grand.' Eugene rubbed his hands together and looked up at the massive spidering scaffold from the site, his eyes adjusting to take in the darkening background, and he wondered how they'd get that lot down before morning. Dusk had spread over it, like a tarp, so that trapped within the stark angles was the promise of an adventure. The day workers were traipsing from the site, and even in the wake of Buck's anger, Eugene felt a buzz of excitement as he watched the men preparing to strike parts of the scaffold, hauling themselves into position. In between the ringing of boots on metal, he heard the rosy tones of a ditty rising into the dusk – 'She's a big lass, she's a bonny lass and she likes her beer . . .'

On the street Eugene had to stop himself smiling as he directed a couple of women out and away from the hoarding and out of reach of the scaffold they were taking down. When the passers-by thinned out and there was no one in sight, he clambered up the scaffold to smoke. As he sat himself down he heard someone ribbing Uri and looked up to see a middle-aged black man, with a couple of grey flashes escaping the hard-hat sitting high on his hair.

Uri was biting: 'You have seen what a pole does to your hand in minus forty?'

'They no have gloves in Russia?'

'Horace, you are one big English gay!'

'I come from Kingston.'

'So why always Yorkshire, rugby, Yorkshire?'

'All right, then, Rocky. You ever lay a toe board out a window at four hundred and fifty feet?'

Horace wrestled with a mess of couplers while Uri told Eugene, 'Post Office Tower? For Horace is Sistine Chapel.' Eugene started a smirk but looked for reassurance to the man working above them.

'Every clip strapped to you. You know how long that takes? The weight of it?'

Uri mouthed, 'Wow!' at Eugene.

'You never seen a right angle till you come here. Admit it.'

'On the gas pipe in Siberia you would not survive. There, I work with men. Supermen. Vikings. Not monkeys with no teeth. You know, Eugene? Horace is so old, he put the scaffold on Big Bob.'

'Big Ben, you imbecile!' Horace finally looked at Eugene and they both laughed.

'That is what I said,' Uri argued.

'And, Uri, Iman is younger than you, me lion.'

Eugene felt warmed by the friction; he leaned in now, enjoying the crackling between them.

Buck had gone to the concrete yard in the vain hope he might catch someone who was willing to cancel ten loads of concrete on the morning he was supposed to be flying to Ireland. By the time he left the site, he had stopped answering Noble's questions. In his absence, Noble appeared, shouting from the ground, 'How much you done?'

No one answered. Instead, Horace shouted up to another black man, working above him, 'Douglas, chuck Eugene a spanner.'

He threw the podger down to him, and Eugene was surprised at the weight when he caught it.

'Look after that, pickney. It commemorate me SOBO award.'

Eugene squinted up at him, then to Horace. 'Scaffolder of black horigin.' He winked.

'Anybody'd think you loved work, Douglas,' Horace shouted. 'This here is a man who had six months off for slipping on a fish-cake.'

'Hush your beak. It was me ligaments.'

'Six months?' Eugene whistled.

'See?' Horace nodded. 'Eugene like me. Come to work even if he had his leg off.'

Noble had moved up a floor. 'Who's looking after the street?' but now Horace was asking Eugene, 'You like girls den, Eugene?'

'I do,' he said, his face scarlet.

'This place round here? It swarm wi' pussy,' Horace sing-songed. 'And what did Buddha say to a bit of batty action?'

'Oy!' Noble had moved closer and now his face was red from the climb. 'Less of this,' he shouted, letting his hand yap. The talking stopped at last. A standard crashed some-where above them. There was a clatter of 'fuck's, and Noble belted out, 'Take a bit more fucking care with them, will you?'

Horace leaned out dangerously above him. 'Why you makin' a fuss?'

'You'll fucking brain someone, you moron.'

A few of the men sucked in their breath audibly.

'If you the expert, why you not helpin' us?'

'Buck wants this down tonight.'

'Because of your foolishness.'

90

'Don't act hard, Horace, it doesn't suit you.'

Horace stared at the scar on Noble's lip and, for an instant, he looked as if he was going to throw something down at him. Noble flinched, then motioned for him to go to the other side of the scaffold where there were fewer men. Horace went over and peered down at him. 'Tell you what, sunshine . . .'

'What?'

Horace jumped down on to the site and landed so close to Noble that he knocked him over. While Noble was still on his back, Horace got up and thrust the ratchet into his hand, '. . . do it your ownself,' and, without using his hands, Horace lurched his head forward, leaving his hard-hat hanging in the air before it crashed to the ground beside Noble's head.

With Horace already a few slow steps away, Noble jumped up and whooping spread like flame up the scaffold. Noble looked down at the hard-hat and kicked it as hard as he could. It spun towards the gates.

'You'd better get back here now, Horace, or I'm calling Buck.'

But Horace didn't turn: he just walked straight out of the gates. The men had stopped working and Noble tried to say something else, but the scaffolders smacked their tools on the poles and the clanging drowned his voice. With Horace gone, other men started to swing down the scaffold and, descending slickly, they slunk like solder off the poles. Then they clumped in twos and threes until they were out of the gates. Only a few stayed, heads down, working steadily on the scaffold. One was Jack, trying to undo a clip. Eugene was all nerves now and jumped up instinctively to help him but when he saw Jack's hands he wished he hadn't.

Babe appeared, a box under one arm and bags of provisions, nosing through the men, looking uneasy, asking, 'What is this ass-tit doing now?'

19

For Della, the bar of the Beacon had been a theatre of sorts. Looking at the faces in the the snug after closing time, she was reminded that many little tragedies had unfolded there and, to keep them all in mind, she had to make her representation of the pub smaller, more manageable, puppet-sized. She thought it best to keep Jack at the back: that way the audience couldn't see his fraying strings or his joints not working smoothly. Jack had tried to keep hold of Seamus; their strings had been a quiet mess for a moment or two, but it was the final pull that had left Jack's limbs loose.

The way that Seamus had jerked out of her life meant that Della's strings had reached snapping point. For a good while after that, she had been just a jumble of limbs and snaggled-up strings, parts. No more. But then Julia had come along with short strings that she couldn't work for herself so Della had had to pull herself together, stretched and useless at first, then with a few knots and a heartbreaking tightening, until – ta-da! – there she was, in front of the bar again, all strings a-working. Only now more controlled than before. No more room for love-slack, and there she remained, her strings straining, polishing the glasses.

She put a glass up on the shelf and thought that this old bar was a dreary backdrop for a puppet theatre. The dun and caramel of the walls had slowly absorbed all colour from the characters who had played parts in this little world. The bar lights above Della's head gave off a weak yellow fume as if they were not really trying, barely creating enough shadow for the landlady's eye to distinguish between faces dusted with work dirt and those finished with the deeper tan of homelessness.

Della, in her own bar, was sensitive to tiny shifts in the air. Anyone could catch the clumsy gusts of threat and flattery that regularly swept through it, but it took Della to pick up the wind change from distaste to disgust. She sensed the vibrations of a fight coming before the argument even began, could almost trace the quiver to a paranoid thought, the rumour of a cheating wife or a lost bet. Fine tunes.

She'd take in snatches from conversations as she scalloped around the bar, collecting glasses. She'd scoop around groups and couples, right at their backs, giving them no room to hide as she picked up code that meant nothing to amateur listeners. From these parts of patterns Della recognized the whole, so that from a 'Don't be daft!' she knew who'd lied, who wished they hadn't and who never could. In her own bar, Della would know what was going on with the lights off, in the pitch black.

They must have been working late. It was after midnight. Jack had slipped into the back, swayed and sat down heavily. Eugene followed and just sat up at the bar; the only movement after that was the black pint slowly sailing up to his lips. Otherwise, he was sitting extraordinarily still, extraordinarily quiet and it was this lack of action that was scrambling Della's signals. His inertia gave off a high keening, like a dog-whistle, she imagined; something she couldn't shut her ears to. She stole a look at his hands: his Seamus gloves were still greasy from his dinner, and Della couldn't ignore them. His modesty was somehow massive, she thought, all-pervasive, unsettling. Like Seamus, he radiated the power of restraint. If you didn't know the type, thought Della, you'd think Eugene was mute. But Della knew the type exactly.

Rhodri was sitting to Eugene's right in the centre of the bar and was already having to hold on tight. Della could see that someone like him could vibrate right out of this scene. This she loved. Rhodri was leaning back in the low cup of his bar stool, his hands behind his head but Della knew that, seconds ago, he had nearly fallen backwards. She poured Eugene another pint, prepared herself. 'Eugene, have you met Rhodri?'

The introduction was an uncomfortable disturbance. It was too late in the day to be introduced to anyone and Eugene's ears still rang from the scaffold.

'He's Julia's friend. What do you call yourself these days?' Della said this loudly.

'I'm a writer.' Without looking at Eugene, he said, 'We've already met, upstairs.'

Della looked at Eugene for his response.

Eugene nodded. 'A writer? That's grand.' Della shot him a look, so he said hurriedly, 'What have you written?'

'Erm.' Rhodri smirked, as if to let everyone know he was going to have to bring this down a notch or two. 'Well, I have a book of . . . let's call them arguments and—'

'And that's what he does for a living,' said Della.

'Very good,' said Eugene, and looked down at the bar.

Rhodri was changing gear. 'Now, the research is a different matter.'

'I think it's been done to death,' Julia cracked.

Eugene jumped. He hadn't known she was there.

'It's precisely that it is so well mined that I chose Wittgenstein. It remains a difficult seam to chip away at but there are still jewels in there. I work Saturdays.'

Eugene nodded and didn't say that he didn't think that was the right way to put it, that this notion of ideas being hard to mine was the wrong shape, mineable was the wrong way of looking at it, that Rhodri would never get anywhere chipping and picking. Eugene didn't let them know that he thought ideas were better thought of as more like mud, things to sink into, take your time over, surround yourself with. They shaped you, you shaped them. Try Saturdays and Sundays.

'And he's a teacher on the side,' continued Della, to Eugene.

'A teacher!' mimicked Jack, and started coughing explosively. Jack had surprised himself by shouting without warning. Everyone except Eugene ignored him, but Jack couldn't ignore this: he'd done it again. He had started shouting out, repeating others, like a fucking wean, he thought. He put his hand to his mouth to keep the babby inside.

Reluctantly, Eugene looked at Jack and stoked himself: he needed to be stronger, not sitting crying in a grimy kitchen over his dinner. He could see that Jack could pull him under, weaken him, so he must not make this a habit, sitting round this bar with these characters. He ordered another pint, this time from Julia, while Rhodri carried on.

'The teaching gets in the way of the research. I wish I could give it up but they keep on requesting me.'

'Come off it,' Julia said smartly. 'Students requesting you? Don't forget, I used to be one of them.'

'And when's this book going to be finished?' Della addressed everyone equally, gathering them in towards the question.

Rhodri leaned back in the cradle of the bar stool placing his foot on the opposite knee. 'Ah, slowly, slowly, Della. *A posse ad esse, a posse ad esse . . .*'

'Latin?' Julia snapped. 'Remember? If you simplify your English, you're freed from the worst follies of orthodoxy.'

She carried on stacking glasses.

Rhodri was leaning with his hands grasping the bar. His knuckles were quite white. He looked at Julia. 'You? Quoting Orwell to me?'

There had been poison in Rhodri's voice as he addressed Julia, and Eugene found himself very interested in it. 'From possibility to actuality,' he said quietly.

The words had come out purely under the pressure of coincidence. They were the words on Uri's sternum, and today, by way of a breaktime lesson, Babe had translated them. Eugene was surprised at the coincidence and sat picturing what was Uri's oldest tattoo, a bad version of his own mother's face and a Bolshevik symbol.

Eugene was instantly sorry he'd said anything and yet he found that he was fixed on Julia. He wanted to decipher her reaction to this uncommon opening he'd made for himself but had an overwhelming fear that he was setting out a stall that he couldn't really stand by. He took a large swig of his Guinness, the kind of swallow you saved for water.

Julia looked away from him, trying to spread the huge impression he had just made on her between numerous small tasks at the bar.

Turning to look at Eugene, Della followed his stare to her daughter and, for an elevated instant, allowed her glances to stitch Julia and Eugene together until, very suddenly, she spun sideways, placing herself broadly between them.

'Clever lad like you must have someone back home.' Della's voice was quick now.

'Yes,' Eugene said, but he looked down at the bar as if he didn't want to betray any more of himself.

'She waiting for you, is she?' Look at me – the thought pushed out with her breath.

'Hope so,' he said, but it was too slick, too cheerful.

Della wound up inside, her mettle tight. Oh, no, sunshine. And she pushed out this silent promise to bind around Eugene. *Not her, not now, not ever.*

20

Noble finally got the wagon driver on his mobile. It was just past eight but the load had already left the yard. 'Harry, can you hold off for an hour or two? We're still shifting tubes from this scaffold.'

'I'm in Peckham now.'

'I'm sure you'll find something to do.'

'The other wagon's not far behind me. You'd better ring the yard. What about this mix?'

'If I haven't rung back in an hour, let some water into it.'

'Your funeral.'

His phone beeped, call waiting, Buck. He must have landed.

More than an hour later, Harry fastened his trousers and pulled sharply at his belt. 'I've got to get this mix over to East London.' Outside, his concrete wagon was still turning, churning out time in slow circles, and he knew the mix would be suffering in the heat.

'Great,' she said to the wall, holding smoke down until after the word had come out.

He was very suddenly glad he wasn't married to this woman and had an urge to tell her so, but he wasn't stupid: he knew he'd be back when his memory had sweetened what had just happened between them. From the window above the optician's he saw the brown patches that made up Camberwell Green in the summer. The light was somehow too much, and from this gloomy bedsit the outside world looked far away, out of reach. Inevitability had dulled everything; it hung over them in the room and Harry would be very glad to get out.

Outside, he jumped up into the cab of the wagon, opened the valve and let five minutes' worth of water pour into the mixer before he set off for the site, just east of Old Street.

A few more scaffolders had turned up at Noble's promise of double-time and the scaffold was almost clear so they would start pouring concrete over the far side of the site and eventually work towards the façade. Floors were going in today. Horace had been persuaded by Babe to come in and finish the job they had started last night. The Singhs were arriving and Noble was bragging to anyone who would listen that only he could find skins at such short notice. He'd called the agency this morning and they'd immediately sent two Polish blokes. One was wearing carpet slippers and Noble was shouting something into his face as Eugene looked out of the shed.

When the wagon finally arrived, Harry jumped down from the cab and Eugene was ready to take a sample from the stream of concrete and assess the mix from the way it slumped in the cone. He walked over to Harry, but Noble was there before him and thrust the ticket from Harry's hand at Eugene while pulling the concrete tamping rod from Eugene's other hand. Eugene just watched as Noble drew back comically from Harry and tapped his watch. 'You already been chucking a mix out, you sly old bastard?'

They laughed complicitly. Without looking at Eugene, Noble said, 'I'm doing the slump test today.'

Eugene shrugged and returned to the shed. Watching the test from the crack in the door, he became irritated that Noble wasn't tamping the sample properly. The concrete looked wet. He checked the paperwork in his hand and saw what Noble had signed for. This was lightweight stuff, not structural strength. He moved into the doorway.

'Noble . . .'

'I told you to fuck off. Get up the scaffold and play monkeys with your nigger mates.'

'It's not the right stuff.'

Noble dropped the cone and took a step towards Eugene. 'This concrete's going in, mate. The lot. Today. Don't make me tell you to fuck off again.'

Harry backed the empty wagon out of the yard and the Singhs were getting ready to poke the concrete under Noble's unwanted supervision. Eugene was anxious and wondered who he should tell. It was roasting now. Another wagon pulled up beside the shed.

Eugene took off his shirt and his pale body reflected the sun's glare. An old labourer swept by with a hard brush that had all but worn away. He must be about seventy, thought Eugene. Buck allowed the old ones to stay on if they were desperate not to leave, even though it bumped up his site premium. The man scraped by, looking at Eugene's hairless body with rheumy eyes behind safety glasses. 'Don't you burn, lad, you hear? You'd be on a court martial in my day if you got sunburn. Self-inflicted wound, see?'

Eugene nodded appreciatively, but promised himself that, no matter what, he would not be leaning on a fucking broom in his dotage. He smiled, trying to make the old-timer feel like he'd imparted something important.

Eugene went round to the front of the façade and found Horace with a book in his hand, his shirt off, sitting in the sun. In his mid-forties, Horace maintained the body of a teenager, fiercely muscled. Quick in his work and slow in his leisure, neither way seemed false. His smile said that he had ample spare time for odd little Eugene and his awkward ways.

Beside Horace, a scaffolder whose every second word was 'Boro was explaining 'monkey-hangers' to Uri. Horace was sitting cross-legged beside them eating dark green callaloo bread that he'd made himself. His thumb was between the pages of the slim book. Eugene read the title, *The Waste Land*, and wondered if it was depressing.

'How're you doin', Horace?'

Horace put the book down and started rolling a spliff with one hand. His palm looked tough, grey and powdery. Eugene knew from working the bigger sites in Galway that scaffolders' hands would be skinned in winter because the poles froze and claimed their palms when they unloaded on dark mornings. With frost came plenty of swearing and random high-pitched screams as five-footers were swiftly passed up a façade and, later, whistled lethally down through cold air. It took a special person to be a scaffolder.

'Ah, lickle Eugene, sit down, sit down.' He patted the battens beside him. Eugene was torn as to what to do. He looked through the façade window on to the pour. Ravi was getting the pokers out to vibrate the air out of the concrete and the next wagon was already on site. Noble was there watching his every move when he should be taking cubes for testing. The Poles were standing beside him. Eugene turned back to the men on the scaffold, pretending to himself he didn't care.

'You always reading, Horace?'

'Reading is everyt'ing and everyt'ing, me Gene Genie. It help stop up the loneliness.' Horace read poetry like other men read the papers. He explained to Eugene that he had gained an English degree in Wakefield prison, and inside he had been able to keep his hard wiry frame. Nobody mentioned murder, but to Eugene, fourteen years seemed a long time for someone who, as far as Eugene could see, was a gentle, open man. When Horace spoke, it was hard for anyone but veterans to keep up with him. His conversations and recitations formed webs of ideas that, for those listening, weren't always related but made great sounds. Eugene listened carefully, and with Horace it was worth it for the shape of the words, the unashamed rhythms and the occasional truths that were dragged out with them.

'Listen.' Horace put down the book and sucked in the weed smoke. '"April is the cruellest month."' He closed his eyes and let out more smoke than he seemed to have taken in. He offered it to Eugene. Being this high up with new friends, the beating sun and the worry about the concrete cajoled him into taking a drag.

'If workers were months, then scaffolders, they would be April. The cruellest. Eh, Uri?' He looked over at the men working through their dinner hour. 'Hod carriers?' He continued as if he'd been asked the question. 'Now, they would be February, 'arsh and unrelentin', and stubborn 'cos them beasts of burden.'

He sucked the joint again. 'Money men, quantity surveyors? June, nothin' but possibilities, blue-sky bwoys, seen?'

Eugene passed the spliff to Uri and lay back, the battens warming him. He was still listening, letting Horace's world work its way around him so that, one day, he might find a way in. He wanted to file some of Horace's sentences and pull them out for a woman some day. Some day when he was older and braver. Some day when there was a woman.

Horace's words beat on with the sun and, with his eyes closed, Eugene didn't realize he was smiling. Horace carried on about work being freedom and about freedom being hard work and finally argued with Uri a little about what it felt like to lose it. He called for silence.

'*Ciúnas!*' called Eugene, trying to help to quieten them, his eyes still closed.

> '"Good-bye now to the streets and the clash of wheels and locking hubs,
>> The sun coming on the brass buckles and harness knobs.
>> The muscles of the horses sliding under their heavy haunches,
>> Good-by now to the traffic policeman and his whistle,
>> The smash of the iron hoof on the stones . . ."

'And this me favourite part:

> '"All the crazy wonderful slamming roar of the street –
> O God, there's noises I'm going to be hungry for."'

They applauded, stamped the boards. Horace, still seated, gave a small bow from his middle.

The weed was strong, but Eugene didn't want to think about it too much, didn't want to feel like he was falling off the world. It was pushing itself upon him but he tried not to consider the physics of a ball spinning, hanging by nothing in the blue, and he laid out his palms to feel whatever was underneath them. There they were, the toe boards: he could relax. Eugene let his worries be taken up by the blue above him and squinted at them from a distance. They seemed so small just now, and all because he felt that these men liked him and, with a joint, had invited him in and made him feel hooked on. He knew that there were thousands of other people around, soaking in the rare city sun, unable to hear any more the perpetual circulation of the traffic. Up on the thermals of his happiness, Eugene thought he might ask one of the lads if he fancied a drink after work, Ravi maybe, and his mind fired up again, floating further out into the general sweetness of the day, becoming part of it.

A few minutes later, the man from Middlesbrough called out to them, 'Watch this! Listen!' He leaned with his hands on the cross brace and looked down. 'Hey, Noble, man!' he cried.

Noble looked up and shielded his eyes.

'Can't wait to get w'or lass's knickers off tonight!'

There was a pause as Horace and Eugene stifled their laughter.

'They're killing me!'

Without understanding the words, foreign workers joined in the laughter; the fun of it was in the man's red face, his tug at the waistband and, most of all, at Noble way down below, miles away from them.

*

Down on the ground, Noble squinted up. He should have known. They think they're such clever cunts, he thought. Go on, laugh while you can, lads. No more than monkeys; monkeys in charge of box-head spanners and five-stone standards. The most dangerous job with the thickest workers. 'What an excellent fucking combo,' he said to himself, his scarred lip curling. Scaffolders were the scum of the earth. They worshipped speed, not accuracy. Without danger this breed couldn't work. They thrived on the whistle of a five-footer as it was launched from a couple of storeys above, and everyone had to suffer the ear-splitting clangs of ratchets and podgers on steel and aluminium that would last through the journey home, through dinner and into bed. Horace got on his tits more than any of them with his answers for everything that no fucker could understand. When the men had presented Horace with a new ratchet for his fortieth birthday – Babe and Uri had had it engraved with 'Simply The Best' – Noble could've puked. He remembered wondering if Horace knew how much he looked like Tina fucking Turner now he was getting on—

Noble's concentration was broken by a clip that bombed to the ground, missing him by inches. It lay a couple of feet away, half a kilo of dead metal, just landed, the threat still in it. He looked up and shouted, 'Whoever threw that is off this job!'

'Whatever you say, me lion,' Horace called sweetly from above.

Eugene lay on the boards, laughing, but when the laughter subsided, thoughts of Buck crept in and what he would do when he got back to find all this. He picked his way down the scaffold at the front of the site until he got to the first floor window closest to the pour. He peered down and saw that Noble wasn't there, just the concreters.

'Ravi! Oy, Ravi!'

Ravi turned and saw Eugene giving him a thumbs-up and a smile. Eugene shook his head and pointed down at the concrete, mouthing, 'It's wrong!' His eyes darted to the cabin where one of the Polish lads had just emerged. Ravi cupped his ear. 'Leave it!' Eugene gave him two exaggerated thumbs down. Ravi dropped his tamp, looking disappointed.

Eugene's frustration wound itself around his creeping paranoia. He jumped down the last level of scaffold to the floor and leaned though the ground-floor-window aperture. Ravi came closer, wiping his hands on his trousers.

'The concrete's wrong. Go and look at the ticket.'

Ravi walked off quickly, already calling to Noble. Eugene watched for a moment, then made himself scarce: being stoned and telling this tale were making him feel naked.

Noble was screwing up his eyes, his phone again to his ear. 'Yes, it's here. Go fucking fishing, will you?' He had to walk under the scaffolders again and could hear 'Simply The Best' booming out from two storeys up. An old black woman's song. 'Hope you're proud of yourself,' he mumbled and then, audibly, 'It's like a fucking zoo in 'ere.' Ravi had stopped work and was quickly coming towards him.

Ravi had the ticket from the concrete yard. Before Ravi spoke, Noble had a hand on his chest. 'What's going on here?'

Ravi's stutter became chaotic under threat. 'Why are you w-wasting my men's time?'

'R-R-R-Ravi! Calm the fuck down – you sound like a fucking nail gun!'

'This is wrong-grade concrete.'

'It will get to strength.'

Ravi removed Noble's hand from his chest and made to move past him. Noble struck him in the sternum with his other palm. 'Who told you to down tools?'

'I am not your puppet,' Ravi said slowly, and he gripped Noble's wrist and stared at the Poles dumbly flanking the other man.

A fight kindled.

A few seconds more and it was raging.

21

The Singhs had left the site as one, Ravi with a bloody nose threatening action against Noble. If Jasdave had not held his brother back, Noble would have been finished. The tamps were left unmanned beside the forms containing the concrete; the floats were quiet futuristic relics.

Men crowded now at the apertures of the façade. Eugene was back up there, shaking and feeling sick.

'You'd have told him, wouldn't you?' he was asking each of them, but no one reassured him quickly enough and his paranoia became suffocating. Noble was panicking, screaming orders at the Polish blokes, physically dragging them when words did nothing to shift them, eventually making one of them stumble over the form and put his foot into the concrete.

'Somebody lend this cunt some boots,' Noble screamed to no one and everyone. A tab end was flipped down on to the site from the façade. Noble stooped to pick it out of the concrete without looking up.

The afternoon heat made the site blister, and Noble and the Poles continued to try to cure load after load of concrete with gallons of water. The last wagon had emptied and, from the scaffold, the men watched Noble sweat and screech into his phone, noisily trying to find help from other concrete finishing firms. Uri followed the others to the cabin at breaktime, saw the sweat staining Noble's pristine cap and heard him say, 'Fuck them bastard Singhs.'

Uri went into the cabin and beckoned Eugene and Babe. They followed him off site and into the Harlequin. As they walked in, one of the strippers put down her *Sun* and, in a thin ivory-coloured wrap, stood looking cheerful behind the pumps at the bar. Eugene felt bad asking her for a drink. He sat down at the little table where the others had gathered.

'Buck will be ballistic,' Uri began.

Eugene had been waiting for just this damning opinion and blurted, 'I should have stopped him in the first place.'

'Always better to leave Noble. Unexploded bomb. Don't worry,' tutted Babe, beetling his brow at Uri.

'You did not sign off concrete that came out like piss,' Uri reminded him.

'Look,' said Babe, 'when Buck is away, Noble is signatory. He is in charge and the puck stops with him. Yes?'

Eugene smiled, despite his new worries, but quickly became grave again. The weed was still with him, giving him flashes of uncertainty when he least needed them.

'He is now showing the Poles around the shed,' Uri said.

'It is just routine,' said Babe, making a face at him. 'But that's my job.'

'Listen. Even if the concrete must come up, there is insurance, *inshallah*. Buck has insurance.'

'You sure?'

'Yes, leave it to me. Don't say a word. When Noble knows you have worries, he poke you like a soft plum.' Babe jabbed a wooden finger from his brown hand into Eugene's belly.

When they returned, Noble and the Poles were still trying to finish the concrete between them. The Pole with the slippers had swapped them for two left wellies that had been in the toilets for weeks. When Noble came in from the pour, saturated, Babe started to question him immediately. Noble spat, 'Of course there'll be insurance! One thing you space monkeys just don't get is that, in England, we do things properly. No fucking wooden scaffold, no dogs in orbit. You get me?'

'OK, OK . . .'

'Anyway, *vashtuk*, you need to start earning some proper corn for me,' Noble snapped, mopping his face with his T-shirt.

Babe scowled: *vashtuk* meant 'vagrant'. He doubted that Noble knew what it meant and he silently wished that his children should shit in Noble's soup, may Allah forgive him.

'Never mind fucking insurance. You need to sell more. We're falling behind. Now is the perfect time.' Noble rubbed the caustic concrete off his gloves. 'Advertise! Do the rounds while Buck's away. Make hay! You know what that means?'

'Of course I do,' sniffed Babe.

22

The evening did not bring any respite from the day's heat and Eugene sat in regret of his afternoon's activities. He hunched on the step in the yard at the Beacon, pulling his biceps round to pick at something gritty he could feel but could not see on the back of his arm. When he squinted up, she was there before him, strongly outlined, and he felt like an animal caught grooming.

'You fancy a swim?'

Her suggestion was so absurd that he was encouraged and offended equally. 'Too hot for swimming, surely,' he said, smirking.

With a small shrug she turned and made her way through the yard to the gate.

'Wait!' he shouted, shocked at the urgent tone in his voice. 'Why not?' he offered more gently, thinking as he turned to get his kit from his room, *I am one sad eejit*. The last time he had been swimming was at the lough where he had pretended to Theresa that he was proficient at front crawl and, with ill-timed breaths and maximum effort, he had demonstrated just how excellent he was at nearly dying.

He mounted the stairs three at a time, already warning himself to calm the fuck down. In the End, he scrabbled in the drawer with the loose bottom for the silkiness of Vincent's white Tuam Stars shorts. He'd brought them in case he could ever get a game of something. He hadn't told his brother he was taking them and now he scoffed aloud at the prospects he had imagined were his when he'd packed his bag a few weeks ago in Salthill. The shorts weren't in the drawer, so he fished in the part of his bag that had been left packed, his thoughts turning to a bikini, a belly and, in his reverie, he knocked over an almost-empty can he had been using as an ashtray. With an almighty 'Fuck,' he hoped she wouldn't hear he used a sock to mop up the amber poison that flowed out. He finally found the shorts under the bed and examined them, hoping to God he hadn't worn them as pants. In his excitement and enthusiasm he was sure they weren't too small in the waist especially if he pulled them down under his prominent hips. His jeans back over the nylon shorts, he chose a T-shirt also from the bag, left there because, even if you'd never met him before, you'd see that a T-shirt like that really wasn't him. Well, neither was swimming, he said to himself, and in for a penny . . . He pulled the T-shirt on and tried to stretch the cap sleeves down a bit. After a struggle, he decided to push them up and over his shoulder bones. The shorts were tight and the constraining mesh bag inside them didn't feel as comfortable as it should if the yokes fitted a fella but he was ready at last and he would do for now. A quick scan over his one towel and he was away.

As they left the yard together, she said, 'I can smell beer.'

'Aye, well, you live in a pub.'

'No, old beer. And fags.'

'I just upended a can on myself.'

'Beautiful.'

To distract her he found himself asking, 'So how's Rod?' He hoped he wasn't showing too much interest in her private life.

'Fine, if you like that kind of thing.'

Her eyebrows were up: it gave him confidence.

'That kind of thing?' he ventured. God almighty, he may as well put out his tongue and pant.

'I'm just kidding,' she said, blushing.

He was positive that it was the hope in his voice that made her reel this back in, and his heart lurched until she turned with a complicit smile, some truth blossoming behind the words making them irrelevant.

His shorts under his trousers meant that he was changed in about forty seconds and waited a good ten minutes for her beside the pool. She turned up with her hair stuffed into a lump at the back of the rubber cap and it made him instantly petulant – as if she had welched on a deal. His mind had made a mermaid of her and this didn't fit, but the costume she wore was sleek enough to see through and her hard belly already gleamed from showering. Standing at the edge of the pool in the shallow end, he wetted his hand and ran it through his hair, over his face. He leaned back and suddenly felt a hell of a lot of freedom in the shorts that had been strangling him a few moments ago. Wetting them had made them billow, and as she dived in at the deep end, he fingered the limits of what now felt like a little skirt to make sure he was still in them.

Even with her beautiful hair in the cap, the goggles, the sideways swipe and the mouth gulping for air that punctuated her stroke, he was stirred by her and had to put his hand down surreptitiously to make doubly sure his cock was not floating free of the ridiculous shorts. The mesh inside them seemed to have dissolved on contact with the water. He realized that it was obvious he was waiting for her to stop to speak to him, and as it became plainer that she was not likely to, he felt that setting off to swim became less and less of an option. When she did stop to speak after ten more minutes, he was once again fighting with the shorts, pulling up and plastering down the various frills and panels.

'What you up to?' She was breathing hard.

In shock at her greeting, he said, 'Nice and warm now, eh?' He sounded like the worst kind of pervert.

She smiled nevertheless, rinsed her goggles and said, 'Come on, then, or are you too hot to swim?' She set off again at speed and he was left laughing at no one. He tried to set off like a man who'd decided to of his own accord and found to his dismay that although he was using a stroke he felt he could maintain with some dignity she had doubled back on him again in his first half-length. His breaststroke was wooden and clumsy, his shoulder clicked at every stroke and he wondered if his arms extended the way other people's did. But he felt that at least now he was moving and he wasn't such a dolt and he hadn't lost everything. He was still a contender. And much louder than was warranted by the space between them, the lifeguard blew his whistle and motioned for him to hop over the rope into the slow lane. Nodding his understanding to the man, he was worried that he wouldn't get up and over the rope that separated the lanes without her seeing and without showing the lifeguard or anyone else his balls. Gracelessly, he mounted the rope, riding it momentarily like a skinny steer, but in bringing a leg over, his foot caught and he almost drowned. Recovering, he had no idea if she had seen him – but she was there beside him almost immediately saying, 'Can't stand the heat eh?'

He laughed, a theatrical aha! that sounded as if he'd discovered something (his hand was down there again, ferreting for the horror of unfettered parts) but she was away soon enough, leaving him to bend close to the water to examine what an onlooker might be able to see if indeed they wanted to know what was so interesting down there.

He was smoking when she came out afterwards and she smelt to Eugene like a dessert, something autumnish. She was wearing a dark brown vest and he thought he wouldn't mind leaning in to discover whether the apple-pie smell was coming from under it, but he didn't. He suddenly felt that she was staring at the sleeves of his T-shirt.

'Fancy some food?'

'Sounds good.'

His voice wasn't his own: he seemed unable to shake the guise of pervert he'd taken on. Without the shorts under his jeans he felt too free and uncomfortable. In his haste he hadn't packed underwear.

She took him via Old Street to a cheap Vietnamese on Kingsland Road where she ordered for both of them and Eugene tasted things he would never have ordered. Prawns and noodles and delicious hot pancakes. Emboldened by the novelty and pleased at his bravery, Eugene told her about Horace and *The Waste Land* and what Buddha seemed to mean to him. About Ravi and the size of his shoulders. The cards they played. After a couple of beers he was in the swing and stretched out his legs under her side of the table, but just as he was comfortable, he saw that she was looking at her phone, packing her bag. 'I'm off to town now to meet some friends. Will you pay? I'm late.' She handed him the money. He passed it back to her without saying anything. She left it anyway but was already speaking animatedly into her phone. She pushed away her chair, gave a small wave and left the restaurant.

Maybe he was still a bit stoned because he felt sick and dizzy. What came to him was his mother and Gloria crying over a boy on the telly who had Tourette's syndrome, forever spitting at the cake on the table, calling all and sundry from a pig to a dog. Even the priest. That was what he felt like, that boy, as if he couldn't stop exposing himself no matter what pain came as a consequence. Alone among the people of the restaurant, he examined his new affections and realized that the track he was cutting was not new. He was pushing Julia into ruts cut by Theresa, and his feelings for this new woman, and the pace and force with which they were gathering, were not warranted by her acceptance of him or any encouragement from her. He was an idiot. Why could he not rely on himself?

23

The sentence had not left him when he got up for work. 'I'm off to meet some friends.' What was he? Was it the shorts? His woeful swimming? She'd seen him getting over the rope. His accent? Must be his job.

He walked across Shoreditch High Street and chose an alley to wind his way to the site because the shade was already needed even though it was before eight. He couldn't shake her words: he was burned, affronted, and still he disgusted himself by inventing scenarios where he'd fit in perfectly among the people she had been so desperate to leave him for.

Babe was touting a spot-the-ball coupon around the cabin when Eugene arrived, shadowed almost immediately by Jack. Babe had looked furtively over his shoulder but loosened up when he saw it was these two. Eugene gestured as if to tip his hat at Babe. Jack shuffled past him and sat down.

Babe handed over the spot-the-ball card for Jack to put his

initials on. Jack said nothing. Babe watched Jack's shaking hand and tilted his head because, instead of initials, Jack had written his name in full, upwards, his signature a plant craving the sun at the top of the page. Babe looked at it, intrigued for a second, but he wasn't concerned. He shrugged – that was probably how he always wrote it. He almost asked, 'You went to school up a tree?' but figured that his good nature would have been stretched as Jack would take his time to understand and respond. He shuffled around the table and on to the next man, but before he left Jack, he offered quietly, 'Trips? Es? Charlie?'

'Chips?' said Jack, aloud, but Babe had moved on to the other side of the cabin and didn't hear him. Jack hadn't eaten for a couple of days so he wasn't altogether there this morning. Charlie? mulled Jack. There had been a steel fixer, a Scot, Rangers fan, but Jack quickly lost the thought and began again to dwell on the night before because last night had frightened him.

He'd been in the bar of the Beacon, just having a couple of cans from his bag because there was no one serving yet. The snug was empty, which was the way he liked it these days, in case he felt the need to shout.

He hadn't seen her come in but suddenly Della was before him, saying, 'Stand up, Jack.' He'd been marched then, but she hadn't been rough, up the back stairs into his room. The mean curtain was drawn and the room was bathed pink with the light easily pushing through it.

'I've only had a couple. I've had some dinner,' he said. His guilt stuffed the pause and then he got it. 'Did I shout?'

Her gaze was neutral, pity cancelling her impatience.

'Jack . . .' She was looking at him with a waiting face. She didn't have patience and it was painful for her but she waited a few more seconds before saying, 'Your trousers.'

He looked down at his bare legs and pulled up his leather coat from the bed.

Last night hadn't been an isolated event. In fact, the last few weeks had been bad for Jack. He was not well. He'd find himself in the yard, a feeble stream of piss slanting at the wall, then splashing back at his bare feet. In the short-hand that his mind now used, he tried to work out whether the poor force of it was the end of a longer flow or the miserable offerings his bladder had been putting out recently. He never took off his underwear so when he found himself outside without his pants it was this jolt in routine that scared him more than the grander aberration of using the yard as a toilet. Worried, he tried to get up the back stairs in haste so that no one would see him. The weight of his belly unsteadied him and pushed him from one wall of the stairwell to the other; he could never find a middle way. He kept losing his voice. For the last couple of days he'd lain in the mid-afternoon heat barking out blanks. When he did make it to the toilet, he stood at the urinals in the Beacon and realized his socks were wet. He didn't drink that night, but he didn't make that mistake again.

Babe could smell fresh booze on Jack as he was doing his rounds. That was what Noble called it, doing the rounds. As much as he hated doing Noble's bidding, the slack beginning to June had left Babe with debts so he used this time to advertise this second job; the more he needed it, the more he loathed it. He felt like Noble's fat little mule.

With hindsight, he blamed himself. From Babe's very first day on the site, Noble had watched him and Babe noticed that he was particularly rapt when he spoke to the men in their own languages. Once, as he was standing over tables giving out stories about Albania ('Having a share of two seas has halved our luck!'), he saw Noble hanging on his words and called him over. Noble looked unimpressed but he didn't move out of earshot. Babe imagined for a long time that Noble kept tabs on him because Buck had asked him to, but as Buck's trust in Babe steadily became apparent, he saw it was something else.

He should have kept his daughter out of it. At any opportunity, Babe would refer to his eight-year-old daughter. He firmly believed, and stated often, that she was the reason he had been brought by the Prophet out of the horror of his homeland, and she needed violin lessons and dancing school now she lived in England. He made it very clear that she was going to be British, to fit in. 'She is my weakness and my strength,' Babe told the uninterested listeners, and Noble listened most closely of all to this.

And then, a few weeks after Babe had showed his uses, Noble made his move. There were a few quiet words with Babe outside the gates of the site, and from that week on Noble handed over coke and weed, trips, Es and speed for Babe to sell. Babe's wife, Fatima, sang blessings for Buck and his 'overtimes', *Radia'Llahu'anhu*, may Allah be pleased with him. Babe had quickly grown used to the money he saved for his family and in particular for his sweet little raisin pilaf, his *kabuni*. Working for Noble? Not really, he convinced himself, assured that Allah in his unbreakable might could see his intention. It was for his sweetie, his *kabuni*, and because of the purity of his motive, he was almost certain Allah understood, so he trawled the cabin with the spot-the-ball card and with his every morning mantra of 'Trips? Es? Charlie?'

*

Most of them sat outside for break that day. Eugene immersed himself in the frictions and goading so that he needn't think about Julia. He turned to Babe. 'So, tell me, how'd you get here?'

'Evgenie, I love you like my son but you ask many, many questions!' Babe feigned irritation while really he valued Eugene's innocence like a collector. It gave him the excuse to tell his story. He did not start with Kosovo and his ragged run with his family from his little town of Velika Krusa to Albania, Germany, France and Holland. Today, for Eugene, he started from the beginning.

'You see, in my father's time, they used to need us – ethnic Albanians were fresh blood absorbed by Serbia – but then,' he snapped his fingers, 'we became a problem for them. A dense clot of poisonous Muslims.' Here, he brandished a fist. 'We had to be cut out!' A slashing movement. 'Dispersed!' The last word was accompanied by a spreading out of both nut-brown hands.

Babe cooked up summers in the Drini Valley and he was content to see that, in the telling of it, Eugene could almost smell the spice rising from the baking earth.

'You have a brother?' asked Babe.

'Aye, younger. A lunatic.'

'My brother is Ordil. Also crazy. We were wild boys.'

Babe picked out every detail and he worked hard to paint a picture of two brown brothers against the blue backdrop and the grey-beige earth of the narrow lanes of maize fields, the shy buttery colour of the young ears of corn, faint, heavy beacons bowing as the kids ran through. He wanted Eugene to see the deep green making the lemons blaze and feel that it was he under the sturdy canopies of waxy leaves, breathing in the dark huts of hot shade they held beneath them. Eugene listened hard.

'Aye. Sounds like us. We were wild enough. Innocent, though.'

'Ordil would eat my aunt's *qofte të fërguara* until his belly ached.'

'What's that?'

'Lamb, minced. And mint. Crushed into discs between this – what is this part?'

'Heel.'

'Heel of her hands, fried and wrapped in newspaper.'

'My brother? Vincent? He'd have eaten the fucking newspaper. He used to try to buy sweets with a handful of screws. Greedy little feck.'

'I always gave Ordil the big share,' Babe stressed, drawing a circle in his palm.

'Aye. Vincent'd take the big share off you and share it back with you, acting like a saint.'

'I can see him licking lamb fat off his fingers, rubbing his hands with a lemon squashed under my bare foot. Then Ordil? He would smoke the rolled-up greasy paper.'

'Sound like the same kind of eejit. Vincent ate the paint off the wall in our toilet back home.'

They laughed together, and Eugene was still smiling when Babe said, 'They found Ordil in a pile of bodies. The women that found him? They had only curds to put on his wounds.'

'You serious?' Eugene was dumbed for a second. 'Where is he now?'

'His last letter was sent from Rome, an airport.'

'An airport?' Eugene was puzzled.

'Yes. You can live there. When I lived in France? There was a famous photo, a man in a toilet mirror. Orly. Shaving with thin foam.'

'You lived in France?'

'Yes, but the French tightened up long ago. Too many immigrants, too soon. Chirac said, "*Il y a overdose.*" People get scared.'

'Then here?'

'Kilburn and the Peace guesthouse until we are processed.'

Babe told Eugene how he would fend off accusatory stares as he pushed his little 'pudding' around local parks. On wet days he'd smuggle her into the afternoon showing at the Tricycle, where he'd watch French films, looking around frequently to show other cinema-goers that he didn't need the subtitles. He remembered watching *Le goût des autres*, trying not to compare Agnès Jaoui with Fatima. If his pudding stirred, he'd take out a container that had once held a roll of film (then the last bit of saffron salvaged from Fatima's mother) but now held Greek honey. He would dip his little finger into the pot and let her suck, her breathing fast, connected to him under his coat. She never cried out.

Babe offered Eugene a swig of his tea. Eugene had a sip and winced. There must have been ten sugars in it.

'And you are Catholic?'

'Sure enough.'

'My *kabuni*, she is Allah's own little Catholic. She start at St Abraham the Poor.'

Babe hoped that the patronage of their father Ibrahim, Friend of God, *Khalilu'llah*, would appease Allah for the next little while until he and Fatima found their feet. Every time she nodded at Jesus's name, Babe would offer atonement towards Mecca.

'She makes Irish dancing with her friend, Niamh.'

Eugene groaned. 'No, Babe. Not that awld shite.'

'Not shite! But you know?' he whispered now. 'They wear the false hair for dancing. I say no way. Fizzy and black! Plastic! Curling, curling.' He shuddered. 'Not on my nellies!'

'Your nelly,' said Eugene.

'Yes, my nellies.'

And Eugene rolled about laughing until Babe begged him to tell him what he'd said wrong, finally giving in to laughter himself. Drained, they sat in a warm silence. Babe looked at Eugene sitting so close beside him and almost told him about selling drugs for the pig Noble until he thought of his *kabuni,* holding hands with skinny little Niamh, and he saw her belonging, back straight as a white beech tree. He saw himself before her, clapping and tapping, enjoying annoying Fatima with his incessant nudging and beaming and her calling him what translated to 'very simple man'. He looked back at Eugene. He'd tell him some other time.

'And violin? "London's Burning" will bring tears to any eyes . . . all of your eyes.'

Eugene didn't wait for Jack after work that day – he didn't want the energy draining out of him, listening for Jack stumbling behind him on his way back to the Beacon or watching him nearly get run over.

Left alone in the cabin, Jack was glad he didn't have to keep up with anyone after work. He felt a peculiarly light but significant exhaustion. Ignoring it, he left the site gate and followed his usual path home.

Jack felt the same exhaustion when he woke up in the beige light of the hospital ward. The first thing he thought was that, for once, he had a real reason not to go to work. It gave him a feeling of worth, as if all his working life had been leading up to this.

A nurse came over. 'You're in the Royal London Hospital. Whitechapel Road. Do you know it?'

'I know it right enough,' said Jack, his eyes closed.

24

No one worried when Jack didn't come into work: the men had long since stopped trying to hold him down with a pattern. Noble was away on a safety training course for the last part of the week and the mood on site was jubilant, despite the morgue of concrete that lay waiting for them. Some of the men took the chance to meet up in the cabin and discuss what needed to be done. Eugene was up and down as the waves of blame passed over him and could hardly sit still. None of them could wait for Buck to come back on Monday. In the cabin, despite their own misgivings, the others chatted, made light of a problem that they knew was not their own and made him feel protected, so he allowed himself to relax a little.

Vincent was coming in a few days, and Eugene's stomach was getting tighter with the excitement. Or maybe it was fear. Since he had moved to London his mind had had difficulty in distinguishing the two.

Friday was the last day Noble was off site so they

arranged to meet in the Pelican at lunchtime. Uri met his girlfriend Matilda, his 'Ashanti!' and brought her. Everyone was filled with violent confidence and vigour; they all had their own solutions to the problem and these zigzagged other conversations. Uri was talking about the kind of tattoo he'd force Noble to have while he was cutting up lines of coke on the table in the back bar. Eugene was mesmerized by their brazenness and found himself picked up by it and carried along. It was pure daylight outside. Everyone had some of the cocaine, except Babe, and under its quick influence, Eugene found himself speaking furiously with the others about what was right. As they babbled together, he added obliquely, 'I've never had that before.'

Uri's mouth would not close for a good minute.

'From now in, we are Dinamo Shoreditch!' said Uri. 'Team United!' He grabbed Eugene first.

'Uri, you're busting my hand.'

'Babe, get into here,' commanded Uri, motioning to the little circle. Uri forced Babe to hold hands also and the three of them looked at each other with a love-laced clarity.

'We're going to get into the shit for this – you know that, don't you?' Eugene scanned their faces and saw a poorly hidden boredom at his worries.

'I tell you now, do not worry. If worst comes, we will tell Buck you were not at work that day.'

'I'm not lying to Buck.'

'Ah . . . *abrar*.'

'A what?'

'*Abrar* is you. Righteous.'

'Get to fuck.'

'Allah, close your ears. Forgive him, he is Irish.' He hugged

Eugene's head and rubbed his scalp through his hair with his knuckles.

'Is this boy not good?' Babe pointed to Eugene, then stood in the middle of the circle and put his beer bottle above Eugene's head. 'This boy is more than good.' He blessed Eugene with his cigarette.

'I always think that Zog is too tall for Kosovans. Kosovo needs a small giant! A king of their own! Eugene, King of Kosovo!' They laughed, whooped stupidly in the daylight.

'Can't I be king of somewhere good?'

Babe looked seriously at him. 'I am pretending you haven't said that.'

They hugged each other. Uri put his tongue in Matilda's mouth while he crushed the back of Eugene's neck until he had to squeeze his eyes shut.

It was late afternoon when Eugene made his way back to the cube shed. He saw Voitek begin a guilty scuttle out of the shed when he spotted him approaching. It didn't bother Eugene because, after the lunchtime amusements, he felt he was in the wake of something powerful and he felt above himself, invincible. He could burn off his enemies. Even Noble. Fuck this little job-robbing Pole.

Inside the shed, he sat looking at the moulds, thinking about how he could really make something of his life in London now that he had friends, good men. Idly he flicked his lighter and a rag soaked in shutter oil caught light in a breath. This lit a mould, which was beside the wall that, over the weeks, had held enough oil to light the entire inside of the shed. It happened within seconds and he sat for a few, just staring at the flames licking round him, letting the danger slow. For a second he found he could enjoy the progress of the flames.

With his coat pressed up against the walls of the shed and finally some sand on the floor, Eugene put out the fire without anyone seeing. His heart was booming and he was sweating, and he stood breathing hard, the plug pulled on the power he had felt. He shook himself and, with his breath beginning to shake, he tried to hold himself in check. Drugs and big ideas. What was he doing? He should be more careful.

25

Vincent jumped off the coach straight into the Saturday-afternoon crowds and Eugene almost expected Theresa to be behind him. With Vincent in his sights and their weekend together spread before him, Eugene opened up, let Theresa float out of his chest, let his feet feel the floor and silently chimed, *My brother would never betray me.* He leaned against a lamp post watching Vincent stare at the people around him, his gaze loping from strange to stranger, his mouth hanging open slightly.

Eugene smiled a lop-sided smile and moved towards his brother because he didn't want to see much more. It was like watching himself. He clapped Vincent on the back. 'What've you got a bag for?'

'The threads. Show me to the Ladies.'

'Come on, we'll get the tube.'

'Listen to you, we'll get the tube. So, big man, what've you got planned for me?'

Eugene winked, then felt he didn't have the right to. They

could have caught a 38 to Dalston or Hackney, but after the trouble it had taken to acquire it, Eugene wanted to amaze his brother with his small knowledge of the Underground.

'How's me mother?'

'Grand. You know, nuts, the usual. Thinks you're a bastard. Glo wants to murder her, that kind of thing.'

Eugene went through the list, asked about mates, made sure that he left out a few names so that Theresa wasn't the glaring omission. He was worried that if he asked about her he'd see pity trying to hide in his brother's face, or that there'd be desperation detectable on his own or, God forbid, both. He would never risk it.

They reached the station, and as they went underground at Victoria, Eugene decided he wouldn't mention to Vincent about the time he'd panicked and almost got locked into the tube at Angel. He wasn't going to tell him about swearing out loud after pushing against the flow of the crowd when he'd switched trains four or five times on the Northern Line, trying to get to Old Street, ending up south of the river in Kennington, utterly defeated by the end points and branches.

Eugene pulled Vincent to the other side of the escalator as people were pushing to get past. He explained that you had to stand to the right.

'Who says?' Vincent was not about to be frightened by the audacity of a silent rule and stood back on the left. He loved a chance to show how different he was from his brother. They followed signs to the Circle Line and Vincent was giggling at the posters that lined the walls, tapping each one as he went past. One showed the cover of a new book with an unsteady font, its title asking *Ever Happy After?* and, under it, high-heels, a bottle of wine. Vincent stuck his chewing gum on the title. Julia called this kind of book 'chick-shit' and Eugene had hoped it wasn't just because Rhodri did.

They squeezed on to the train when it arrived and Vincent seemed to be talking too loudly so, with his hand, Eugene signalled for him to keep it down. Vincent poked Eugene's embarrassment by starting a song. Eugene went white. They caught a bus from Liverpool Street to the pub.

'What d'you call this?' guffawed Vincent on seeing Eugene's room.

'The End.'

'The End is fucking right!' Vincent looked all around him while Eugene put on the new jeans and top that he'd bought for Vincent's visit. He'd chosen something he'd never have worn back home and, with Vincent's giddiness annoying him, the outfit felt like fancy dress. He put it on nevertheless.

'Can I have a wash at least?'

'No, we're meeting Uri and his mates and I don't want to be hanging round this shite-hole waiting to bump into Rod Stewart or the likes o' Jack.'

'You live backstage of a pantomime or what?'

'C'mon to fuck.'

Eugene took him up Kingsland Road and into the cheap Vietnamese he'd been to with Julia. He ordered exactly what she had ordered when they'd been before. Vincent had wanted a kebab, but Eugene wanted him to try something new, leave home behind him for a bit, so he ordered for both of them. The starter was cold and Eugene told Vincent that these rolls were supposed to be. The thin rice paper felt like clammy skin.

'I can't eat something that looks and feels like a dead man's cock.'

Despite himself Eugene laughed and was forced into ordering a bowl of fried rice as the waitress took away the food.

Uri was already there when they went into the Dun Cow on the corner of Hackney Road and Shoreditch High Street. As soon as he entered, Vincent almost turned around to walk out but Eugene dragged him to the bar where he was served by a six-and-a-half-foot transvestite with the seat out of his trousers, the cheeks sprayed pink. They ordered, and Vincent said, 'He's painted his arse! You'd better get me a short one.'

'D'you think he does his bollocks?' Eugene winked at his brother, and was pleased that the place had made an impression on him. 'Just wait. He loves Uri.'

'I'll bet he does. He wants to have a word with himself.'

Uri was standing in the corner with Matilda. He introduced himself, and Vincent looked down at his hand as if he could still feel the meaty paw after he'd let go of it. Eugene saw Vincent looking at the tattoos on Uri's neck and hands as he was introduced to Matilda. Matilda's words were English but the tune was distinctly African. Vincent smiled at her and Eugene laughed as he read the blatant question on his brother's face: how had this tiny woman ended up with Uri, with that nose and a head like a breeze-block?

The four chatted easily, and while Uri told Eugene his one hundredth dirty story about Noble, Matilda was giving Vincent a brief history of Ghana. The giant pink-arsed man-woman was playing music now and his candy-floss wig bobbed in time to 'Monster Mash'. Uri bought them tequilas and told them in bloody detail about what would happen to Noble if he ever went to Irkutsk. Eugene went for more beers.

Over at the bar, Eugene could hear Uri's thick *l*s. Vincent was doing some kind of accent now, probably for the sake of a joke. He'd known that they'd instantly like his brother. Vincent was his good half: the half Eugene couldn't do. He was the perfect conduit for everyone's good feelings. With new people, Eugene would short-circuit: a couple of silences would shock each other, and in the static that followed, unsaid words would zap uselessly from the back to the front of his mouth until they lost their energy and sank through his tongue. He looked over his shoulder. Vincent seemed happier, more alive, and this disappointed him: it had Theresa written all over it.

Uri stood with his arm around Matilda whenever she was in reach. He saw Vincent looking at her and asked him, 'You have girlfriend?'

Eugene was at the bar so Vincent modestly admitted that he did. Uri gave a dirty laugh and Matilda tried feebly to push him away as he grabbed her, tighter still.

'She is Ashanti, Ashanti tribe. Queen.'

'Very good, very good,' said Vincent, not knowing whether it was or not, already regretting his admission to Uri.

Uri pulled him close and winked. 'And for tonight, for good Irish man, I have snowstorm in my pocket.'

Eugene and Vincent came back from the toilet and Vincent made an O with his finger and thumb to show Uri he was ready for weather like that whenever he wanted to blow it his way. Pleased, Uri pressed a tight little pill into each of their palms 'For later.' He smiled like a pirate.

Matilda returned from the toilet, suddenly claiming she had to visit her aunt.

'Where is aunt?' boomed Uri.

'At church. We are all welcome.'

They laughed; it was late. Matilda looked dolefully at Uri. He went to the toilet and when he returned he announced firmly, 'We all go to church. Aunt is waiting for you, you pack of godless wolves. One more drink first.'

The taxi dropped them at the wrong end of London Fields. To get to the church they had to cross a dark park. In the poor light, the fence around the tennis court had a military look. Uri tried to climb it but his huge shoes gave him bad purchase and he hung there a couple of inches above the ground, shouting, 'Johnny Rambo, he is here!' the fence bowing deeply away from him.

A few drunks moved from prominent benches to avoid them; a dog walker retreated, took a longer route home. Uri was showing them how to click their heels in the air, to one side.

'No, no. This time is good.' He fell heavily on his final attempt to show them how to do it properly. They pulled his bulk off the wet ground, and when he got to his feet, Vincent got on his back. Uri started to run as the others laughed. 'Yippee, kayay, motherfucker!' rang out over the deserted playground.

Inside, the church was flashbulb white. The singing hit them in the chest and, all around, the people seemed to be much higher than them, swaying with sleepy, reverent eyes or sweating and pulsing out their love of the Lord with quick claps. Vincent was still on Uri's back but slid off silently just inside the door. Matilda scanned the rows for her aunt and started walking down the aisle. No one turned to see the three white faces standing at the back.

Matilda beckoned them down to the front of the church, and while the pastor sang not five feet away, each of them introduced themselves to Dorcas, who, in her late fifties, was dressed in a tight floor-length wrap and material crown. Confronted with the aunt, Uri shouted, 'I am from Russia, from Siberia, like tiger – arrgh!' and he held up his hands as claws to help her understand.

They said goodbye as quickly as they'd said hello and hurried out. Uri clapped his way up the aisle, smiling and nodding beneficently – he turned at the back to give them one last look at his tiger face. Matilda dragged him through the door and, as it closed, a couple of whoops snuck through to mingle with the singing. They continued as if nothing had happened.

Matilda led them to Dalston through back-streets. Uri walked on his hands now. Under a streetlamp he held a pinch of coke under each of their noses and they took it obligingly. Eugene sniffed and blinked down at the gutter. The grey-yellow glow that bled down the camber of the road now heralded endless opportunity. He jumped on to Uri's back. Soon, Matilda was pulling them into a small door with an awning above it. Eugene and Vincent blinked up at the word 'Afrinoco' and wondered what the steps led down to.

There was a packed restaurant, spice fragrant and laced with the hard pungency of fish. They walked through it to get to the club. Uri slapped the shoulders of a few of the older men, and Matilda talked to the people behind the small bar in the corner, laughing, her head thrown back. Uri waited for her at the top of the stairs. Downstairs was ultra-violet. They laughed at each other's teeth. The barman had just started work and needed warming up. He waited for them to finish laughing before he took Eugene's order.

'How is your girlfriend? Good like this?' Uri asked Vincent, hooking Matilda round the waist.

Eugene swivelled from the bar. No smile.

'Girlfriends, Uri, girlfriends.'

Eugene turned back and ordered more tequila to hide his despair. His brother didn't often lie to him but when he did it was like this. With abundance. With silly plurals and stresses, as if practice was something that other people needed. He turned back to them and fed his tablet to Vincent in the hope that it would fill up the part of him that hankered after Theresa. Vincent scrabbled in his pocket and returned the favour for his brother.

A few more tequilas and the drugs allowed Eugene to ride up the steep hill of his suspicions and survey what he knew to be true. Vincent was happy, that was all. He wouldn't play such a trick on Eugene. A party off Brick Lane was mentioned and they headed for the address. It was a warehouse just off Bacon Street and they went straight upstairs because they couldn't get into the downstairs rooms. Eugene climbed higher and took a last look: no Theresa.

His face was in his brother's. He'd grabbed his sleeve. 'Do you love her?'

'Love who?' Vincent shook his sleeve free to crane at a girl lying on a bed speaking into a mobile phone. Eugene didn't force him to turn round and show his face: instead he chose to listen to Vincent and, in thanks for these words, he planted a kiss on his brother's cheek and planned for a night without Theresa between them.

Vincent moved over to the bed, and though she was still speaking into the phone, he was asking the girl a question.

'I'm divorced, not single.'

'And is he here tonight?'

'You'd be nowhere near me if he was,' she said.

Vincent moved in to kiss her and Eugene watched so closely that he had to stop himself making the moves with his own mouth. Vincent pulled him forward and Eugene surprised himself with how he crushed her body into him as he kissed her. For once, everything was enough. It didn't even hurt when Theresa slipped into his mind and then into his mouth through his memory. He put his fingers into the girl's hair when she was kissing Vincent and held his brother's hand across her bare belly.

The light was coming in to rob them of all this when Vincent earnestly entered her number into his phone. The three of them were very reluctant to leave each other. They found Uri and Matilda, and made extremely important plans to meet up later. Promises and promises.

Eugene had led Vincent away from the party the wrong way. After half an hour, he had found a broken pram left in an alley and had pushed his brother, his arse almost touching the ground, within half a mile of the Beacon. He ran at top speed, taking it on to two wheels and tipped him out into the road. They entered the pub by the back, Vincent saying, 'I would have had her tonight if you'd have just fucked off.'

'She wanted to marry me. It was so fucking obvious.'

They laughed up the back stairs. Light was just filtering through the grime on the kitchen skylight. Vincent couldn't believe there was a shower in the kitchen. He got into it and laughed like a cockerel. He joined his hands in prayer and, in a mangled Cockney accent, shouted, 'I now pronounce you man and wife.'

'Shut up to fuck, or fucking Roddy Doyle'll be up!'

In the dim kitchen, half-cut, the quiet was an itch, their laughter the scratch. Eugene struggled to put his hand over

Vincent's mouth until they were both clanging around the cubicle.

He put two pounds in the meter and, as the lights flicked on, he explained that Della had a deal on the electric, which meant she couldn't take the meter out. He was undressed in a second and had already stepped out of the rosette of his clothes when Vincent came in. Eugene got into the bath and sat down, even though the tap had only filled it an inch.

'What are you doing, you eejit?'

'Having a wash, you tit.'

'In that?'

They laughed at each other until Eugene pissed himself in the bath. The water wasn't high enough to cover it and his laughter pushed it out in amber arcs. Vincent had to sit on the toilet in front of the open door his head between his legs.

'We're going to be late if you don't stop fucking around,' Eugene said, trying to sound threatening. 'You've got to be on the coach at three. That leaves us . . .' he peered at his watch '. . . nine hours.'

'Shit – we'd better hurry up.'

The bath was still running so they didn't hear Rhodri come into the kitchen. Vincent saw him, though, and poked Eugene in the back while Rhodri stared at him with a flat, angry mouth. Vincent stared back. Eugene looked over his shoulder at Vincent's blank face. He turned off the tap.

'What's up? Have you shat yourself or what? You'd better put that lid up if you have.'

Rhodri walked round the table and pushed his face into the bathroom. Eugene turned, saw him and gave an instant high-pitched scream. Rhodri jumped back out of the bathroom and swore, pushing the door closed.

*

'So hold on, how comes you sometimes call Uri "Gary"?'

They were still in the bathroom, coming down, but nicely, gently. Gliding; no steps. The clock showed 6 a.m. The sun was barely registering through the skylight in the kitchen. Vincent was shaving in the mirror-tile above the sink. Eugene was dressing, moving in and out of Vincent's view.

'That's what Noble calls him. Went from Uri Gagarin to Gary. There's this Bulgarian bloke, Illian – he's Ian. He calls Sergei "Sir Gay". Thinks he's hilarious.'

In the cabin, even without Noble's help, nicknames grew like yeast. Because Jack had been 'Princess' for years the fun had been worn out of it. One of the scaffolders was a Finn called Pasi who became 'Popsi' then 'Pepsi' and stabilized at 'Shirley'. He didn't seem to mind, but Eugene had wondered if this huge man would be quite so easy with his name when he found out where it hung in the web of what was what.

'And what do they call you? The half-wit?'

From behind, Eugene slapped Vincent's cheeks with both hands. 'Come on! Stop poncing about – we only have today left.' He headed for the End.

'Then it's a good job we started it yesterday!' Vincent shouted after him.

Eugene led Vincent through the back yard and into the alley. It seemed colder now it was daylight and the sky was dove grey behind the weak sun. In the middle of the pavement, a few pigeons picked at the edge of a pile of puke while Eugene and Vincent looked on. In this scruffy street, Eugene suddenly realized he felt safe. It was a small revelation that, after the high of the laughter, made him want to cry. He blamed it on the drugs wearing off and the natural light.

In their optimism, the two of them had dressed to go to another party; they wanted to carry it on. Teeth chattering, they laughed at each other at the bus-stop where a couple of cleaners were waiting in tabards to get to work. In the cold, Eugene began to feel a little lost and put a pin back into the map of last night.

'Why were you trying to shift the girl I was trying to shift?' They had their hands in their pockets, shivering.

'She wanted me, mate. I let you stay there 'cos I felt generous. Have you got her number? Ring her, tell her to meet us in Spitalfields.'

'You do it, fecking Robbie Williams!' said Eugene, pointing at Vincent's outfit.

'And have you seen yourself? Daniel O'Donnell does London.'

Eugene laughed, punching him in the arm.

The bus turned up and Eugene let Vincent on first, proud of his part-ownership of London, happy that, without saying it, they had only had to wait a couple of minutes for a bus, even on a Sunday morning. They were only on it for a few stops and, now in the warm, Eugene couldn't shut up: as well as minor landmarks, he was pointing out places where cabs had dropped him off and where he'd bought the blackened halal chops, where he'd had a piss after a pub.

Vincent took all the details in and suddenly felt sorry for his brother's excitement in these small things. It made his smile ache. He hoped no one was listening. He needed another drink. Eugene left it until the last minute to pat his brother on the back to get off the bus, showing how used to all this he was.

They jumped off and found themselves hedged in by pedestrians. 'What's this, then?' asked Vincent.

'It's the start of Bethnal Green Road. You could call it a market. A market like you've never seen.'

They merged with the shuffling queues. People had set out stalls on the pavement and were selling, it seemed, anything. Vincent stared at the motley collections spread out on towels and rugs, suitcase lids and bin bags. The air was contaminated with hopeless whiffs from sheets stretched alongside bedspreads that sucked the smells back in like damp magnets.

The hawkers were mostly old, a bent woman with an emulsioned face, some in costumes, involuntary fancy dress. The punters were mostly young with naked midriffs, old hats, hair jutting diagonally. Excited by the mix of people, Vincent shoved Eugene into the person in front and kept hooking his moving feet. Eugene replied with a jut of his arse into Vincent's stomach. No one was in a rush; everyone seemed to be standing still or kneeling. Even the vendors were sifting through their neighbours' rubbish, and Vincent was drawn in by their interest. Some had goods on carpets and Vincent bent to open a miniature caravan, gypsy inside, her full head clumsily painted with the colour meant only for her scarf, staring fixedly at her pearly future. He pointed to a rug that had soaked up a sump.

'They can't be selling that, surely to God?' he said to Eugene. He touched the name 'Audrey' hung awkwardly on a chain of questionable metal, never to be claimed by anyone but her. Eugene wondered if there was a Theresa or perhaps a Julia in there. Coming out of a crush around a computer-games pitch, Vincent kicked a bag. CDs sliced through weak plastic and the dumb currency scattered into their path. No one noticed. Further on a Caribbean holiday was remembered on a barometer, ridiculous in the damp; frocks that had been lifted; plates with their nuclear families or extended straggle of saucers; an orphanage of cups. Vincent

weighed a wrist-width drill bit with a look of disbelief and
picked over wrenches with their insect jaws rusted in a
permanent bite. Everywhere you could smell fatty cooking.

Vincent pointed. 'What would anyone be doing with a
single shoe?'

'Not single, divorced,' said Eugene, winking. 'Look at the
heel on that – it'd make a good lump hammer.'

They moved a few steps at a time and Eugene checked
Vincent's face now and then to see if he was impressed.
There was nothing like this back home. People would be too
ashamed. Vincent kept kneeling to feel the crazy objects on
sale. In a box of cameras without guts or eyes he found the
Mahon crest, their name waving under a fiercely blue lion,
pasted on to a wooden block. He bought it. Eugene laughed
at him as he stuffed it into his back pocket.

They rounded a corner, and Vincent saw scores of
pitches lining the floor for yards ahead. This stretch was
different again, heavy plant and bicycles mixed with
lifetimes of irrelevant flotsam. He laughed, amazed,
nudged Eugene. The floor was heavy with useless machines
trying to be understood by healing fingers; car seats
moulded to no one there; cogs; corkboard. Shuffling past,
a tiny man wore a coat as old as Eugene, its lapels and
shoulders flat with grease from his long hair and beard and
small hours in greasy cafés. It looked like sealskin. He had
black fingers and his bowed nails moved tenderly around
a padlock. On this side, the sellers were mostly men, East
European. As he scuffed by them, Eugene looked down
and saw that each shoe looked as if it was filled with three
fists. It made him want to stretch; made him feel young
and perfect. Vincent nodded towards a man and, in mock
distaste, said, 'Half pissed.'

'Twice shy!' Eugene used his new camp voice, pursing his lips. He was surprising himself.

It was getting busier. They had no choice but to carry on with the slow, peristaltic urge of the crowd, stopping to flick through records that should never have been made, videos to make you feel bad and better. At each corner, men who looked like mercenaries stood guard over fake Marlboros and, leaning against walls, unopened packs of cigarettes with darkly aspirational names like 'Combat' or 'Richman'. Vincent and Eugene snickered as they pointed at the titles. A mercenary let out a loud, foreign bark and they jumped, thought he had seen them poking fun.

Quickly, a fight broke out. A dark-haired man, his shallow forehead passionately furrowed, pushed the mercenary over his stash and sent the purse at his waist skidding to the side, money everywhere. Another little man was on top of him like a rat as a few people screamed and scattered but more just looked on. Shaken, Vincent and Eugene pushed out of the crowd, over the road, and into the folds of another crowd. They found themselves in the massive mouth of a railway arch, the bricks velvety with soot. People were selling in here and, above them, dirty gowns decorated the arch like pretty bats.

Away from the fight they felt invincible. Eugene watched the violence so that he would know what to do if anything happened to him; used it to grease himself up, make himself more slippery in future. Vincent was already listing the things he'd seen there, practising for when he got home. Eugene wondered if he'd be telling Theresa about his visit. It made him low; he hadn't brought Vincent here for that, and the easy truths of last night were worming their way back underground.

Eugene's phone rang. It was Uri. Matilda was going to bed and he was too cold to come out again. Eugene gave him the usual stick, called him an old-timer, said he couldn't take it and that he'd see him at work. At the same time, Vincent was shouting in the background, 'Halleluiah, Rambo!'

It was half nine in the morning now and both Eugene and Vincent needed something to help them make last night into today.

'They said to say goodbye to you.'

'Are they not meeting us?'

Eugene saw his brother's excitement wane and said, 'No . . . but that means we can go to the pub!'

'At this time?' Vincent grabbed him round the neck and kissed him.

They fell into the pub. No one seemed to care that the music pumped, night-time loud, and the boys grinned at each other as they ordered Guinness.

'I'll get these,' said Vincent.

'Put your stinking euros away.' Eugene smirked.

'You must be raking it in. I haven't spent a cent yet!'

The pints arrived. They both drank and Vincent said, 'You can't beat a black breakfast.'

'Right enough,' said Eugene. He got out the roll-ups and they went to sit at the front window. Happy in anticipation of his drink, Eugene carried on, 'You're on your holidays, you can't be paying.'

Vincent removed the family crest from his pocket so he could sit down. He put it on the table in front of them. A big daft lion, its tongue sticking out. 'All I can say is you must be earning good money.'

'I'm even saving.' Half of Eugene's pint had gone already. 'Listen. Della knows a bloke, known him for years.

He's picking up derelict council flats at auction further east and south and selling 'em on to his pals. She's got a few houses. Knows what she's doing.' The bar was beginning to fill up.

'I'd live here in a fucking second!'

'Really?'

Eugene was surprised. The Guinness was doing its job, making ideas into good ones. A couple of pints later and Vincent was reminiscing about the night before. Eugene huffed a smile through his nose, tried to make out that he'd had better nights. 'Come on. I hope I can get you to Victoria before you're pissed again.'

Later, beside the bus, they shook hands.

'Well, mate, see you soon.'

Eugene raised his eyebrows in doubt.

'I'm coming over, Eugene. I'm telling you. Get looking for a place. I'll tell them at work on Monday.'

'You're still off your head,' he said, to hide his hope.

As Vincent got on the crowded Sunday bus, Eugene became heavy with the relief that her name had not been mentioned. Then he panicked, patted down his pockets. 'Stupid fucking lion's still in the pub.' He looked up at Vincent's face in the window: it was happy, relaxed. Not a bother on him.

26

The thing about fishing, he thought, was that it gave life its proper tempo. Back from his trip, Buck cruised up Kingsland Road in a cab. Just off the plane at Gatwick, his mind was reluctant to let go of the time he'd had – the boats tethered, waves gossiping beneath them, the lapping of the water at his feet before they shoved the boat out at dawn, the lough ticking, lap, lick, lap, lick. Time borrowed from water. That was what stayed with you after you'd left it. Buck's friend Patsy had taken his own cab to Forest Gate but Buck knew he would still be feeling the ripples of their trip. It kept them going, year on year.

Patsy's face had been a picture as he held up his last catch yesterday. He'd looked like a kid.

'If you could only see yourself!' Buck had said.

'I'm surprised, that's all!'

'You caught a fucking Killarney shad!'

'I know!'

'And we're in Killarney.'

'Surprise!' shouted Patsy.

They'd drained the hip flask between them before setting off back to the hotel and stayed silent in honour of the sweet melancholy of the last night of a great trip. To Buck, this was what was trapped in a single malt: the taste of good things that are just about to pass. Though he was back in London, he couldn't have been further away from the site.

The vanilla fumes of the air-freshener were sickly, and the taxi sped on. Corners taken too tightly swayed the chunky talisman hanging from the mirror, until through the ebony beads and blue feathers, he became faced with the strokes of grey that flashed by the windows on the run from Hackney Central to Clapton. He felt them close in on him as they passed the bus garage and drove towards the old end of Mare Street. The taxi rounded Clapton pond and, in a couple more minutes, Buck was outside his four-storey Victorian terrace. Bought in 1975, the house had become his own by steady hard work and, despite Deirdre's protests, they had stayed in it because of this. He paid the driver and tipped him well, and before he opened his front door, he suddenly felt a need to look back, grasp for the last of the waves he'd left in the taxi. He wanted to keep a hold of the calm energy of the lough, steady and cool. He got out his keys.

Buck opened the door and shouted, 'Hello,' into the hall, but nothing came back, so he thought about how much more he'd enjoy the relief when he knew things were as they should be here at home. The greys after so many greens, he thought. That was all.

He made his way downstairs and into the kitchen, where Noble waited with an empty plate at the table while his mother, Deirdre, leaned into the oven. Deirdre was handsome, with a block of black hair that squared around her face. She turned to him briefly, and he saw that her short forehead and the thin bridge of her nose gave her the look of an elf, even now in her fifties. The cliff-grey eyes were picked out by the black of the hair but the dark pink of lips stood out miserably as the face's lament that the mouth and chin were just too large for the finer features above it. Noble turned to greet his father while Deirdre straightened but swivelled to face the stove.

'All right, Dad?'

'So it's all gone OK?' Buck asked him.

'Hello to you too,' said Deirdre, into the steam above the pans.

'I'm only after asking 'cos I've been away.'

'I don't want him like you.' She pointed a spoon at Noble, then Buck. 'Not everybody lives for work and money.'

Buck shot Deirdre a warning look. She was blocking him because she knew he needed to know things were all right. There would be no helping hand from her to shrug off his bad feeling. He sat down at the table and softened his face, egged on Noble to tell him more. Noble swallowed.

'Look!' Deirdre was pointing over angrily now. 'Look how worried he is!'

'Worried about what?' Buck implored, the mantle becoming unbearable. The weight of it put him in mind of the dead otter he and Patsy had dragged to the shore at Lough Leane.

'It's been fucking mad.' Noble was starting to babble. 'It was the Singhs, see?'

'Why did you not tell me when I rang?'

''Cos he knew that this is what you'd be like!' Deirdre spat.

'Them Singhs, man. Moan that the mud's too stiff, breaking their backs, givin' 'em blisters. You add a bit of water? It's running away with them. You cannot fucking win. We're well rid.'

Buck scraped his chair, saying calmly, 'Tell me what's happened.'

'The only blokes I could get to help me were skins, Poles, and wait till you see these idiots. The one who can string two words together turned up in fucking carpet slippers!' He looked again to his mother. 'Can you Adam and Eve it?'

'I can indeed, son,' she replied.

'They sent the wrong stuff but . . .' he held up his hands, palms to Buck '. . . between us, me and the skins, we cured it, we got it finished.'

'What did they send?'

'Low-grade lightweight stuff.'

'For floors?' Buck began to pale.

'It looks perfect. It'll harden up.'

Noble noticed the willingness to listen vanish from Buck's eyes.

'That's not the point.'

'You pay enough insurance,' Deirdre snapped.

'We'll have to take it up.'

'Don't talk soft.'

'You want me fucking sued?'

Noble searched, but sympathy was now untraceable in Buck's face so he pushed on. 'Eugene wasn't in the shed.'

'Where was he, then?'

'Pissed? Who the fuck knows? Not one of those cunts offered to help me.'

Deirdre cut in, 'You cannot put that kind of responsibility on a young lad.'

'So who signed it off?'

'You wanted it done!'

Buck's voice was tight now. 'Not load after load of the wrong concrete!'

'Somebody had to sign for it.' Noble's face was towards his mother now. She looked into the steam above the pans and stirred.

Deirdre didn't notice that Buck couldn't sleep that night. Buck couldn't rid himself of the rise in his chest: she had taught their son her games and the two of them had ended up playing by the same rules. Knee-jerks and plenty of blame. There was never a straight answer from either of them, always excuses.

He was on site by first light, staring at the mess of concrete, and wanted to put his head in his hands when he saw that some of the grey gruel had flowed over the forms at the side of the pour. Beside the concrete stood the Singhs' coloured tamps. Old man Singh had taught Buck the names of the colours in Punjabi when they were in Mile End Road, *jamni, sungtari, gulabi,* and he remembered trying to teach Noble these names at home with building blocks. When Buck had looked up from the bricks, Noble was playing with a new toy. He'd never get a firm like them again.

He went and sat in the cabin and unlocked the filing cabinet where he kept the insurance documents. He daren't read them. First he'd call the yard and sort out exactly what had been ordered and, since the cubes hadn't been taken, he'd need an engineer to do some core tests, confirm the grade and strength. It was still only six. The enormity of breaking out the concrete and getting rid of the grounding and starting again with a firm of strangers put Buck's head back in his hands.

He dragged the calculator over the desk towards him. He tried to work out worst case and best case, how far they were behind and how he might recover some of the money and, more importantly, time he had already lost. He must have been at this reckoning for a good couple of hours because he jumped when he heard a voice. His eyes had been screwed to the terrible figures. Too many noughts already and he hadn't factored in knock-on implications.

'Did you have a good time back home?' Eugene's question was abject; a bleat.

'Seems a million fucking miles away, what with this.' He thumbed violently through the window behind him, towards the maimed pour.

Eugene looked at his boots for a few seconds, then asked, 'What do you want me to do now Voitek's in the shed?'

Buck didn't answer: he just switched papers in his hands. Eugene kicked at a flap in the worn lino of the office floor.

''Cos that shed's not big enough for the both of us.'

'Get out of it, then!' Buck barked.

Eugene knew it was more than just impatience but he refused to register what else there was so he continued, upbeat. 'Do you want me somewhere else?'

'I'm busy with this just now. You'd better ask Noble.'

This Eugene couldn't ignore: it hit him up the gut. 'I didn't sign it off, Buck.'

'No, I know well you didn't.'

Eugene was winded. Buck swivelled in his chair and presented his back to him.

Eugene left the office. He wanted to ask one of the others to go in and see what they thought of Buck, reassure him that he wasn't the source of Buck's anger. In the cabin, there was a carnival feeling that made him feel more isolated; the men were on a high because they were being taken out tonight by the marketing man from D'Orion. The hotel chain was paying for food and drink for the entire night for those who wanted it. And those who wanted it were all of them, it looked like, as Eugene scanned the cabin. Noble was buzzing round the room, poking people, jumping on them, and he wasn't put off when he had irritated them. He seemed jubilant instead.

The atmosphere and Noble's childish excitement grated on Eugene. Noble sat with the Polish lads, Voitek and Ignacy. They were both fair with light blue eyes and high cheekbones. Voitek had a patchily shaved head as if the clippers used to do it were nearing the end of their useful life, while Ignacy's fine silvery blond hair hung down over his forehead and ears. Noble slapped them both on the back and was full of chat for them, and Eugene stared as they turned their eager faces towards him, Noble between them, his own blond head chin-up and strong – *f* he looked like a farm-worker in a propaganda poster, digging his way to the front. Eugene turned away.

When he was alone in the End that night, it was hard for Eugene to believe that Buck wasn't just angry with him. When first light came he felt less desperate, and by the time he got on site he was sure he'd imagined Buck's sharpness. There before anyone else, he took a cup of tea into the office. Seeing no one he turned to leave – and almost tipped the hot tea over himself as well as the floor when Buck appeared in front of him.

'I have one already,' said Buck, sidestepping the mess.

Suddenly brave, Eugene offered conversation from the door of the office as he dropped a manual on to Buck's desk. Buck came closer to him and, in his eagerness, Eugene saw this as an invitation.

'My brother was over that last weekend there.'

The pause was excruciating, but desperation pushed him to continue: 'The eejit was asking for work round here.'

Buck said nothing at all.

By midweek, Eugene was monitoring all interactions with Buck. He felt that this was the only way he was going to become skilled in gauging how much of the relative blame was being channelled to Noble by his father. There was certainly no obvious love being lost between them and he found an infantile comfort in this. He saw Buck smile on Thursday but that was at the safety man, and if anyone was going to get a smile that awld snake was. He managed Thursday night sober in the End by reminding himself of this.

Friday found Buck in the cube shed. Eugene stuck close. He'd nearly swept a hole in the wash-out area and bumped into the old man with the rheumy eyes, who bore him no malice for the sharing of his work, but Eugene resented him for taking the shine off the sweeping he was doing to impress Buck. When Buck left for the cabin, Eugene did too, but wished he hadn't as the first thing he saw was Buck handing tea to Noble. Eugene scanned to find a third party in the relay but saw no obvious candidate. He'd faint if Buck had made the tea for Noble.

Shaken, Eugene moved to the sink and heard Buck telling Noble his laces were undone. Everyone knew how Buck felt about health and safety. Nothing out of the ordinary. Eugene suddenly feared he would cry.

'You heard the one about the Albanian prostitute?' Noble had no qualms about what he said in front of his father.

Eugene turned away, flushed with embarrassment.

Buck laughed like a drain.

That night Eugene went west. He ate nothing and drank his way from Leicester Square to King's Cross.

27

The kitchen was never going to be a daytime room, much less a summer room. It wasn't defined by leisure or enjoyment. In no way was it a Saturday room. Eugene read today's headline again because he thought there'd been a misprint: '170th Crack-house Raided'. The picture under the headline was supposed to show how proud the police were about this. Eugene thought they looked smug about their own stupidity, with their mid-brown hair and pale faces. Fat, middle-of-the-road clones who were glad that they didn't stand out in any way from each other. The colourless English, see-through, thought Eugene, and then wondered why he was angry and why this bitterness was leaking into places it didn't usually. He continued sceptically, reading about the success of Operation Kudos and the teamwork between the *Hackney Gazette* and the local police.

Eugene hadn't seen any evidence of this but he had seen coppers picking on a Spanish beggar; a slight, Victorian-looking girl who had sat silently outside the off-licence, the policemen standing over her as she gathered up her books and, when she had one, a blanket. They stood around her, protecting the community from the embarrassing shambles on the pavement, shifting the books with their feet, giving out their air of we're-doing-you-a-favour-here. Eugene had slowed and stared because he wanted to let them know he was watching them but they never looked up and, of course, he never tried to make them.

He smoothed the pages of the *Hackney Gazette*. This weekend was killing him. He started on the paper again, from the beginning. He had no way of knowing that his name would be in these pages soon.

He flipped over the page to the kids' birthday pictures. The little square photos, each filled with a face from vanilla to cocoa; the page looked sickly, a box of chocolates set within the squalor. He flicked past them and wondered if, as time passed, the sweeties would melt through the pages, reforming into the more brutal stories of the borough. Further in, he paused over the picture of a man who had set fire to his daughter; a hostage situation in a house next to Hackney Central had turned into a blaze that had nearly taken out an entire row of houses; a baby had been found in a bin bag. The picture was of the crime-alert sign that indicated where the baby had been found. Eugene couldn't see the writing in the photo but wondered how they'd phrased it: 'BABY IN BAG 7 a.m. 24 July 2000'. Among the grisly stories he felt stricken again with ordinariness. He felt he had a perverse inability to reach any extreme, even the profane, and that made him wonder about himself, what he was capable of.

When he had first arrived in London, before he'd even left Victoria station, Eugene had been shocked by one of these signs, big and toucan-bill yellow, shrieking out a crime that had been committed right there. It had forced all of the particulars down Eugene's throat and he had suddenly realized that knowing these details meant you couldn't escape the horrors and that you had to share the sickness. Hackney blared yellow in every other street, the signs shouting out what people were up to round here, a shocking yellow brag of a sexual assault or an attempted murder. Eugene found the signs barbaric and upsetting. He felt the same about the *Hackney Gazette* but he read on, and he did this because he thought that these stories, if he could swallow them, might immunize him against the worst of London.

He sighed. Free time made him feel a failure. He had been down to the yard for his first couple of fags and now sat at the kitchen table, waiting to want another. Outside the grip of work, he floundered until Monday creaked around again.

Work meant that he didn't dwell on the questions. Old ones: how had he felt before Theresa? New ones: could Julia really love a man like Rhodri? Old ones tangled with new: what would he do if his mother died? Was he really that much like his father? Would he be more able for things if Vincent was here with him? There seemed to be no end to the questions he could ask himself. He was becoming immobilized by them; they had even lost their shape as questions. He no longer thought of answers to them but, rather, seemed to be made of them now, like an old golf ball – open him up and underneath he'd be a hard brown rubber tangle of unanswered questions, perished and sticky and clinging around each other. He longed for Buck to understand him.

Before Vincent's visit he'd tried to use the weekends to explore London, but found that he skittered along the surface of the city, skimming things, stopping briefly to scan but never long enough to be looked at. He wandered, searching out things that were familiar, and tried to stay out of the pubs, finding himself staring into women's faces, wondering whether he was really any further away from Theresa than when he'd lived down the street from her. There was always the feeling that he had a special failing all of his own that meant he couldn't move on.

He'd been up since half six. It was nine now and he was already exhausted by the thoughts that the weekend always made room for. He didn't know where to go except the kitchen. He sat at the table. It was gritty with sugar. He heard Rhodri's door go. He braced himself for pretence and relaxed again as he heard him slip down the back stairs.

Rhodri's door went once more and, again, Eugene stiffened. He heard shuffling feet coming towards the kitchen and kept his head down until he was shot a sideways 'Morning.'

It was Julia and she didn't look at him, just shuffled sleepily over to the sink and, after she had let it run for a bit, bent to drink straight out of the cold tap. Eugene wondered if she was strong enough to ignore him after this initial greeting. Deciding on these matters made life impossible for him. Give me work, he prayed. She was wearing a T-shirt, and as she had gone past, he had picked up a sweet smell: booze, but with a milky pleasure to it. The T-shirt was too big to be Rhodri's. An old boyfriend's? It was worn thin and clung closely to her broad shoulders. As she leaned over he saw the outline of her breast and, with her head in the sink, he took the chance to stare at it. Just before she stood up he saw that her pants had been exposed, white and small, just cutting into her athletic leg above the curve of her bottom. If only he'd known that! He silently kicked himself in the time that he should have used to think of something to say. She picked up a tea-towel, looked at it for a second and decided to wipe her mouth on the back of her hand. She didn't glance at him so he gave up dangling and faced the table again.

She faced him. The water had splashed the thin T-shirt and it was pinking her stomach. Stretching her arms above her head she asked, 'You want tea?'

He looked at the full cup he already had in front of him and put his hand over it. 'Aye, that'd be grand.'

She moved to the cupboard and he felt her energy leech his as she passed behind his chair on tiptoes to clear the high back with her buttocks. She filled the kettle while Eugene worried about how long it would take to boil and what he would say until it did. He downed the tea he already had. She reached up above the sink and banged hard with her palm to get the skylight open. It only took two thumps. Eugene was glad she hadn't asked him to do it because he thought he might not reach it. She was public-school length, he thought, never been deprived of anything. He wondered what Della had dabbled in to give Julia such a start in life – those long bones, the money she'd always need.

After she had made the tea she put his in front of him.

'Do you mind if I use the shower?' she asked him.

'Not at all, I'm away for a smoke anyhow.' The thought of sitting in the room where she was about to have a shower caught him up the middle and made him jerk quickly to his feet.

A half-hour later and she was coming down the back stairs where Eugene sat, again with his fag and his paper. Her hair was wet and she smelt now of citrus. 'I'll see you later, then,' she said.

'Right so,' said Eugene, being himself a little now he knew she was leaving.

She had almost closed the door to the yard when she poked her head back round and looked at him directly for the first time. 'I'm going to pick up some books from town. Want to come?'

Eugene listened to himself accept her offer. He surprised himself but her look had somehow made him comfortable and steady. He toyed with the idea of coming out in the Tuam Star shorts again. It's what Vincent would have done. 'I'll just get changed.'

They chatted easily after leaving the yard. The first natural pause was a diversion to Liverpool Street station for them both to buy tobacco. He watched her hand take change and, from her open palm and the lie of the fingers, deduced an ability to charm but a reluctance to do so. They left the station and walked the eerily empty streets from Bishopsgate to London Bridge. Without people, the banks and finance buildings seemed ridiculously grand – a waste somehow, thought Eugene. As they strolled along beside each other, he noticed that Julia would readily offer observations that were personal, giving slick opinions and lending her own interpretations without seeming weakened by them. He wished he had courage like that. If he gave opinions he felt some of himself come away, so he stayed quiet, turgid with opinions that would never be aired.

She was pointing out the towering buildings behind the tiny church of St Ethelburga. She put her hands on his shoulders to position him so that he got the full impact of the differences in scale between the new aching power of the tower in the background and this roadside church already in miniature. She let him take it in for a moment and explained that this little chesspiece of a church had survived the Great Fire and the Blitz, only to be devastated by a massive IRA bomb in the early nineties. He saw in her face that she was suddenly worried about his reaction to the politics and he wanted to tell her that she needn't worry for, in actual fact, he would hold aside anything he held dear for her to reach into him. Instead, he made out like she wanted him to, that he was comparing the little church with its surroundings, and he let his mouth open in an awe-fixed smile.

And so, although Eugene was all would-you-just-look-at-these-buildings?, his insides were dancing because she had touched his shoulders and now she was acting just outside herself, like a tour guide, and for these attentions he suddenly felt he loved her. He looked back at the church and blinked hard. He'd spent too much time alone recently. He'd be in love with Jack next.

She was reading from a plaque now, but Eugene let the words run away and followed them to the nape of her neck, down her back.

When they reached London Bridge they stopped to look over to the South Bank and she pointed east. 'Up there, around there, see that? Where the Neckinger reaches the Thames? That's Jacob's Island.' To their left was Shad Thames. '*Oliver Twist* was set around there. Used to be known as the Venice of Drains.'

Eugene liked this and repeated it. He had seen *Oliver!* on the television – Seamus had been there watching it, an act of contrition, but both Vincent and Eugene knew he was itching to serve out this cinematic penance and fuck off out of there. They wanted him desperately to get out and each of them sat on their own mushrooms of will. With Seamus there, the comparison to Bill Sikes felt obscene and loomed around them. Eugene held a silent passion behind the cushion as he willed Bullseye to disobey Bill, his heart busting when Bill killed Nancy. The cushion came up in front of his eyes when Fagan's treasures disappeared into the slime down there in Venice because he was still of an age where treasure might make the mattresses clean and his father not be sick in the middle of the night. Though he didn't say these things to Julia, he felt that it wouldn't be long before he could. For now, he wanted her to point to something else and stand right next to him while she was doing it. That'll do, he thought.

They looked across to the South Bank from London Bridge.

'The national bird of London. The crane!'

Eugene smiled at the side of her head, then gazed to the cluster of tower cranes along the bank of the river, saluting every which way like a drunken army. Julia talked excitedly about the number of them, then dipped angrily into an argument about economic implications for London's inner city. She was fiery and knowledgeable and he had caught alight with her interest in all of it. He wondered if her father was a builder, an architect, maybe.

They walked along the river, past the Globe and the London Eye, and jumped on a tube at Westminster. Eugene marvelled at the number of weekend tourists and, for the first time, felt closer to London than these visitors. On the tube, he made his own observations about the destinations on the Circle Line and watched carefully for signs that Julia thought him above himself. He was terribly aware that, sometimes, people who didn't know him took the shyness and the oddness as the worst kind of slyness; took the fear in his eyes and pieced it together as mocking. Not her. It almost felt like they were from similar casts or were in some way in step and somehow, just somehow, it seemed to Eugene that she was glad to be the grease to his uneasy machine.

When they arrived at the bookshop in Piccadilly, he waited while she picked up her order from a counter on the fourth floor. He looked up and felt giddy. So many floors for a shop that sold books! He felt that there was meaning in the worn steps, something worthy in the pounding human interest in words, long and hard enough to keep forcing people up these stairs, their hands smudging the brass banisters, their feet causing the stone steps to wear into a sag at the middle.

She came back down, smiling widely, with several books in her arms, and he couldn't help thinking that he didn't see this kind of ease about her when she was with Rhodri. He asked her what she'd bought and she showed him, explaining almost apologetically that she liked nature poetry. He thought how he'd like to take her down the lough, show her the ancient tree stump armoured with pennies shoved into the spongy wood by the kids around the way.

'Do you like poetry?'

He looked at her very seriously.'I like poetry that I've read.'

This made her laugh loudly enough for her to put her hand over her mouth, and that made Eugene very happy.

'Rhodri isn't into poetry. Says it's anti-pragmatic, whatever that means.'

Eugene enjoyed the derisory note that had crept into her mention of Rhodri's name. It made him feel brave. 'I got a kick in them once.'

'What?'

'The anti-pragmatics. It was wild sore.'

She didn't laugh out loud this time and he began to worry that he had misread things. Still smiling, she walked away. He hoped to God she wasn't offended and scolded himself for jumping in too quick, trying too hard. What was he doing?

Julia walked down an aisle. She moved away to make out that she was scrutinizing books, when really she was taking time to assimilate this strange quiet man. She needed to analyse why she liked him so much. Did he know he was funny? Did he mean to be? Why did she hope so? She was rerunning the way he said things and felt as though she was watching a spell unfold. His eyes affected her spine and he smelt beautiful, of work and patience. The Beacon was full of toil but this was something else, something above the brick dust and soap. She needed to slow down, be careful. He was lonely, friendly; the first begot the other, no? She went back over to him. She started to open the books to some of her favourites, showing him the poetry slowly, monitoring his response.

Eugene could feel her love of the words and he was put in mind of a welder's torch, oxyacetylene, he mused, looking sideways at her again. It could cut through anything. She could blind me. He watched her in the knowledge that she didn't care whether she was being watched or not. Brave, stiff-necked. He tried to figure out how he could feel so weak and so strong in one moment: like he'd been skinned and dipped in salt, but sweet salt. The weekend was filling out, the corners packed and the hours plumped by Julia and her talk of blackberries and ploughs and bog men. Eugene could get comfy.

After a while, he stopped speaking but his silence didn't stop her and he found that, soon, they had smoothly moved on from Ireland and buried men to another book and love. She pointed at the title of a poem, 'Twice Shy'. He smiled, because the name fitted so well, and he bristled pleasantly, thinking of Uri saying, 'All the hair of my body is up.' Imitating her doughtiness, he told her about Uri's translation and it delighted her.

'Twice Shy', she informed him, was a love poem, but that was all she had to say about it. She merely guided him along the words with her finger, pressing on at the most moving parts, stilling the words for him. She slid along the page, pressure reddening the point of her finger. 'Our Juvenilia/ Had taught us both to wait/Not to publish feeling.' He was desperate for messages and, wide open, was shocked by this warning. He was childish. He was the one who had published too much feeling and the mistake flashed up in his face. Blinking hard, he held his breath. She pressed on hard and, again, her fingernail blushed at 'Mushroom loves already/Had puffed and burst in hate.' His heart closed: these augurs were dark. She hated him. In silence they read to the end. She must have felt his want because she quickly drew him back up the lines to 'A vacuum of need/Collapsed each hunting heart.' A detour to hope. Light. He soared, wanted to punch the books off the shelves.

She went to the next floor for a couple of minutes, and when she came back down, they left the building together. Once on the street, she presented him with a bag. She had bought the book for him as a present and, in response, he became dumb with what seemed to her to be a grave gratitude and she worried that she had strained something delicate.

She tried to lighten affairs by taking him to the cheap Vietnamese again. She made to order for them and he quietly said he'd choose for himself, and when it came, she watched anxiously as he couldn't eat it. Things slowed; they seemed to feed off each other's stiffness until they were out of the restaurant again. They had loosened sufficiently by the time they reached the Beacon. She worried again about the gift of the book, but after a few jokes from him as they neared the yard (maybe born of relief?), she was almost satisfied that the gesture had not been too much. Nevertheless, she felt that he had left her too quickly at the back door to the bar.

Della watched Julia take the stairs two at a time. She'd been watching them walk slowly through the yard and into the pub and quickly brewed what she was going to say to her daughter. Julia reached the top step.

'Oh! Mum, you scared me!' and she laughed at the shock.

'What are you laughing at?'

Her mother's voice was nasty and Julia began to feel strangely guilty. She looked at Della's mouth. A grim line ringed white.

'Where have you been?'

'I've been showing Eugene round.'

'He's a grown man.'

'So what?' said Julia, lightly, confused at her mother's attack. 'Grown men get lonely too.' She wasn't prepared to give up her good mood.

'That's what I'm talking about,' said Della.

'What?' Julia gave in and swung into her mother's argument. 'You were the one who wanted him here!'

'You leave Eugene to his own devices. Taking Rhodri for a fool.'

'Since when do you give a fuck about Rhodri?' The underlying threat, her mother's falseness, had made her raise her voice, but Della kept hers low.

'I could say the same to you.'

She looked at her mother incredulously. 'There's something wrong with you, you know that?'

28

Closing the door to the End, he imagined that he heard Julia retreat into Rhodri's room. He smiled, felt secure, even generous. Was he finally moving away from Theresa? By the time he walked to work on Monday he was thoroughly convinced that he had taken the whole business of Saturday, of Julia, too seriously and realized he had lost the knack of feeling neutral since he'd left home.

By mid-morning, he had recalled her laughing at his joke many times, and the tenderness in those repetitive clips had distracted him to the point that he almost swept under a pump that was being moved across the site.

'Watch yourself!' Buck bellowed, from the door of the office, and with Buck's back turned, Eugene could have broken the broom in two. The ire in the other man's voice had been too fierce to interpret as care.

That night he retreated to the End as he was sure he could hear Rhodri laughing and instantly imagined Julia doing an impression of him (maybe in the shorts?). He didn't sleep until 4 a.m. He didn't see any more of her for a couple of days and settled a little, felt warranted in recapturing Saturday's events with a faint contentment.

His strategic appearances to be working hard wherever Buck might be on site were finally rewarded when Buck shouted out his name. Lifting his head he turned and was glad others were in earshot.

'You might want to sort this lot out.' Buck pointed to some of the concrete that had already been broken out at the corner of the site. Eugene went scarlet and looked at his broom.

That night, he definitely heard her in Rhodri's room: Rhodri was laughing, sounding like a horse, and she was comically defending something or other. He wondered how he'd felt so comfortable the other day.

To make absolutely sure that he had the right to go and get drunk, he waited a little while outside the door to the End. Her clear, wry laugh stabbed at him in the dimness and he locked his door dramatically to thrust himself into their awareness. Glancing over his shoulder, he caught her peering out through Rhodri's door looking unamused now. The corridor offered little light but he saw her grin broadly and, with Rhodri's voice lilting in the background, she rolled her eyes and pulled a face. He smiled back and considered touching her as he brushed past, but was relieved to find that he hadn't once she closed the door. Downstairs, he downed a pint in one, knowing he would have done the same if she hadn't peeped out of the room but that it tasted sweeter because she had.

One more pint, and he went out of the bar to use the payphone. He felt strong enough now to ring home; wasn't afraid that a mention of Theresa from Vincent or his mother might cripple him. He felt he had new blood. From the pay-phone between the house and the bar he rang his mother's house first and got over the usual questions of ablutions and money-spending, then moved on to Vincent. 'And where's laddo?'

'Off down Reapy's for a few.'

Reapy's. Eugene tried not to make a meal of this titbit, actively assaulted the possibility that Vincent might be meeting Theresa.

'The lads from work?'

'He didn't say.'

Eugene tried Vincent's mobile. It rang off. Eugene retrieved his pound coin and nodded to the memory that it was impossible to hear a thing in that pub.

He decided that another pint would let him think, and four or five later he lay perfectly still but restless under the blankets in the End, trying once more to cash in on the bonus he'd gained by seeing Julia earlier. His doubt about his brother and Theresa had devalued it, and despite his many drinks, after a few poor dips into sleep he once again felt the sun come up.

Friday was hard. He was exhausted from the extremes he had allowed himself over the week. The men at work, unchanged to anyone else, seemed to Eugene to be showing themselves as false prophets, and he spent time alone beatifying his brother and longing for him to come over and save him from strangers. He looked up and there was Buck, coming out of the cube shed with Voitek, happy to take the time to chat with him. Eugene flicked his fag violently through the site fence, thinking, *Friday can fuck off.*

29

Uri flounced into the cabin wearing jogging bottoms. Eugene wanted to laugh because they were too tight and the material too thin and made Uri look like a cartoon strong man. Uri, it seemed, couldn't care less. He slapped Eugene on the back and winked. 'I have a special surprise for you tonight.'

Babe came and sat beside Eugene; they seemed to be the only two who weren't excited about tonight.

'Buck isn't pleased,' said Eugene.

'Would you be pleased if your son was like this?' Babe lifted his chin to Noble and the Poles. 'Why he is being so friendly with them?'

'Fucked if I know.'

'I don't like it.'

'All I know is that some galoot is doing my job and I want to know why.'

Uri straddled a chair backwards. It looked like a child's seat against the billboard of his chest. The billboard said, 'Dire Straits'. 'I have special medicine for you tonight.'

'Not tonight, Uri.'

'*Ty che galuboy*, Evgenie, hmm? Why – you gay?'

Eugene smiled weakly. Uri was hard to put off.

'Uri,' Babe caught him by the wrist, 'you look after those two tonight.'

'These Polaks?'

'Just keep your eyes on them.'

'And stay hanging around with that *pizdobol*, that fucking liar?' he said, biting his thumb at Noble.

'Don't let Noble make trouble.'

'And what about little Evgenie?' Uri chucked him under the chin.

'He will take care of you, you unlucky idiot,' said Babe.

Work seemed not to bother anyone for the rest of the afternoon. For Eugene, the clock seemed broken but the end of the day eventually came around. Before they left the site, some of them showered, most got changed. Eugene was unenthusiastic but, cajoled by Uri, changed into some jeans and a checked shirt. Mohammed, the Somali security guard, wore a kind of smock that, Eugene eventually worked out, was printed with the words 'Retro Snob' and Uri put on a three-quarter leather jacket that made his legs comically slender in the jogging bottoms, until he changed into some other trousers and a pair of black patent shoes with three zips. They were his dancing shoes, he said. What is the point? thought Eugene. He stared at the shoes and their useless zips and tried to throw off his despair among the crowd of men. Uri, beside him, smelt as sweet as a teenager.

As the crowd of them wormed their way to the gates, Uri split off and popped his head into the cabin.

Buck was still fixed on the calculator. He looked at the numbers on the little screen, 25,000, and counting.

'You will join us, Buck?'

'I'm still waiting for a phone call, Uri.'

'It is your final answer?' said Uri, very pleased with himself.

'Final answer.' Buck humoured Uri, but felt divorced from the rowdy gang outside. He groaned under his liabilities when he longed to be reeking of aftershave and ready for anything.

'He says he is not coming,' Uri said, as he passed down the steps. Eugene was eager for an audience, any audience, with Buck. He put his head through the office door. 'You don't fancy a pint?'

'Is it only one you'll be having?'

Eugene smirked even though Buck wasn't looking at him. 'Shall we have one for you, then?'

'Whatever you want.'

Buck's answer was flat and weary, yet it had been an answer, and Eugene ran down the office steps, shoving his head between Uri and Horace, making a jungle cry that surprised them as they went towards the gate. He pushed through them, bouncing ahead. 'You smell like a pair of hooers,' he shouted, jogging backwards, then turned and ran in a zigzag, pulling in his behind to escape a kick from Horace.

30

The next time Jack woke up, Buck was there. He didn't immediately trust this as fact so just stared at the familiar face and closed his eyes slowly. He'd learned not to trust his treacherous eyes in a the last few weeks despite their service over fifty-odd years. They'd become his enemies very quickly, and a pang of sadness tried to thrust through the morphine.

Since he'd got into hospital, it had seemed to be always night. Even in the bright daylight there was the featureless fear that night brings. A couple of days ago he'd managed to catch the attention of an auxiliary nurse. *End of July*, she'd said, but with nothing solid to wind that round it had meant little to him. He gave up trying.

Jack never wanted another night like last night. It had nearly finished him. He hadn't been able to breathe. The metal laundry bin beside his bed had a busted lid and he jumped awake each time it closed because, instead of sighing shut, it rang out its broken clangs at the wrong hours. A raucous cuckoo that had finally, at 4 a.m., gagged on the twisted worms of dirty sheets. The fear was with him as it had presented itself – not in waves but in one giant wave, fixed. A wave that wouldn't crash but just loomed. Everything existed full of horror, impending, just hanging there, huge and terrifying. A new drug had turned the heat down in Jack so that for now, in the daylight, his fear just simmered.

Buck stood awkwardly for a couple of minutes until Jack said, his eyes closed, 'Get a chair.'

Buck pulled one up and sat down, and Jack didn't change his face but pulled out his snuff tin and, painfully slowly, turned the lid and the bottom away from each other. Buck wanted to grab it, open it, hurry him up, get it over with. The lid finally came off and, his hand shaking, Jack scattered it up to his head, leaving a trail like gunpowder on the sheets. He took two great pinches.

'It was Seamus's money.' The sentence barely finished before the coughing began.

It unnerved Buck. 'Don't try to talk.'

Jack shook his head, grimaced in frustration, tried again. 'It was not my money to give.'

The sense of what he was saying was mounting and Buck gripped hard on to the possibility that Jack was talking nonsense. 'You don't have to worry about anything in here – they're doing all they can.'

Jack shushed him feebly, trying to lift his finger to his lips. After an empty grab at the pillow his hand found his ear and he touched it gently, telling Buck to listen. 'The money. Seamus's. Not mine. He left it for the wean.'

'Come on, Jack, will ye? Don't talk like that. Rest.' Buck pushed against the implications of what Jack was saying, but he understood enough to be angry about what this meant, the weight of it. Buck didn't know who she was, or the wean, but he did know that he'd taken off with their money. The fact lay across his shoulders for him to carry into the future. Buck saw Jack sag, the news out of him.

A nurse stopped Buck on the way out and asked if he was a relation. Metastases, she said. Bits of floating cancer from his lungs had gone into his brain. Little terrorist crabs eating his mind. She drew a picture. Cancer, crabs. Buck had never made the connection. Morphine was being given to keep his breathing low, to stop the coughing, and they'd given him something to stop the seizures that always accompanied this. For a second Buck felt relieved and smiled – all these drugs, Jack didn't know what he was saying.

'He's pretty lucid this morning, though,' she said brightly.

Buck nodded, his smile fading as the nurse told him that at this stage of the illness he could visit Jack whenever he liked.

He walked down the corridors, oppressed by the smells and the light green ill-looking walls. Buck hadn't smoked for twenty years, but with these old bones dug up, he begged a roll-up from a crushed little man at the doorway and looked out on to the melting traffic of Whitechapel Road where his eyes conjured up the kid, an unknown child for Seamus wound up in the cruellest twists of his past.

31

Eugene had woken with Vincent's name spilling out of his mouth and, very suddenly, he knew this much: things were not good. He felt for the crusty blankets on his bed in the End. Not there. The comfort that comes after the brief hiatus of morning memory didn't turn up either.

He fumbled at it, but his mind seemed to have ended its relationship with real time: his memory was inert, grounded with a broken propellor that he was trying to spin manually. So, instead of a wide vista of last night, with yesterday in the background and tomorrow before him, he had to wait for some other faculty to spread out his past for him. What else could deal with the day before and the whole mess of maybes that had got him to here? It was here that he was. Slavering, in somebody else's bed.

If he could get up he might feel better. But he couldn't, not yet. Rousing himself seemed unthinkable. He tried to start again, crank it up. He'd have liked to know where he was but his eyes stayed closed and on the red screens of his eyelids he saw eggs. There were eggs now. Tough eggs that weren't ready to hatch. From inside came tappings, promises, but when he tried to pick them up, break them open, they'd hush and still. He had a word with himself. Patience, sir. Sit back on top of them again and wish them open with a hard stare from the old mind's eye: look at the crazy white eggs 'cos when they hatch, out they'll run, cheep and chirp, getting to here, getting to now.

He sat up and snapped open his eyes. From the shine and size of it, he reckoned he must be in a cell. He needed a friend.

'Can I have a cigarette, please?' He said it to the room and his voice sounded deeper, as if a lot had happened since he'd last heard it.

He started to move but he could barely turn his head. He was dazed and battered and he fizzed as he always did after too much of something. His vision was coming at him from two different angles and the light in the cell was nauseating as it continued to reflect off the stainless steel of the toilet bowl and the tiny sink. He didn't even know if anyone could hear him. The hatch at the door opened and Eugene got to his feet and looked through the slot. The black almond eyes looked fair, kind. They were young, Asian, perhaps Pakistani. Maybe Indian. How was Eugene to know? But Eugene was very worried about this fact somehow. The eyes continued to look through the spyhole at him. One side of his face felt massively swollen. He opened his mouth to test his jaw and felt some dried liquid crack as he stretched his skin. He scratched the area and there were dark brown flakes under his nails. There was dried blood around his ear. He looked at his hand. Two nails were missing. He pressed the sore beds as if to ask them where the nails had gone.

'You can't smoke in there.'

The slot was fully open now. Eugene guessed the officer was young, about twenty-five.

'Is there anywhere you can smoke?'

'On the fire escape . . . but the sergeant says I don't have to go anywhere with you.'

'What do you mean?'

''Cos of your charge.'

'What charge?'

'You're in here on a racially aggravated assault charge.'

'You what?' Eugene swayed. He sat heavily on the floor and weighed his head in his hands, felt the right side of his face numb, big and waxy, like a fatty side of meat.

The locks turned and the young officer didn't look at Eugene but beckoned him. Eugene got up and followed. The policeman led him on to a fire escape and handed him a cigarette. Eugene lit the cigarette, shaking more than usual.

'Racially aggravated assault?' he said to the policeman, separating the words, giving them room to make sense. He was trying to make out if any of them was applicable to him. To Eugene Mahon.

The policeman looked at Eugene's open face and Eugene stared back, desperately seeking evidence that the policeman didn't believe Eugene could hurt anyone for such a reason. The policeman showed him a painful mix: that he wasn't convinced but neither was he prepared to be unconvinced. What had happened? An invisible band squeezed his throat; a feeling that would not be leaving him any time soon. Injustice was tight. At least, he hoped it was injustice. He pressed his face tenderly.

Back in the cell, he sat on the floor again. Slowly, his memory creaked, the propellor started to circle, its blades rusty, and he suddenly felt he should protect himself, stand away.

He remembered a doctor. A doctor had been in the cells. Eugene had been asleep on the floor. An officer had been with him. The doctor hadn't touched Eugene.

'Are you all right?' The man in the foreground had bent over him, framed by fluorescent light, his head a featureless outline; a flat black pawn. The officer had stood in the background.

'Yes,' said Eugene, thickly, not knowing what the right answer was.

Rewinding, he couldn't get things up to speed. What had led to this? His legs were killing. He couldn't straighten one of them. He pulled down his trousers and gasped at several raised blackenings, each run through with bright and dangerous-looking red, and when he touched them it felt as if rubber balls had been pushed under his skin. The policeman looked at them.

'Where are these from?' Eugene sounded confused, and the policeman looked away to avoid the question. Without answers, Eugene became precarious and emotion pushed up into his face, making it feel twice its size. He stopped asking questions and let out some tears. They ran through the dried blood on his jaw and presented themselves as pink on the white-tiled floor of the cell.

32

They let Eugene out that evening and he stumbled south from Shoreditch police station without laces in his shoes – he'd just bunched them up with his phone and his keys. He put the belt on round his waist under his shirt, too stunned to find his belt-loops. Stopping only when he got to the river, he finally realized he'd walked the wrong way. He looked at the pink hung-over sky and saw the cranes Julia had pointed out, now making Nazi salutes to the west. He was slowly acknowledging that all he had were the policemen's opinions of what had gone on last night, and without the grounding of his own memory, he walked, wobbling on the slack highwire of their reports.

There were only two other numbers besides Vincent's in his new phone. He called Uri first. He answered immediately.

'What the fuck happened?' Uri cried.

'Didn't you see?'

'I only see that fucking little Tartar beating you outside the stripper club. The bouncer, he must see something! Go to him.'

'But before that? What they're charging me with – it's serious.' Eugene was trying not to cry but his voice was betraying him.

'This is too bad,' Uri said earnestly.

Eugene composed himself. 'What started it?'

'I have not one clue.' Uri's voice was strained.

'Where did Noble go? Voitek?'

'I do not know, Eugene.' Again, Uri sounded uncomfortable.

'Then I'm fucked.'

'Wait. What you say to *polizia*?'

'I told them I couldn't remember.'

There was a silence, then Uri said, 'They no bring lawyer?'

'I didn't ask for one.'

Again, silence.

'We will work out on Monday. Buck will help.'

Eugene lurched at the thought of Buck knowing. 'I'm not coming in. Tell Buck I'm sick.'

They resolved to talk on Monday and Eugene clicked his phone shut. He was about to ring home but remembered the time and, anyway, he felt if he told Vincent or his mother, it would make things real.

Because he had no choice, Eugene called the third number. 'Genie, you can't 'alf run when you want, can you? Your little legs, going like the fucking clappers.' He cackled as if this was a prank in the cabin.

'Have you any idea what happened? They've made some really fucking serious charges against me, Noble.'

'Like what?'

'Assault, resisting arrest.'

'Mate, you should stay off the booze. It doesn't suit you.'

Eugene clenched his jaw, forced himself on. 'Did you see what started it?'

'I wish I could help you, mate, but I'm in the dark, like you. I scarpered. Couldn't stick around with the Poles, could I?'

'Right.'

'Lucky lad like you, you'll get away with it!'

Eugene clicked shut his phone.

The only chance he had was the bouncer with the face like an old settee cushion who sat on his chrome stool from midnight to morning outside Green's. Eugene turned his back to the river and, feeling utterly lost, walked north then east to Bishopsgate.

As he walked he railed at his own stupidity. He thought he was being punished for the wrong reasons but he wasn't aware that he was being taught a grander lesson: that London was a hoarder of superlatives – it couldn't stomach the mediocre so it had made him one of its worst. He hadn't been different enough. That was all he was guilty of.

Horace's words echoed through his mind: *All the crazy wonderful slamming roar of the street – oh, God, there's noises I'm going to be hungry for.*

From Bishopsgate, he took a right when he got to the clock at Liverpool Street and walked the almost empty streets, past the chalky spire of the church in Spitalfields and down Fashion Street towards Brick Lane. He looked at the street name, Fashion Street: even fads could curl a groove out of London but not him – he wasn't heavy enough. For the first time, he sincerely wished he'd never met Theresa: he wouldn't have been in London if she hadn't ruined home for him. He dithered on Brick Lane about which way to turn and a sob punctured him. It had always seemed that London switched the streets round overnight especially to get him.

*

The arteries off Hackney Road and Shoreditch High Street were already labouring with evening traffic when he reached Green's. At first the bouncer seemed to recognize him and Eugene felt encouraged but quickly realized that it was the mess of his face that had prompted the involuntary smile. The man sucked away his chance with a drag on his fag.

'All right, mate. You see what happened last night?' He pointed at his face.

'Didn't see a thing.'

'It was right here.' He pointed to the pavement, a yard away from the man's chrome perch.

'Nah.'

'This is the only part I can remember!' His voice, pitched too high, embarrassed him and, Eugene saw, it had been for nothing.

'Sorry, son. If it goes off inside there's CCTV, but out here, that's different.'

He walked along Great Eastern Street. Looking warily around him, he felt as if even the buildings were staring at him; small childish windows, uniform, doing nothing wrong, like arched mouths singing their unanimous hymn of *nau-ghty nau-ghty nau-ghty*; a curved sandy-coloured tenement with all of its windows bricked up looked happy to be blind, Eugene thought, but the bricks were uneven. Some were being sucked backwards, forcing the building to see again. Much crueller, he thought.

He crossed the high street and left those buildings for the seediness of Commercial Road. A handful of skinny women huddled in the early light and peered, emotionless, at his swollen face. His legs were so stiff now that he could barely walk, and as he neared his turning, a milk-float passed him. He stopped to look at this pug of a machine, very much from the past, the place where Eugene desperately wanted to be. It lurched off and stopped again a few yards in front, then continued its short, arcing journey around parked cars; each arc accompanied by what sounded like a slow groan of realization, as though somebody was showing it, over and over, where it had been going wrong.

33

The engineer looked over the pour and whistled through his teeth. 'How comes you kept pouring?'

Buck felt his shoulders rise towards his ears. He didn't want a meal made of this. The engineer was a small, pasty man, an annoying, sniffing, whey-faced little hee-haw, he thought, but then he reined himself in. It wasn't this fella's fault. As soon as he had seen the concrete, the engineer had turned his feet out to the sides and folded his arms in readiness to stand and talk about the cases he'd seen and how this one ranked. Buck wanted him to drill the cores and get off his job.

'Well, pal, it'll have to come up.'

'I know it's got to come up. These are for the insurance.' Just take the fucking samples, thought Buck, and shut your hole. While the diamond drill pulled the cores from the structure, the engineer insisted on relaying stories of bankruptcy brought about by flouting the laws of concrete, intended strengths not reached because of too much water, not enough cooling or curing, until Buck had to find some more important work to do. He faked a call on his radio but when he came back it was if he'd never left, the engineer winding up with 'You cannot cheat with concrete.' The man was on his hands and knees now. 'Everybody knows you can't rush the cure.' He got up. 'The insurance will want the whole lot, I bet. Freeze-thaw, the works. What do your documents say?'

Buck wasn't about to tell him that he didn't want to read them, and in the silence the engineer defended himself by instructing Buck: 'You'd better check.'

Buck wanted rid of this shit-sucking fly of a man.

After gathering his tools together, the engineer slid the last core from the lifter tube and held the bony sample under his arm. He put out his hand to shake Buck's. Buck grabbed the scrawny paw and the man smiled as if he'd won another battle in the wonderful kingdom of concrete.

In the office, Buck got out Gerry Reilly's number. He hadn't been in touch for a while but Buck had followed his progress in the papers. Sunday supplements hadn't done him justice, Buck thought. He had looked austere, way too serious, but the story told how Gerry had changed human rights law. Serving writs to politicians was stiff business indeed and Buck guessed it wouldn't have been right to have him smiling. Buck remembered him on the doorstep, fresh from Monaghan with a suitcase he couldn't carry. He'd called Buck not long after, in the middle of the night, asking how his Afghani was because there was a case he was looking after where the man needed work. He'd promised Buck faithfully that the man would work like a dog. Buck remembered scrabbling in the dark but failing to pull together enough to make an argument.

Gerry had brought the man down to the site – he hadn't had much work back then. He introduced Sumir. The man's eyes were black and pinched into a squint. He didn't smile; his face said, 'Fuck you for helping me,' and it offended Buck, but he had seen that face many times since then and knew now that the expression came from being away from your family. None of them could ignore Sumir's black eye.

Gerry had looked at the Afghan and pointed to the eye. It was obvious to Buck that Sumir wanted to explain himself. Gerry was patient, but after a minute or so of the man feeling around for the right words he had explained to Buck that he had tried to use his vouchers from the dole office to buy aftershave when they didn't take them for that kind of thing. Without the right words the woman behind the counter had found him threatening.

'What can he do?' Buck remembered feeling like a shit for asking someone else about a man standing right there in front of him.

'From what I can work out, he can lay bricks and shout,' Gerry had said.

Sumir had now been with Buck for fifteen years. He worked through the dark if Buck asked him, and over the last year had run a small job on the Holloway Road for O'Halloran's.

It wasn't his usual, but Gerry might be able to help Buck sort out what he was liable for.

For a moment after he puts down the receiver, Buck allows his eye to hover over the past, letting it focus on people and events, then follow consequences as they roll into the present and place themselves, flap, at his door. If Eugene'd been there, fit for work, he would never have signed the concrete off.

Buck's eye on the past pulls back further, wowing open, then tightening into a spotlight. In it, he sees himself, and he is ashamed because he knows he is close to tears. He has Seamus hard by the shoulders because he doesn't know what else to do.

'You nearly killed the poor bastard!' he shouts. Seamus, under Buck's hands, hangs from his own shoulders, limp and blinking, and Buck lets him go because here is a man who doesn't know how to stay still enough to be sorry; side-stepping, shuffling, sifting stuff through fingers that will never quite grasp what they've done.

34

The next day Buck dragged himself to the site to find Noble already there, giggling at the computer.

'I'm making a poster,' his son answered, to a question that Buck hadn't asked.

He got the body from the Internet; a picture of Jean-Claude van Damme's torso and he chose it decisively with a click, smiling, and, with a prurient groan, said, 'Van Damage, I think.'

The picture showed a sideways shot of the martial artist, greased up, a couple of stripes of camouflage for the studio, holding a curved knife in the foreground to head height. Over Jean-Claude's head, Noble pasted the photo of Eugene that had been taken for his identity badge, muttering, 'You shoulda known you were gonna be famous. It's in your blood.' He laughed into his shoulder. He finished with 'Mate, you have been Van Damned.'

Under this uneven hybrid he typed 'Free the Galway One!'

Large, bold.

Noble was fitting up the posters as Buck walked into the office. Eugene's confused stare met Buck from the neck of a man's naked body.

Buck shivered as if to confirm that Jack's news had been an omen. Jack had let a bad genie out of a bottle and all Buck could do was watch it billow.

'See? I told you not to let him on site. Trouble.'

'What's happened?'

'Pissed, probably on drugs, caused some trouble with the coppers outside Green's. Probably get bird.'

Noble saw Buck narrow his eyes. Disbelief was always his first reaction. He looked back to the comical chimera in front of him. 'Anyway, fucking Billy the kid 'ere,' he thumbed at the photo of Eugene, 'just rang in sick. He's gonna be a fucking millstone to us.'

Buck sat in his chair, feeling heavy. He'd ask Uri or Babe what had happened. Noble was gathering up the posters and whistling, and when Buck looked at him, he couldn't help thinking that this was all his own fault.

Noble went into the cabin and sat with his new sidekicks, Voitek and Ignacy. The two boys had been at his heels all around Shoreditch before the trouble had started.

Noble's phone rang, the tone a fly buzzing, getting louder. ''Ello, sweetheart.' A gap. His mouth open, then a wink. 'Oh, shut up!' He laughed filthily.

He nodded at the two lads, who were still hanging on his accent, his eyebrows raising and lowering, tongue out. He put the phone down and looked around, excited by his conversation. Those who'd been listening couldn't understand and those who could hear him didn't want to know.

He whispered to Voitek, then swivelled to Babe at the sink.

''Ere, Babe!' shouted Noble. 'Listen to this. These boys are learning.'

Babe was making the tea. He looked over good-naturedly for the sake of the Poles.

'Voitek was so fucking pissed the other night . . .' He nudged Voitek, prodding him to perform. Voitek screwed up his face and shook his head. Noble whispered to him again.

'I said, Voitek was so pissed the other night . . .' He pushed him gently with his shoulder. Silence, so he jabbed at Voitek's stomach.

'I was so pissed . . .' Voitek sighed, then gave in and, at Noble's prompting, stood up to recite '. . . I got my cock out for a shit.'

The sentence lilted upwards at the end and his face was scarlet with uncertainty. Ignacy looked on, giggling, impressed by the brand new words that were coming out of his friend's mouth; their friendship allowed a little of the responsibility for them to fall on him. He settled into an open-mouthed grin.

Noble clapped gleefully, flicking his eyes over at the table where Horace and Uri sat in conversation. Eugene's absence was strangely conspicuous. None of them looked up.

At the sink, Babe forced a smile and turned back to the tea. Across the cabin, Uri grunted and, without turning to him, Noble said, 'Don't forget, Uri.'

Uri turned to see Noble with his finger to his thick, scarred lips. '*Pizdobol!*' choked Uri, then stared at the table.

Blackmail was poison to a paranoid man and Uri hated guilt. That was one of the reasons he had made friends with cocaine. The more he felt, the more he put away. He had acquired the name 'The Pelican' from his frequenting the pub of the same name but, more importantly, it reflected the piles he could stuff into his beak. What had happened to Eugene, and the silence forced on him by Noble's threat to sell-out Matilda to Immigration, had undone him so he'd tried to do himself back up with more coke. He had cowered in his room until Eugene finally called to ask him what the fuck had happened, and even after that had lain wide-eyed, and spent the ripening dawn stiff and hurtling on his bed, arms close to his sides on a bedroom luge that the pure coke would not let him get off. Imprisoned, he thought incessantly about what a *zasranec* he was, what a fucking arsehole! The kid wasn't used to it! He should never have given Eugene such high-grade gear. Not cut with plaster, like usual, it was from Holland, medicinal-grade cocaine, and it had blown away Eugene's record of events.

He knew it was bad luck to hang around Noble but Babe had been worried about Noble's influence on the young Poles.

'I am an angel over them,' pledged Uri to Babe, one hand on his heart, the other fluttering at his shoulder; a stubby tattooed wing.

Reassured, Babe had gone to see his *kabuni* dancing in Bermondsey with a ceilidh band over from Kerry. The odd group had moved loosely together all around Shoreditch, Uri keeping a good eye on Noble throughout the night.

It had been late, perhaps two, two thirty, when it happened. The first thing to catch Uri's attention was the windows of a black car that slid by them at a crawl down the alley off Rivington Street. He was intrigued by the enigma of what looked like darkened glass. The passenger window was open a crack and he tried to see inside.

Behind Uri, Noble was carrying Voitek on his back, staggering and loud, Ignacy behind them, slapping his countryman's behind. Eugene was up for anything, out in front, trying to chat to a throng of girls in short luminous skirts, amid the crowd that thronged the narrow pavement. Uri was following them.

As the creeping car passed him, Noble bent and shouted through the window, 'Oy! What you looking at, you cheeky cunt? You looking at their arses, you fucking pervert?' Then, like a horse and rider in reverse, Noble had nudged Voitek's legs with his elbows and Voitek, already the obedient beast, had kicked the car.

The car stopped immediately, only a meter in front of Noble. The door opened directly on to Eugene, who was not much taller than the skinny Chinese-looking bloke, who got out in trainers and T-shirt. Without saying anything he pushed Eugene violently back into the crowd. The crowd of girls complained loudly, and others further back, drunkenly.

In the short time it took Eugene to scramble back to him, the man swung out a baton obliquely and people started to push, trying to get out of his way. Eugene's face was a mask of misunderstanding, and as the guy closed in on him he shunted him back in the chest and he toppled into the car. Uri reckoned that it was not for another minute that the driver got out and screamed, 'Police!'

But things were already bad. There was scuffling, and Eugene had crashed into the velvet-roped barrier of the Embassy nightclub just before the arch at the end of the alley. He cried out from the ground and Uri could see that the copper was smashing the cuffs into Eugene's hand, which was covering his head. Uri shouted, 'Stop! Eugene, it is police!' but he was drowned by screams. Eugene was flailing, then caging his arms around his head to protect himself from the sharp open jaws of the cuffs and the short, brutal swipes of the baton.

Eugene was on the ground but Uri couldn't get to him, his huge bulk squashed by the panicking crowd. He looked back for an escape, to try to open up the crush from another angle. He saw Noble and the Poles making their exit down the alley and on to Curtain Road.

Eugene managed somehow to push the copper off and scramble through the straggling mass. The policeman matched his speed and was up and after him. Uri burst out of the crowd, wondering why only one of the police had chased after Eugene and why there had been no badge, until it was too late. The last he saw of Eugene as he reached the end of Rivington Street was the small, elastic figure of the plainclothes policeman behind him. Eugene had stopped running, had his back to the copper with his hands up.

He took his legs out first and Uri winced as Eugene crumpled. He then started on his head without any reservation. He was short enough to use the baton as a club. Uri watched helplessly. A fat old man with badgered hair was looking on from a stool outside the strip-club. Uri watched the beating as the bouncer shifted on his stool and blew smoke up Hackney Road.

Uri had panicked then. He headed quickly south down Shoreditch High Street and ducked into the overlit petrol station to get his breath. A second later, Noble and Voitek fell through the door, followed by Ignacy. Noble was breathing hard.

Uri threw his hands into the air. 'Fucking man, why did you do that?'

Noble pressed air to the floor, telling Uri to keep his voice down, but his face was hard and closed. 'Do what, Uri?' The startled Poles blinked in the artificial light behind him.

'Shout at policeman! Kick car!'

'Not me.' Noble put up his open hands.

'I heard you shout. That is why the car stopped.'

Noble came up close to Uri and whispered directly into his face. His breath was sour. 'Your girlfriend, Uri, she got her papers?'

Uri was stunned and fell silent. Matilda was here illegally.

'Eugene must have done something. They don't attack people for nothing.'

Uri's heart was out of his chest with the extra strength of the drug and it pulsed out a rainbow of bad chemicals; yellow guilt, scarlet anger and white, white paranoia.

He pushed Noble out of the way. A sickly pink mess, Uri headed home.

35

After the weekend, Uri was glad to get to work but irritated also, knowing that Babe would blame him for Eugene's predicament. He came from the toilets to the cabin and Horace saw a white streak on Uri's lip; a third track to his deep philtrum. Horace made a sniff to let Uri know. Uri pinched his nose with his thumb and forefinger. Prison was a university of gesture.

'Man, you want to give that shit up. It don't make you high no more, it just make you long.'

Uri didn't need instructions in the ways and whys of cocaine. He didn't need religion or other people's ideas or ways of thinking. That was why he had left Irkutsk, and with this in his mind he gave Horace a thunderous look, but Horace was not put off. He took up his book again. Turgenev.

'Lookit, I underlined this part just for you, Uri. "A nihilist is a man who does not take any principle on trust, no matter with what respeck that principle is surrounded."'

Uri understood this because it was direct translation, barely clothed Russian with strong grammar bones, and he felt an extra charge because he had an opinion: he agreed. 'Yes! I am happy to trust nothing. I will live longer than you!'

The last person Uri had trusted had been found by a work group outside the perimeter fence of the prison, frozen in a sitting position, his arteries cut, hidden under a scarf, his hands behind his back, holes where his kidneys had been pilfered. Eaten. He was a 'cow', his parts provisions for those who had escaped from the camp. A lesson.

'Respeck – that's the key word here.'

Babe chipped in, 'Paranoia! Having no trust, this is the perfect petrol for nihilism.' He wagged a finger in the air.

Now Uri was getting confused and flustered, and he struggled furiously to accommodate the word 'petrol' into this sentence. A word he knew! '*Poret chush' tak Trotsky!* Bullshit like Trotsky! That is all you talk.' He was getting even more irritated by their academic discussion with the news about Eugene burning away at him. Let them talk on. Let them wait. He would punish them with it.

Horace went on, 'And that stuff gonna mek you more and more paranoid. Your brain him writing cheques that you body cyan't cash.' Horace and Babe gave each other a high-five.

He snatched up the book and read Turgenev's friendly nicknames that were in bold on the back. 'He is no "Soft Pear", he is no "Gentle Barbarian" – he is devil. Dostoevsky named him "Devil" and devil he is. He push Russia into slavery from slavery!'

He made to spit at Horace's book, but Horace knew him well enough not to flinch.

'No one put my mind in prison again,' Uri said obdurately; a promise made heavy through repetition.

'Except the cocaine!' Babe quipped.

Horace wouldn't let go. 'Turgenev, cha! He changed history through words. Literature actually move t'ings back then.' He shook his head. 'Turgenev's brain, it weighed two kilos. Two kilos!'

'Yes,' Uri spluttered, 'because guilt is most heavy!' He banged the table.

Babe stood. 'No, Regret is heaviest, like lead. Cocaine keeps regret away. Uri, you keep going like this and when you die, your brain will float off like a balloon!' and with the outer tips of his fingers he flicked up the sides of his temples. Horace congratulated him with a touching of fists.

Unable to keep quiet any longer, Uri lowered his voice, leaned in. 'Shut up of balloons already. Eugene is in big fucking trouble.'

Della had sent Eugene up to Highbury to Ferdinand & Ferdinand, a firm headed up by a second-generation African called Cornelius who specialized in race cases. The copper had snapped Eugene's card with the hard round head of his baton, so Della had reluctantly lent him fifty pounds. She was emptying the meter above the fridge when Julia came stretching into the kitchen.

'Well, your friend's gone and done it now.'

'What are you on about – *my friend?*' Her voice was still gravelly with sleep.

'Eugene, last night. He's on a racial assault charge.'

'Who says? Jack?' She snorted and carried on walking to the sink.

'He's just borrowed money from me. They're arranging a

hearing. Bow Street Magistrates.'

Julia turned, but tried to snuff out any glimmer that she was about to take her mother more seriously. 'What happened? Eugene?'

'Yes, Eugene.' Della stood up and played her best mummy card. She lived to play and win these increasingly infrequent hands. 'You never know people – you see? Even when you think you do.'

And Julia looked unsteadily at Della because, behind the sibilant front of this satisfied little speech, she heard a rumble that she felt had great potential; news that you couldn't escape from, gathering at the horizon.

36

A Friday-night show blared from Noble's room down the hall. Buck hadn't been asleep but he was in bed and Deirdre was letting out ribbons of breath beside him. He answered the phone before the first ring completed. It took thirty seconds to discover from Gerry's readings of the facts that the insurance was not going to pay up. He thanked his friend anyway.

Buck got up silently and looked down at his wife. He wanted to wake her and tell her he was sinking because of their son, but he knew that before she'd heard him out she'd buckle and bend his words until his every course of action looked like a line of vicious attack against Noble and therefore her. He wanted to open up the map of his relationship with her and Noble, lay it on the bed and point to the junctions where he felt he'd taken a wrong turn, where she'd given him wrong directions. Work out a better route. He wanted to tell her how he'd like to scalp that eejit of a son of hers and that silly little bollix Eugene. He wanted to explain once and for all how her back to him in bed used to break his heart, that he'd tried not to be stiff with the boy, with her, but the unsaid did what it was good at and stayed where it was.

He went downstairs and got his business folder from the cabinet and glanced around the dining room at the walls covered with photos of Noble, Noble and Deirdre, Noble and Deirdre and Deirdre's mother. Buck in the odd one. There was one of Buck and Patsy, right at the back of the cabinet, a fish between them.

Noble had always wanted more of everything and Buck's perverse reluctance to give to him varied inversely with the strength of Noble's desires. He was ashamed of his son's needs, wished he'd keep them to himself. Buck had the love that Noble wanted. He had it all right. He knew he had it. It was just never quite ready to be given. When Buck thought of his son he wanted to wash his hands.

He got out his papers and spread them on the table. The loan on the business was definitely going to have to wait, at least for a couple of months. He wouldn't be telling Deirdre because she was always ready to fight when Buck forced her to be part of anything that wasn't a sure winner. There was Noble's money, to get him a nice house, out of East London. It was Deirdre's mother's way of having her hand in their business. A little debt she could use when she felt her hold on her daughter was weak. She would intermittently deposit money: surplus rents from a row of mews houses, now flats, that she had long owned in Islington. The account was governed by Buck and Deirdre in their son's name. Back when their relationship was less skewed by their son's existence, they'd both dump money into it. With only one signature needed, Buck had borrowed from it after the '91 crash and had managed to pay it back without anyone asking questions.

Buck was making his coffee and pouring it into a flask when Deirdre came into the kitchen at 5.30 a.m. He kept his head down and hoped he was not silently priming some instinct she had to protect the boy.

'You been to bed?'

'Not really. Had to sort some stuff out. For the job.'

'Don't forget we're going away next week.'

'When is it again?'

'The seventeenth. My mother is worse than Noble.'

'Eh?'

'You know. Excited. Planning.'

Buck already felt the ocean between them and was saddened to realize that he was no longer troubled by the idea of a life alone. Deirdre was taking Noble and her mother somewhere ferociously hot. They seemed to like to go places where there was no peace, where everybody was always shouting. He didn't ask where it was this time.

'She still saves money for his holidays. Those little bags from the bank.' Deirdre laughed, a ticklish girlish laugh, to herself, way, way across the waves.

Buck packed himself up a good chunk of ham and some soda bread that one of the electricians had shipped over for him. Ten years in London and the sparky would only eat his mammy's own. Buck went up the stairs from the kitchen and stood at the door to put on his boots. He thought of how he'd put it to the blokes, but knew it didn't really matter.

Though he'd normally stay in the office in the mornings, Buck's troubles took him in to the men. He busied himself at the sink and put his sandwich in the fridge, all the while straining to seem as if he wasn't listening in to the urgent whispers at Babe's table.

Babe stood up, sat down and then stood up. 'I will pretend I was there! I should have been there!' He clapped his forehead with a rough palm. 'No. Stick to the truth.'

'Policeman trying to kill him in front of Green's. Beating him! *Mordu nabil!* Blood and mess, mess, mess.' Uri made circles with his hands in an effort to beckon the words he was looking for. 'Eugene had hands up! Not fighting!'

'What started it?' Babe asked.

'This I do not know.' Uri's voice became lower as he worried that the real story was smouldering like strong incense in his belly and that Babe would smell it sooner or later. He went to the toilet to damp himself down.

'Trouble come to man as sure as sparks fly upwards.' Horace breathed it and sucked his teeth. 'You can see it in a bwoy like Eugene.'

Buck headed over to their table. 'Trouble, then?'

'Looks like that,' said Babe.

'Where is he now?'

Uri came from the toilets and smuggled himself in behind Buck.

'Uri? You know?'

'Why will I know?' Fresh from the toilets, Uri was taken aback by Buck's sudden appearance and now a question.

'Pissed, was he?' Buck asked, scanning their faces.

Uri was sweating and he wiped his hand over his face as if he were holding a flannel.

'I know, I know, I should have gone with them,' moaned Babe, looking at Buck with one eye from under his hand.

'Just what we fucking need,' said Buck. 'Listen,' and every one of them leaned in, beckoned by the rare need in Buck. Uri sat down.

'Insurance won't pay.'

'Sit, sit.' Babe motioned to Buck and pulled Uri's shirt for him to make a space.

'All my cash is going to have to go into breaking this out and getting new stuff down with a new firm.' He smoothed his hand over the back of the chair but didn't sit. 'This could fuck me up. To the tune of about ten grand.'

'Losing the Singhs. Very bad luck!' tutted Babe. They all nodded.

'I need some overtime from you lot.'

'Anything!' said Babe, and the silence meant he spoke for all of them.

'I'll pay you, you know that, but it'll be a ways off yet.' He crouched in the midst of them now.

'Do not worry!' said Babe.

'It'll be pure dunkey work.'

'We can break it out easily. Pieces of piss,' Uri said from behind.

'Not a bother, Buck. Just let us know,' Babe said.

Their loyalty threatened to take Buck over so he stood up again to give his chest room to expand. Noble entered, whistling, sticking up his posters above the sink, oblivious. Buck put his hand on Babe's shoulder and Uri's neck. He didn't squeeze: he knew his big hand weighed enough to say what he meant.

37

In the smartest clothes he could find, Eugene made his plea of not guilty to Bow Street Magistrates Court and hardly believed it himself. He wore a round-necked dark jumper and a tie, the tie practically invisible, making an awkward bunch under the wool, as if it was the thought that counted. Apart from avoiding Julia, the kitchen, the shower, the very idea of getting washed and changed had seemed quite ridiculous to him since the arrest. He sat in court smelling himself, frankly wondering why he had ever bothered with washing at all. He looked down at his left hand, the one that had shielded him. It was turgid and the knuckles were hidden by the swelling. A deep cut traced a ragged line from his little finger to his wrist. As Eugene held up his hand, his fingers clawed as if defeated, and he scrabbled at his memory, dredging, lumbering through the sludge of that night. He remembered Uri holding a huge pinch under his nostrils that had numbed his face from the nose down and removed him from the evening, until he was brought back by the beatings to a hard ringing floor, scuffles, scuttling. His 'Not guilty', uttered a moment ago, seemed tinny and unrealistic.

The lawyer had said how lucky he was to have a clean record, which meant they could go to Crown Court – not everybody sides with the copper there. This lucky feeling wasn't all it was cracked up to be, he thought. The angry lumps from the cruel head of the baton, which had bled under his skin, were pushing into the hard bench. They throbbed along with his head, and as the charges beat down on him he absorbed them, folded them into his story, a new chapter, the one where Eugene, it seems, is able for all of this.

In his dazed state, he arrived without a hitch at the Beacon and he realized, with a lump in his throat, that it was taking too much notice that had got him lost on tubes and down alleys. As he put his key into the lock, he looked jealously at a weaving circle of swifts, filtering the midsummer sky for insects.

The pale end-of-evening light seeped through the blanket at the window. He sat, barely breathing, in the End in the dark. He didn't want to go to the meter because he didn't want to see Julia. There was a sharp knock at the door and he didn't make a move to answer, but soon enough the knock came again, louder. She must have pre-empted his worry as she shouted, 'It's me, Della.'

He opened the door a chink and Della handed him the *Hackney Gazette*. What he could see of her face was serious.

'You'd better have a look at this before you go back to work.'

She'd opened it to the right page, folding the news out to him. 'Tower Hamlets Resident Arrested For Racial Assault'.

They'd got his name wrong, calling him Seamus Eugene Mahon. A small mercy. He looked at the names and wondered how his mother had thought it wise to stick those stinking labels on someone else.

His phone rang, and Cornelius brutally passed on the news that there was no CCTV of the attack. Eugene felt relieved. He didn't tell Cornelius but, because of the stealthy erosion of self-doubt, he no longer wanted an independent record of the night's events. Off the phone, he was left with the feeling that Cornelius had been looking to him for reassurance. He nearly laughed out loud. The good news was that they could use Uri as a witness. Eugene guessed he should be glad, but the upturn seemed perverse in this run of downturns.

The next morning, Eugene met the barrister who was going to represent him and was puzzled for a moment when he saw her. Everyone in the Highbury office had been black. She was an exceptionally short Glaswegian woman, a tiny thing with freckles and a high forehead and a look of foreboding, which Eugene worried about for the courtroom.

'Sorry I'm late,' she offered, across the office. Eugene was impatient to determine whether this fluster was an exception to, or the rule of, her working life.

'Shona McArdle.' She was tiny – looks like a wee babby, thought Eugene.

She explained that she'd rushed straight from another case, and Eugene watched this little bird dragging a huge pull-along chest for her robes, the wig sitting at a confused angle on top of the case. Animated by its journey across the floorboards of Cornelius's office, it seemed to Eugene to be asking, 'Are we there yet?' When the case shuddered to a halt, Eugene thought it seemed relieved. Shona offered her hand and Eugene felt the calluses on his palm rise up to meet her smooth one. He might as well have had hoofs.

She sat down. She opened a stuffed briefcase and began to rummage and, watching her, Eugene immediately began to worry about her confidence. Her red hair was scraped back and he could see her scalp through the comb furrows. He tried to detect whether the freckles that crawled up her forehead had made it under her hair.

He looked at her and cursed his compulsion to see things through others' eyes. When his mother was on time, she would pick him up from school, brash and clattering, wearing a short skirt amid a sea of Catholic calf-lengths. He'd feel himself tighten as she came into view and he became a funnel for everyone's opinions about her. That same squeeze was on him now as he imagined what a judge, jury and prosecution would make of this tiny barrister's soft, soap-ad voice and fumbling childlike hands. You could get two hands around her waist.

'Cornelius has briefed me on this . . . on you . . .' she said, as she fussed through the pages. Like a pining lover, Eugene hoped that Cornelius still thought about him when he wasn't there. Did he care enough to pick the right barrister?

'He knows that PC Lee's my favourite.' She smirked, and Eugene hoped to fuck she didn't think she was funny. He didn't want someone like her to have to rely on their charm; it would destroy him to have to sit through that. Eugene was an expert on, and a great believer in, working with what you'd got and no more.

'Mr Lee.' She pointed to the page. 'He's not getting away with this again.'

'So you think we've got a chance?'

'Of course we have. This bloke doesn't know his way round a Crown Court.'

She leaned over and looked as if she might touch him. Eugene was still unsure.

'I've seen him lie before. With a jury, Lee doesn't stand a chance.'

Eugene smiled weakly.

She became grave and he was glad of it.

'There are some questions we need cast-iron answers to.'

'Ask away.'

'Without a record, why did you run from the police?'

'He never said he was a copper. Not before he'd given me a hiding.'

'Cornelius said he hit you in the head with the baton?'

'Fucking hard.'

'That's good for us.'

Eugene already had trouble with her use of 'us'.

'Lee says he distinctly heard an Irish accent calling him "Chinky cunt".'

'You can count me out there.'

She closed her notebook. 'I promise you that I'll do the best I can.'

But Eugene was afraid that promises were for those who didn't really believe in what they were saying.

He'd never promised anyone anything. In a few weeks he'd be promising to tell the truth, the whole truth and nothing but the truth, and the prospect pegged him out like a groundsheet.

38

Babe and Uri tried to make sure they maintained Eugene's good character if Buck asked a terse question about him. It was obvious that it irritated Buck. Friday came and Babe was worried as the sun crept through the scaffold up to noon. Eugene wasn't at work again and he couldn't help but feel responsible.

It was he who had forced Uri to look out for the lads. Uri might have left otherwise. Eugene would surely have followed. Babe was even more worried about the new allegiance between Noble and the Poles. Babe liked the Poles, even had an idea he could help them; pull them out of Noble's dirty hands. He had been the first to notice Voitek's carpet slippers when he'd arrived. It had cut him up because it had brought his past up close, and he wondered if his brother had found himself in a similar predicament.

He would give Voitek a couple of wraps to sell, *inshallah*, get him a bit of pocket money before his pay came through. These guys from Poland were usually open to anything.

Maybe he had a *kabuni* to care about. Too young? He would ask him, get to know.

Babe spoke to Noble. 'It will increase sales.'

'More *kishka* for you, more *kishka* for me,' was Noble's attitude. *Kishka?* Babe hated the stinking sausage that some of the Georgians brought in to eat but he kept his mouth closed.

At lunchtime he handed over ten little envelopes to Voitek, closed his calloused hand around the young lad's and explained procedures, prices and a cut, and even threw in a half-joke in the little Polish he had. The boy smiled, his cornflower blue eyes revealing, for an instant, that he felt cared for. Babe went back to the others with a little more optimism about Eugene's situation. It gave him the same feeling as his *kabuni* on fire with talent in Bermondsey dancing the Packhorse Rant. While she danced, his pudding constantly searched for his eyes as she circled. The music was Celtic but she didn't realize that it shared the folky bones of Kosovan music, and the similarity brought out more smiles in Babe. Thinking of these little joys and the helping hands of Allah, Babe felt good. They'd work things out between them.

For one thing, Uri was going to be a witness. He had one previous British conviction from several years ago, but it was a minor one where he had hit a policeman with a – 'You know it, a brush!' Uri had made a sweeping motion. 'A brush that is wet!' Not catching on, they shook their heads and he huffed with frustration and searched the cabin and finally went to the toilet.

Even Eugene had smiled when he returned shouting, 'This! This! With this I used to hit policeman,' a dripping mop in his hand.

Alone in the cabin, Babe counted out the extra wraps on

to the table. He folded squares of a *TV Quick*, each little envelope showing half a word or three or four of a soap-star's bleached teeth.

'What are you doing?' asked Uri.

'He needs extra money.'

'Who?'

'I am giving these to the Pole. The one with the bedroom shoes.'

'Aye aye aye – blow my cock and make a wish.' Uri shook his head. 'Drugs are making you soft here.' He pressed Babe's chest.

'And you here.' Babe cupped his balls, his thumb resting over his cock.

'Never!'

'It could be Ordil.'

'You need to be harder.' Uri pointed to his own chest.

'So do you.' Again Babe grabbed his groin.

'I am serious.'

'And I am more serious. Maybe my brother has slippers somewhere.'

39

Nearly a week away from work and the End felt more like a cell than a place to rest. Eugene knew he had to go back to the site, and on the Friday that he did, he was sick. He'd stopped eating his normal three meals a day and in the last couple of days, apart from Guinness, he had only had a half-sandwich that Shona had shared with him in the office in Highbury. He began to think that pleading guilty might not have been so bad. Get it over with.

On his way through the site, he could feel the foolishness of a Friday lunchtime, and easy laughter reached him from the inside of the cabin. Just inside the gate Eugene saw that this place, whose smells and sounds had become comforts to him, had turned on him. The work, the endeavour of it all, seemed grotesque in the late-afternoon light and he almost went back to the Beacon, but something on the fence caught his eye, and when he turned, one of the posters slapped him in the face.

'I'm not from fucking Galway!' he screamed inwardly, and

he ripped it down so violently that it hurt where his nails used to be. He looked round to see if anyone had noticed him. With the poster still bunched in his hand, he made the long walk to the cabin, and as he went through the door, Noble cheered and applauded and coaxed the Poles into doing the same.

Horace jumped up. 'Shut your fucking mouth, man!'

The Poles snapped their arms back to their sides and Noble stopped cheering, but he let a few more claps flutter out before he dragged the Poles up and went back out on to the site. Eugene didn't give any sign of it but he was relieved to see Buck wasn't there. He crossed the cabin and sat at their table with his back away from the door. Uri stood up and put a hand on his shoulder; Babe crouched to put an arm around him. Horace's stoicism forced him simply to stand beside Eugene, while Eugene leaned on his bruised elbows and covered his eyes.

In the afternoon, Eugene was back in the shed. The smell of the shuttering oil, an old friend, seemed to have turned its back on him. It made him feel nauseous.

When he could avoid it no longer he went to find Buck. He walked into the office with his head down and Buck looked above his glasses, then turned back to what he was doing.

Eugene started haltingly, 'I suppose you've heard.'

'Indeed I have,' he snapped.

Eugene knew then that he would never be able to explain what had really happened, and the weight of disappointment made him wonder if he'd ever move from that spot. 'I'll be in to help tomorrow. Make up some time.'

Buck gave Eugene a stony look and a sharp silence with the salutary sting of a well-earned punishment. Eugene almost thanked him for it. He was about to leave when Buck said, 'Jack's in hospital. He asked for you, he's ill. It won't be long.'

Eugene was not shocked by the news but it was bad all the same. It made him feel sorrier for himself. 'For me? Where is he?'

'The Royal London, Whitechapel Road.'

'I'll go and see him,' said Eugene, obediently, but Buck didn't look up, just made a noise as if it was all the same to him. Eugene took another step towards the door and what Buck said next was urgent, as if everything else had been irrelevant.

'And stay away from fucking drugs. I thought you of all people had more oil in your lamp.'

Eugene felt there was nothing left to do but cement his guilt by saying nothing, putting his head down and closing the door.

For the rest of the day Eugene didn't come out of the cube shed. He didn't know that his friends had considered going in but had decided between themselves that they'd leave him to have some time alone. Eugene stared straight ahead at the singed walls: he was caught on the barb of a fact and struggling to be free of it was killing him: Buck knew about the drugs. Uri was his friend. It wasn't him. Was it? So who else knew? Doubt took small bites out of him and so began a steady, silent corrosion. The next time he looked, half of him had gone.

He stood up, thinking sharply, What if I did it? He sat down again. I'm no use at all with the drugs. And maybe he didn't know as much about these men as he'd thought. I'm a mug. A fucking stooge for strangers. Faced with these

wheedling half-truths, he scorned himself. There was some
relief in shutting off trust, a chopping off, a violent closing
down of his reliance on these men. Friends? Ha! He was
alone in this. He had pushed himself on these strangers and
they had used him to keep their own positions. You'll stay in
London now, son.

He left work without telling anyone and went to a pub
where nobody knew him, so nobody doubted him, and after
a good few hours he stumbled back to the Beacon. He wasn't
sure how he'd got there, and when he collapsed into the End
at two in the morning he lay on top of the covers capable of
only simple childlike thoughts. With them came childlike
tears, full and unrestrained. With a keen-edged self-pity, he
swiped at himself, enjoying each cut. He missed his father.
He missed Vincent. He missed Gloria. He missed his mother.
And still, after everything, it was Theresa who cut him the
deepest.

40

Eugene's first clue was the blank taste of the glass of water he kept beside his bed. It had too much time in it, too much daylight, so he tasted the bad start to Saturday before he saw it. He pulled aside the blanket at the window and winced at the glaring butter-thick light that clearly stated midday. Outside looked warm again, hot even, but the End was cold, as if it had a hermetic hold on everything you didn't want. His heart jumped as he sat up, but then it dragged him back with a deep thud, still beating time to sleep.

He'd been dreaming of prison. Surrounded by other prisoners, it seemed natural for him to show them what he was made of, and he pressed in hard with his battered nails at his sternum to create a jagged opening. Through the rough slit, he loosened the skin from the flesh, eventually pushing his entire hand into the pockets between the muscles of his chest and his skin. Next, he got his nails and then his fingers and then his whole hand, palm to bone, under the slabs of chest muscles, loosening them from the ribs, and pulled them towards his shoulders where they rested heavily; he had to lean back a little. A tough rip at the sternum meant he could creak open the cage of his ribs, and he looked down, as if to 'check that this was what he was really like. This dream had teeth. It frightened him. It had been so vivid that it followed him fully formed into his bad start, but the relief that follows a bad dream flowed weakly, then ebbed as his real life rolled in to meet him, and the sticky slick of his bad luck crawled into the space where options used to be. He had told Buck he'd be in to help.

He heard someone in the toilet and an eel of fear flicked up his gut. His body was jangling, but his brain was inactive, insulated from the present; a part of it still pulsed with sleep. He needed no more inspiration than that to get him to standing, and he breathed quickly as his heart tried to keep up with what was happening. Late was what he was, stuck without a plan, unwashed and in yesterday's dirty clothes.

He sat down again on the edge of the bed and his situation cramped in his chest. If he went in to work now he'd have to deal with jibes, Noble's snide comments and worsening looks from Buck. He shook his head quickly and pushed the heels of his hands against his eyes. He gave a high groan. There was already a headful of clamouring alternatives. Saucepan sounds. 'Phone in sick' was loudest and the one he least wanted to listen to. He almost stood up, but he thought that if he did call in sick, a thing he had never done, he'd spend the whole day worrying himself inside-out about whether or not they'd thought he was lying. He imagined their faces pinching tighter with suspicion. No way. He sighed because he was faced with lying, and lies lagged him till he felt he was wearing Vincent's coat. Too tight across the chest.

The toilet swapped occupants and he strained his hearing for their signatures. It was Rhodri who took a piss now, a weak tinkling. He's sitting down, he thought. The door closed, a muttering into Rhodri's room, then Rhodri was gone down the back stairs. If Eugene had got up at his usual time no one would have been vying with him for the toilet. There was never a soul when he got up at five thirty to wash. Staring around the room he let out a low, vicious 'Fuck' because he didn't want this: he didn't want his morning rituals to be under the pressure of others, squeezing his simple secret sequences into a solid chore that he couldn't hide. Blame stuck in his throat with nowhere to go. It turned on him: it was his own fault.

He waited for the gasp of the flush to subside before he opened his door a crack – he really didn't want anyone to know that he was still there. Furtively, he watched the corridor for a second before slipping out. On tiptoe with his hand on the curled handle, he spotted her. He let his heels fall to the floor.

Julia had been reading – her book was still in her hand and she was rubbing the other over her face with a casualness that aroused him. She wasn't wearing a bra. She had on shorts and a vest, and in so few clothes, her privileged length was drawn out. A cool drink of water, he thought. Although he had actively avoided her, a thirst rose up in him and he drank her down in the few seconds during which she hadn't noticed him. He knew he wouldn't have the luxury of her being unaware for long so he stood as still as he could. She stopped when she saw him and looked at him steadily.

'I know about it,' she said.

'No, you don't.' The force of too many lonely hours pushed this out of him; out of his character.

She didn't reply. She was thinking. He was mad to know what she had to decide. She was immobile for too long. Too long, but he didn't try to change what was happening: he just let his eyes hover about her in his abnormal way, never looking directly into her face. She turned back to her room without a word and looked over her shoulder. Book still in hand, she beckoned with her head towards the bedroom. He wouldn't let himself register her meaning, although now he was staring hard enough to melt away any ambiguity.

She waited. 'Well?' she said.

He thought she sounded annoyed and still he didn't move.

She guessed at his black-and-white reading of the situation and threw him some colour. 'Are you coming or not?'

Eugene didn't know how to let go of the toilet door.

41

Without the morning to ease him into it, the afternoon seemed brutally bright. Eugene caught a 254 across from the Empire. It was packed but Eugene had never been on a London bus that wasn't. As he glanced at all the other eyes on the bus he saw nothing but menace. He couldn't wait to get off. When he reached the bottom of Whitechapel Road he jumped out and walked back up to the crumbling façade of the Royal London Hospital. He wanted this visit over with.

Eugene made enquiries at Reception because he hadn't dared ask Buck for details of where Jack was. He found the right floor, and as he walked into the ward he was hit in the face by a warm smell, the smell of something that had recently been internal. An odour that should never have made contact with air. Some of the patients were conscious so he resisted the urge to put his hand to his face.

It had been pleasant outside, autumn playing hard to get. In the ward the air was hot, and in his two jumpers, Eugene started a slow swelter.

He looked down the rows of faces for Jack's. Most of them were male and many glowed ochre on their arranged pillows. The ward was full, and it seemed to Eugene that there were beds where there shouldn't be. A clang from a metal laundry bin startled him, but the man in the bed beside it didn't flinch. He was under water. Out of it. It was Jack. He didn't move, his hands like yellow clasps at the lip of the cover. He also saw the obscenity of Jack's bare chest through the open pyjamas – which must be a dead bloke's, he thought. Jack didn't own any. He walked over to the bed and stared at him awkwardly. Whatever it was that was killing Jack, Eugene could almost see it crawling under his skin. He blinked away the feeling of hurry-up-and-die that had shamed him during his father's final illness and forced himself to look hard at the sleeping face.

Princess, thought Eugene. The name hung over Jack's ravaged body: a sweet pink piss-take.

Jack finally opened his eyes but showed no sign of registering Eugene's presence.

'Get a chair,' he said, closing his eyes again.

Eugene walked over and jerked one from a sticky spiral of plastic seats beside the nurses' station. The metal legs squealed as he did so. The nurses looked up at him, and a new spritz of sweat pricked his skin.

Jack lifted his scrawny legs in an effort for his visitor. His bony knees made sharp impressions through the blanket, and the cover made a saggy tent across his knees and up to his groin. Jack still smelt of fags. They were part of him whether or not he could get out for one any more. What hair he had left was tainted. Even the blanket looked yellowed. He was trying to speak but his voice was, at first, almost impossible to hear.

'Keep you away from that one there.'

Eugene leaned in. 'Which one?' He looked around the ward.

'Your woman behind the bar.'

'Della?'

'No. The wean.'

'Julia?' Eugene was confused.

'Keep you well away from her.'

'Why?'

Jack stayed silent.

Eugene tried chirpiness. 'Is that what you've brought me across London to tell me?'

'Just keep away from her and that's all.'

'I'll do what I like, thank you very much.'

But Eugene could feel the suck of some powerful truth that was about to sweep through the ward. He waited for it, listening, as if for the excited keening whispers of tracks telling you the train was coming.

'I'm just warning you because you'll be sorry.'

'Sorry about what?' Eugene pulled at his collar.

Jack finally opened his eyes. 'Sorry when you find out.' He tried pushing himself up the bed and winced in pain.

Eugene looked around the ward, wondered if he should call a nurse.

And if Jack had kept his eyes closed, Eugene might well have called a nurse, told her that Jack was rambling, not making sense. Eugene might not have believed Jack at all. The nurse would have advised him that Jack needed to rest now and Eugene would gladly have taken her advice to leave, lightened by a duty done, and would have walked down the long, sick-green corridors past sorry-looking strangers. He might have found himself smoking on the street, determined that after the trial he'd give it another try, or maybe not try so hard with Julia. Either way he'd have been making a plan.

Instead, Eugene had tiptoed around Jack's bed to the cabinet. He stood over Jack and very carefully poured the full jug of iced water into the hollow of the blanket above Jack's groin. He did it slowly because he wanted to pour all of it, completely empty the jug, but he didn't want to make a splash. Didn't want anyone to notice because if anyone had stopped him he had no idea what he might do. Not one.

When the jug was empty, Eugene silently put it back on the cabinet. The ice cubes huddled in the hollow above Jack's groin as if they had a moral objection to passing through the cover. Jack had pulled in a perilous breath, but accepted all of it without moving.

When Eugene actually found himself outside, he stood, embarrassed to be taller than the other smokers in their wheelchairs. With each suck-in of the smoke, he felt more and more blessedly neutral, relieved that he could finally let go, that there were no more plans to be made.

42

The same afternoon, Rhodri had burst into the room, hysterical. Julia was reading, stretched out on his bed.

'I am not fucking having it!'

Her first jolting thought was that he must know something. The bed under her felt guilty. He picked up a cup and threw it hard at the bed beside her but the old mattress absorbed the force; a saggy *mea culpa*. He started packing randomly, anything and everything, into a holdall. Julia didn't dare move.

'The fucking cheek!'

The book slipped out of her hands.

'Do you know what they're accusing me of?'

Julia breathed again. Of course it was about him.

'Gross plagiarism. Paraphrasing the Lizard's paper on Foucault's influence on foreign policy!'

The Lizard was Daniel Fournier, a cultural heavyweight, now emeritus professor who had, for a time, tutored Julia. She adored him.

'I asked them if they'd even considered the idea that he might have seen the abstract I put in for the BPA meeting two years ago.'

'But you didn't give that talk. You didn't even go.'

'Yes – because, if you remember, I was ill.'

Julia remembered. She had been kinder to him back then.

'But the abstract was accepted! It's a publication! Let them get out of that.'

Julia was unable to look at him.

He pulled down an army duffel bag from behind the door and continued to pack furiously. 'Well, if they think I'm going to hang around – I cannot wait to get out of that fucking shithole.'

He stuffed his kimono into the bag and put the cup on top, pushed it down petulantly and drew the string.

'Anything that smug fuck has written, I could have written, and they know that.'

'You didn't actually say that to them, did you?'

Rhodri threw the bag at the door but it was heavy and landed, sadly, a couple of feet away.

'Yes, I did say that – and why the fuck shouldn't I? Johnny was right. UCL was definitely a move backwards.'

Prudently she chose not to remind him that he'd had no choice.

'Fucking Establishment-crippled wannabes. I'm going to my mother's.'

Rhodri pushed past Della on the stairs.

'Oy! Now then!' she shouted after him. She'd give him a fucking hiding if she could be bothered to run after him. He'd hurt her leg with his ridiculous bag.

'What's all the noise?' Della demanded.

Julia was standing outside his bedroom and Della immediately snatched a whiff of relief, dust settling over a cover-up. 'What's the matter? What have you done? Julia?'

'What?' It was loud but Julia pushed her nails into her palm when she should have reacted quicker.

An accusation began to arc. 'You haven't!'

'What?' squealed Julia, but Della was going too fast for her.

'Not Eugene!'

'Mum!' It was meant to be angry, *boom!*, a grenade but fear fizzled it before it reached the ground and it puttered on the landing into a big awld beg. Julia blushed deeply in the dark. 'Nothing happened!'

A slap, and Julia began to cry.

'I should have told you.'

Della shouted this as if it were Julia's fault that she hadn't, and Julia looked back at her through thick tears, blinking – what? what? what?

43

Standing on the hospital steps, he nearly sang. Jack had done him a favour. A huge favour! Eugene had held the old facts in his hands on the ward and then realized what it meant: that there was only one thing to do. One way to go. Everything was so clear when he left the hospital. It made him stand still outside Whitechapel tube station, bright with astonishment, his hand up to his neck, appreciating the mechanics of his throat as he laughed out loud on the street. A couple looked at him and he continued to smile in their direction. He felt magnanimous after his revelation.

He went back to the Beacon, avoided the bar, avoided the kitchen and locked himself into the End, already fixed on his new motive. He slept like a baby.

When he woke up he found that, during the night, notions had fermented to a pure and clear idea, like the poteen Seamus had kept in a tartan hot-water bottle in the outhouse. He got out of the End quickly and had his first fag walking towards Liverpool Street. No smirchy kitchen, no yard step:

he was going west. He was going to show Theresa that he knew how she felt about him. He'd buy her the book that Julia had given him – after all, without Julia and yesterday, he could not have seen this so clearly. Theresa would think he was very clever to notice it like that, with a poem. She always wanted words. Good words that someone had sat and thought about, then given over for everybody to use. A library for feelings. Plenty overdue. He'd tell her that. Very casually. He didn't call Buck to tell him he wasn't going in.

Out on the street, the weekend welcomed Eugene like an old mate. It was a beautiful day and he felt like a pioneer in the glassy light – early autumn's bold effort to rival summer. London looked washed down and gleaming, ready for the tourists, and he was going to fit right in with the shoals of visitors. He filtered lithely through the crowds in the station, happy to be part of the thick current, but also relishing the fast freedom of the short-cuts that Julia had shown him.

He entered the Circle Line crush and felt like grabbing the hands of the bustling passers-by, who were walking at weekday speed even though it was Saturday. He wanted to tell them that he knew now what he had to do and – oh! Wasn't it a relief to know your purpose? He wanted to explain that the only way to pull yourself clear of the wreckage was to get back into the smouldering hulk. Theresa was waiting for him.

Once on the tube, he beamed at the passengers opposite, wasn't put off as their gaze slid off to the left or the right. He watched the tangle of wires flash past the windows, mostly black, but some red to show that, even down here, there was hope. He changed to the Piccadilly Line and reached Piccadilly Circus in no time at all. As he emerged into the sun he was laughing at himself for being such a fecking eejit all along.

When Theresa used to punch him and bawl at him to smash through his silences, he should have pinned her hands down, got her by the wrists, the neck. She'd have resisted, that was her way, but then she'd have relaxed, satisfied. Become his. That's what she was looking for: an unlocking. He'd fumbled too long. Being still didn't get a bloke anywhere. Now he felt sprung, light as wire, strong and grateful, and here he was; it was in the way he moved. Grace. It was as if someone had shown him a short-cut in a sum.

He strode into the bookshop in Piccadilly and smiled his way around the stacks, rubbed his hands over the warm flat brass of the banisters. His calluses gave dull little tinks as he placed his hand on the agreeable metal. He'd held Julia's hand yesterday in the bed, placed it with his own warm hand between his thighs. The confluence of their feelings from the baths to the corridor to the bookshop and, finally, to Julia's bed sank through it and flowed away the moment they had got close enough to make use of them. He didn't need Jack to tell him what was wrong and right. Theresa was the one for him, and if only he'd fought for her sooner . . .

He leaned against the flow of the crowd back towards the bottom of Regent Street. He bought an ice-cream, and crossed the road to Piccadilly Circus, nearly getting run over. The driver honked violently and Eugene gave him a thumbs-up. He sat on the steps around Eros and looked up at the statue. Licking the ice-cream, he felt more permanent and freer than Eros and he was sorry that Eros seemed unconcerned by the contradiction of his expectant metal wings. He looked back to the cone and felt certain in the knowledge that there was one person to love, no matter how much they abused or rejected you. So easy! Without a choice things were so straightforward.

London could show him what it wanted. It was no match for this epiphany. Theresa still wanted him and he could admit now that he had not let go of a single hair of her head since leaving home. The clarity was staggering because, for all he really knew, Theresa was still waiting for him at home. Waiting and willing him not to love anyone else. He felt through his jacket for the book. His pride could have been the death of him. He shuddered, preferring to see his new clear angle on this. He'd been rewarded for his suffering. His pride had made investments of all his dark feelings and they had gained interest.

He thought of Job, poor Job. Eugene liked the Old Testament. God had really had a hand in things back then, and when God was involved, the pictures and messages were always clearer to Eugene. Vincent always chose to draw Job. The chalk white didn't work as Job's leprotic skin on the light paper, but he had made up for it by giving him a large, red, child-sized grin – Job squatting in the middle of the page, happy as hell, it seemed, to be plagued. Eugene would choose to draw Jonah, leaping, ecstatic, from the mouth of the whale, his outstretched limbs, Eugene hoped, showing how he loved his new freedom. Today, he felt empathy with the stick-man of those guilt-strangled Sundays, and straightened his back now that his own spirit had been galvanized by a dark imprisonment.

He finished the ice-cream cone and wiped his hands on his top, happy to be certain about something at last. He'd tell Vincent later. Tell him about the trial and tell him that when it was over he was coming home.

The rickshaws wobbled their weighty cargo to the right of Regent Street, avoiding its grandeur and traffic, plumping instead for the plentiful shade in the low-rise buildings that lined Soho's streets and alleys. He followed them.

Eugene had hated Leicester Square when he had first seen it a few months ago. Couldn't wait to leave. He'd thought that the buildings surrounding it were a vulgar chain of chains. The square itself was just a venal pit for punters. Today, he finally saw its allure: its bustle and the vivid encouragement of the signs on the fast-food shops and huge cinemas. He saw the green as a resting-place where a man could cheerfully take a break from his situation or dry out in the stale shade.

Walking further south, his hands in his pockets, Eugene felt a swelling in his chest as he crossed Trafalgar Square. When he had first walked through it, his heart had been empty; the people and swarms of pigeons had done nothing to dissipate the pomp-ready emptiness of the space. He walked further south, and along Whitehall he saw strength, not threat, in the buttressed Gothic blocks of the regimented government buildings.

At the end of the day, entering the dusty tube station at Piccadilly, he skipped down the steps. There was a lull in the crowds but he would happily have waited for families to lift down prams and for old people to sidle down the worn, dirty steps.

Changing at Holborn for the Central Line, he darted through the doors to the tube while they were still opening and, with matador hips, chose a seat at the end of the carriage. At St Paul's, a slender young girl came into the carriage, wearing a fitted vest and wide cool gauzy trousers the colour of putty. He smiled at her and she looked away.

He didn't take offence. He looked up and down the length of her and noticed that Theresa had shoes like the ones she was wearing. The hem of the trousers obscured the heels so he wasn't sure if they were exactly the same. He leaned forward smoothly from the waist and gently lifted up the trouser leg to take a better look.

44

Back at the Beacon, Eugene allowed his smile to pull him up the stairs. On his way up, Della looked at him sharply from the bar – 'Julia's gone, don't be looking for her,' – but he shrugged, wondering why she was telling him this. The kitchen and the End were silent.

In his room, he tried the law firm. Eugene wanted to share his new verve with his Shona, tell her how well he was going to play it, but her phone switched straight to answer-machine. Eugene wished he was the firm's only concern but it didn't dampen his spirits. Neither had the woman on the tube. She had shouted at him and called him a name, but he forgave her. He had had to wait for the tube to pass slowly through the weekend tomb of Chancery Lane before he was able to get off at St Paul's. The woman and others in the carriage had talked loudly about him all the way to the next station but he simply thought ahead to going home, back to her. Telling Vincent he was coming back to Ireland. Where he should be. He was certain. He'd floated off the tube like an air-hockey Jesus.

He dialled another number, his breath staying high in his chest as he waited for Vincent to pick up. He hadn't spoken to him since his visit. Vincent answered.

'How are you, sir?' Eugene asked, excited.

'Where the fuck have you been, sir?'

'There and thereabouts, you know.' Eugene could taste the words. Big lumps of goodness.

He was savouring them when Vincent said, 'Your woman's having a party.'

Eugene felt a snap inside his head. The words lost their flavour.

'Said I'm to invite you.'

'Who's your woman?' Eugene said stupidly.

'Surely to God you know!'

Eugene couldn't say the name.

'Theresa, you *amadán*!'

'Aye?'

'So you'll come over for the party, the twenty-eighth?'

'That depends on the job, mate. I'll be in touch.'

'Hold on, what's your news?'

'Ach, nothing.' Eugene swallowed, then said, 'For a man who's moving to London you sound pretty far away.'

Another pause.

'I'd do your head in over there, wouldn't I?'

'You would indeed.'

'You'd better make it to the party.'

'I'll try me best.'

They said their goodbyes in their usual way.

'Good luck.'

'Good luck.'

'Good luck.'

*

237

The next day, Eugene was the first in the cabin. Horace didn't want to be the one to tell him that Buck had called him a waste of fucking space for not turning up on Saturday. Over their tea, Eugene casually told the guys that he was going up to Highbury – 'Off to see Cornie. Make plans.' He winked.

'Did you let Buck know?' Horace asked tentatively.

'Ach, he'll be fine about it.' Eugene left whistling, but as he skipped out of the cabin they looked at each other uneasily, already gauging Buck's reaction from the apprehension on each other's faces. They were making a collective move to escape back up the scaffold when Buck came in and asked for Eugene. They had to tell him that Eugene had gone to the solicitor's.

'So Ignacy's going to have to cover! Even the Poles are busting a gut and Eugene's swanning off when he fucking feels like it!'

Buck's anger was slow to rise but stayed up there when it did. It was already up there when he appeared from nowhere behind Voitek, who was chanting by rote, 'Charlie? Trips? Es?'

'What are you doing, boy?'

Voitek jumped, then stared at Buck as if he were his dead Polish mother. He pulled his hands behind his back.

'Show me your hands!' Buck pulled at Voitek's arms, jerked them round to the front of his body. The wraps of cocaine flew out of his hands to the floor.

'What are they?' Buck asked, but the set of his mouth showed he already knew.

Voitek weakly pointed at Babe. Babe stood up smiling, his hands up to calm Buck. He needed time to make up an explanation but as he approached Buck he knew it was too late.

'Get off my job.' Buck spoke evenly.

'Buck . . . Buck . . . Buck,' Babe clucked. He wanted to contain him until he had something solid to say that might make a difference. He made to put his hands on Buck's shoulders.

Buck screamed, scaring him, his face dangerously red, 'Get off my fucking job! I will not have this!' and he kicked the wraps at his feet across the cabin floor. Uri looked frozen, concerned. One had spilled.

'This is my job, do you hear? MY JOB! Do not take me for a cunt! You and you . . .' he pointed at Voitek but prodded Babe hard in the chest '. . . need to be off this site in thirty seconds or I'm calling the fucking police.'

Both men walked quickly towards the door of the cabin. Buck was close behind them. Babe stopped to change into his shoes.

'Fuck that!' cried Buck, and pushed Babe aside. He kicked his work boots out of the open door and clear into the middle of the yard. Babe walked out of the cabin in his socks. Buck followed to make sure they left the site.

In the wake of the outburst, everyone in the cabin looked guilty. Uri swept up the coke at his feet with his hands. He stood up, as if he intended to follow Buck, but sat down again, the siren of truth going off inside him.

45

The last few days before the hearing were not so much filled with work as lengthened by Eugene being there. Every cacophonous second bothered him as the working day marked its own time with the clank of steel on aluminium. Time seemed to go backwards and the roar of saws went through him. The bad concrete was still being taken up, the relentless drills and jack-hammers serving as testament to its perverse reluctance to budge. Even his friends grated on his jangling nerves – he found himself easily wounded by their jokes and was exhausted by being on edge – he began seeing things out of the corners of his eyes.

Since Vincent had said her name, all Eugene did consistently was drink. And that was in silence. No Jack, no Julia, no Rhodri. Della seemed to avoid him, and that was fine, but the emptiness of the Beacon pushed him to other nameless pubs after work. What had happened with Julia had worsened things, but it was Theresa who had ruined him for good. The idea of prison stretched out; it had become probable to Eugene. A very particular horror had nested in him and he began to look at it with a distracted fascination.

In the cycle of these thoughts, he realized his phone was ringing. Slowly, he took it from his pocket: Vincent. He made it silent because he didn't want any more reminders. He put his phone away because, right now, he needed someone who didn't know him.

It was dark when he rounded the slight bend of Commercial Road as it reached Shoreditch High Street. Although there weren't any other pedestrians, Eugene couldn't help but feel that everyone knew he didn't belong there. He was conspicuous, even to himself. On the walk from Brick Lane, there had been several places where his determination had run aground. He had stopped, taken breaths, set sail again through the crass, sulphur-bright night.

Fifty metres from Shoreditch High Street, he saw a clutch of them, standing together under the lamplight, heads and hands and some handbags touching. He was jealous of their unity, their trade secrets made to keep out men like him. They seemed to swarm under the light like languid moths. Their smoky breath plumed from a common chimney.

Eugene walked towards them but stayed on the opposite side of the road. When he drew level he stopped, fidgeted. He didn't cross the road, he just listened and watched in his hovering way. He grappled with the snapped threads of their clipped conversation, carried short by the cold wind that had got up since the sun went down. The keenness of the air made him want to close his eyes.

Suddenly one turned and, with her cigarette wand, chose him. He froze. She walked over to him and before she said anything she surveyed his head. He felt like a bull, she the farmer. He wondered for a second if she was going to pull up his lip, inspect his teeth, feel his bollocks, and all the while, her slow blinking stamped him an outline. She wore rings of all sizes with jet black stones but they couldn't pull him down from the eyes and he noticed very quickly that her eyes said she was already in debt where kindness was concerned. It gave her a look of don't-even-bother. She smelt of too much perfume, good over bad over good.

'Fifty quid, all in.'

He put his hand into his trouser pocket, showed her his money. She started walking towards Shoreditch station and he followed for what seemed a long time down the middle of the road, then an alley. Head down, he watched her heels; he was transfixed by the routine irregularity of her steps. It seemed she had one leg shorter than the other and, for a second, he wished she knew the silly things, like his mother's name. They took a right just after the station entrance and she started walking across a patch of grass to a high-rise block.

In the lift, neither bothered to talk. There wasn't a hint of nerves or curiosity about her. He didn't know it, but the length of his trousers had already given her direction. She motioned carelessly for him to get out of the lift and made him wait until she found her key – a banal act but Eugene contemplated that he could love this woman just because her attention was absolutely elsewhere.

Inside the flat a chipboard partition further separated it into two. Entrances to both sides were padlocked. To the left, he smelt more of her and her perfume. They went through the left-hand door. He immediately looked to see if there was a window that could be opened. His nerves were getting to him. She beckoned him to yet another room and sank on to a mattress without a cover. There was no blanket, no sheet. Knees bent now, level with her chin, shoulders rounded in between, she sat on the mattress, which offered no resistance. Then she undressed, like a dog-tired child, messily, with uncoordinated abandon, as if she was trying to break a habit. He stared, like a glutton, until she told him to get undressed. He did as he was told and then he lay down. She sighed and lay down beside him. He rested his head in the cup of her neck and swallowed his own truncated breaths.

Not knowing what else to do, he looked at her and her face said he was going to be a problem.

'Do you want me to talk a bit?'

'No.' God, no.

Finally, impatient, she forced him, without a smile, to palm her skinny thigh, but after a few moments, she got up to go to the toilet. It was in the half-flat next door. She slipped on her shoes and a towel and, without looking at him, said, 'You'll still have to pay.'

'That's all right.'

She had already left the room when she poked her head back through the door. 'Don't take anything, will you?'

He had never felt so heavy and was aware that a sediment had collected in him, threatening to push him through the floorboards. He didn't speak any more, and eventually she went out, leaving the door open. He got dressed, looked around and threw the fifty pounds on to the bed. A lump came to his throat and he felt a flimsy token of himself bump and jag, like a loose kite, around the paper-thin walls.

46

Eugene opened his eyes and kept still, letting the black feeling fill him. The trial started today. Just above his dreams, his memories glittered in the background. He was back in his mother's living room.

He lay back in front of the fire. How could he get out of school? The flames tightened his cheeks as plans looped like rope, figures of eight, wound back and forth around the possible and the probable, until he had a perfect and brilliant idea.

He stole his mother's purse from her bag. He carefully folded it into his coat before getting on the school bus. He was deliriously happy because he knew that once the theft was discovered in the homely smelling austerity of Sister Concepta's office, everyone would be shocked, no one would know what to do with such a bold child and he would have to be sent off immediately to his mother at work. It went without saying that he would be asked never to return to school. With the purse in his hand on the bus, he smiled as he directed these scenes to their unique conclusion.

Here was what actually happened. His mother was telephoned and had to lose a shift at work to come and pick it up. The bus-ride took her more than an hour, and while they waited, Eugene overheard Sister Mary-Dennis whisper, 'She can barely look after herself.'

Of course he wasn't allowed to see his mother: it would upset him. He'd heard her, though. She was apologizing. When she'd gone, his teacher made him stand on a chair to tell the class that he'd been born of an idiot. He whispered it so that he didn't really mean it: 'My mother is an *óinseach*.'

He dressed and went downstairs. He swallowed a whisky that he nervously milked out of the optic in the dark bar, and pulled at his collar; his tie was strangling him. Horace had lent him a suit. It fitted nowhere. The trousers trailed on the floor, no matter which shoes Eugene put on. He would only have one drink: that was what he thought as he watched his arm glide up to the optic for the second. He had become obsessed by what the jury would be like. If he could just get across to them in a look, a stance, that he could never do what he was accused of . . . He needed a fucking crucifix.

'You know a man by his actions,' Seamus used to say.

He'd spent the night in the raw black, twisting around in bed, trying to keep in synch with the agonizing turns of his thoughts into dead ends. Trying not to counter his fate.

In court, Eugene hunted down the jury and spotted an old woman's hair first. By the time she had met with the rest of the members and finally taken her seat, her hair was like a harried cloud, only slightly covering a face that shone with innocence and belief. Belief in national institutions. In her small, square shoulders, Eugene saw the law being upheld.

He covertly scanned the other faces. Four white, three young. He gave up on the other five. He did the maths and came up with the odds. The pay-out? He was fucked.

Shona shuffled in. 'Looks like we've got a good jury.'

Eugene stared at her, wondered what on earth she could be thinking.

Between the swearing in and lunchtime Eugene had to sit on his hands because the small impression Shona had made on him amounted to nothing when the prosecutor, perfectly formed for rugby and fucking, allowed his voice to roam through hills and valleys of learned intonation, ending square in the face of the jury, the voice not afraid of their nearness, layered tones using the height of the room. Eugene searched the jury's faces, silently pleading that they wouldn't be swayed by the powerful rhetoric, as the prosecutor allowed his prize argument to rest in a valley to graze and fatten before the jury. Gentle bullying. An art, thought Eugene. If I lived a hundred years, I'd never be able for that kind of talk.

In the afternoon, the photos of his injuries were handed round as exhibits. Della had breathed in sharply when he'd shown her his head and his legs; she was not free with sympathy so his knees had buckled when he heard the whistle out of her. Behind the bar with his trousers down and his back to her, he'd had to hold up his bollocks while she photographed the backs of his thighs.

'How the fuck did he get up in there?'

Eugene had cried like his sister when he saw his face in the mirror the morning after, and the tears could barely make it out of the slits of his eyes. Now he flicked through the photos in his mind and tried to gauge their effect on the jury.

When it was Shona's turn to perform, Eugene drew his hands up over his groin. Lee was in the witness box again. In the middle of the floor Shona held a telescopic baton.

'Can you show the ladies and gentlemen of the jury how one would use an instrument such as this, PC Lee?'

She handed it to him and he fiddled with it, seemed to brood over it, making it look like a clumsy gardening tool. He ended up twisting and pulling it from both ends when he, Shona and Eugene all knew that he could have it fully extended, fully lethal, in less than a second.

'If I may, PC Lee . . .' Shona read a tract from the Metropolitan Police training regulations that stated quite clearly that there were no instances where it was justifiable for a policeman to use this weapon about a person's head. She moved on, as neatly as she could, addressing the jury. 'I present Exhibits Three A to J, and the doctor's report, Four. It's a lengthy report. Allow me to summarize. "The resultant injuries from this weapon centre around the accused's head. There are two contusions and oedema in no less than eight areas around Mr Mahon's skull."'

Shona cocked her head at Lee in an attempt to unsettle him; a childish interrogatory rug-pull. 'Unrestrained force, PC Lee. Is this something you use often?'

'My life was in danger.'

'A lethal weapon? Coupled with unrestrained force?'

'I was very worried for my safety.'

'But you attacked from the back and the side. I particularly refer the jury to Exhibits Three C and F.'

Eugene didn't dare enjoy Lee's discomfort. He couldn't wait for Uri to testify. This was the part that he had clearly seen, outside Green's, where the unrestrained force had taken Eugene down and Uri was very sure of what he'd seen.

'*Mordu nabil!*' Uri had said – beaten to a bloody pulp. Cornie had tried to keep Uri calm, made him practise, focus on the fact that Eugene was in front, with his hands up.

'He had already resisted arrest and shouted racial abuse. I was worried about what he was capable of next.'

Shona looked perplexedly at the jury – Don't bother with all that! thought Eugene. 'I find it difficult to understand, PC Lee, how such a man, in such a position, is a threat to your life.'

Eugene held his breath. Lee squirmed slightly and looked absent as he rifled to find a victim's face, a victim's words.

47

Della was counting out change when Julia stepped into the bar, but she didn't miss a beat, asking, 'You want a drink?'

Julia dropped her bag, and while Della went behind the bar, Julia sat herself on the stool next to the one that Della had vacated, pulling it towards herself a couple of inches. Before Della returned, Julia felt she could hear the tinkle of a tune-up, that an awkward dance was to start.

Della came back with two china cups and poured brandy and a slug of Lucozade into each.

'So,' breathed Julia.

'Now,' her mother said. And she swigged from her cup.

Julia stared at Della. 'Tell me about him.'

The cup stayed at Della's mouth.

'Everything,' said Julia.

'I didn't know everything.'

'Something, then.'

Della sat very still for a moment. 'He twitched in bed.'

'Not that.'

'What, then?'

This dance needed practice. Back to their beginnings, they started again, slowly.

Julia learned that Della was not allowed to put her cold feet on Seamus in the bed; nor was she spoken to if she stood behind him when they played cards after hours. Julia remembered drawing a daddy for herself and him being torn off the page the next day.

'What did you think?'

'I don't know. I thought you were testing me. Making me stronger.' They laughed, but Della had to swallow hard and drained the thick-tasting brandy from the china.

'How did you keep it up?'

'It was easy. Keeping him out of your life.'

'No, I mean you. Living here. Without anyone else.'

Della sat back and her face betrayed a naïveté about the answer. She took a deep breath. 'Sometimes a new bloke'd come into the pub and I'd think I'd see an oddness that I could work with or an awkward shoulder like his, but they'd always end up talking where he wouldn't, and after him, I didn't give second chances.'

'Why did you want someone who ignored you?'

Della looked surprised. 'You can be loved without words, you know.'

They retreated for a few moments, figuring out the next steps, and Julia let Della know the weight of a dead father while Della listened bravely, pressing her shoulders back against a contrite slump that she had managed to keep out of her back for twenty years. Della tried hard to stay in time: she didn't want to rush this and, keeping with the beat, she found the courage to say, 'And he's so like him.'

'Yeah?'

'It's been murder.'

Julia stalled. 'What do you think'll happen to him?'

'I have no idea, but the Mahons could do with some fucking luck,' and Della stood to get more brandy.

The frankness seemed to sink beneath them after this, and in fear of drowning they returned to steadier, more buoyant memories, things they were allowed to recall without effort, but these didn't support them comfortably. They were still making an effort, and with the brandies stacking up, they got back to the dance, and the dance became slicker and there was no longer a lawless daughter and her bitter teacher but, for this evening at least, in step, two bodies trailing their pasts, twirling and even smiling, warming up the cold space that had been held for so many years by a ghost.

The clock above the bar struck eleven. Julia had been drinking for a good half of the day.

'I'm going to court tomorrow.' She was slurring slightly.

'You sure you should?' Della drained the teacup. No one would have known Della had taken a drink.

'Sure as I'll ever be.' She picked up her bag. 'I won't go upstairs.'

'I'll call you a cab.'

He had slept in the suit that Horace had lent him and cared about it now, too late. On spotting her in the gallery, he felt his stomach flip at the thought of what she was about to hear. Her face was turned towards the entering judge, and when she finally turned to him, and he found the courage to look at her, she was already looking away. Now this was what she'd remember about him. Eugene gasped at what his self was turning out to be and was convinced that everyone could see his head shaking on his shoulders. It had come around quickly. His time.

'Mr Mahon,' sang out the prosecutor.

Eugene felt the pause before a hurtle.

'Your statement says you can't remember what happened.'

Full of words, Eugene kept silent.

'But you do remember that you only had four or five drinks. Is that right?'

'Yes.'

'I'm sorry,' the prosecutor lathered up the jury with his smile, 'which was it? Four or five?'

'Probably more like five.'

'All expenses paid. Friday night. One of the most vibrant quarters of London and you limited yourself to five drinks?'

Things were sliding.

'Yes.'

'Now, I'm not a psychologist, Mr Mahon, but the faculty of memory is a robust one and it takes great force to switch it off.' He made an alternator movement with his hands towards the jury; his voice was varnish. 'Could that force have been an excess of alcohol or something a little stronger, perhaps?' He held his palm up and pulled it to the right for them.

Eugene floundered silently while daring a look at the jury, then watched as the prosecutor pumped on – he's a fucking piston.

'Let us mop up another pocket of resistance, Mr Mahon.'

I bet she loves this bastard with his pockets and all.

'You realized PC Lee was a policeman only after he had attacked you. Is this correct?'

Eugene nodded. The prosecutor waited, shook his head and smiled at the jury, then at the floor.

'You must answer, Mr Mahon,' boomed the judge.

'Yes.'

'Even though, by all accounts, PC Morton had shouted that they were policemen as soon as he emerged from the car.'

'Objection, your honour,' interrupted Shona. 'The account of Uri Vajarov has not yet been heard.'

'Sustained.'

The prosecutor smiled as if objections were what kept him getting up in the morning. He changed tack. 'Once you realized that PC Lee was a police officer, you continued to run away from him, didn't you, Mr Mahon?'

A pause.

'Yes.'

'What exactly were you running from?'

'He attacked me.'

'When a racist resists arrest the officer is forced to control the offender if violent.' Once more, he addressed the jury, not Eugene.

'Are there many Malaysians in Ireland, Mr Mahon?'

'I don't know.'

'Let me ask it another way. Would you reserve the word "Chinky" for anyone who is Asian?'

A map of embarrassment crept up around Eugene's neck. 'No.'

'Just for those with slanty eyes? Yellow skin?'

Eugene felt three heartbeats pile up. 'No, I wouldn't.'

'There must be a type of person that you stick this label to, Mr Mahon, since it was so readily available to you.'

'It wasn't.'

'You mean you hadn't used it for a while?'

'No. I haven't never used it.' 'Haven't never'? Well done, son. That one's for you, sis.

The prosecutor visibly shifted gear, but Eugene was

wondering whether she would notice the 'haven't never' and if there was ever, anywhere, any reason that these two words would be put together.

'Working on a building site, Mr Mahon, you must be surrounded by racist comments.'

Eugene didn't answer.

'Mr Mahon?'

Eugene swallowed. 'Yes.'

'So, perhaps you have picked up a few of these turns of phrase from others without noticing. After all, construction work has never been more competitive, has it?'

'I work with good people.' The statement was ridiculous. Tricky bastard. Eugene's cheeks raged in his sallow face. Why didn't he do a handstand? Juggle a bit?

'Old immigrants are often the first to attack the new, aren't they?' He turned to let the soundbite settle among the jurors. 'Why aren't you working in Ireland, Mr Mahon?'

Eugene was too angry to speak. He was afraid he'd cry.

'Do you have family here?'

He was not going to slip up again.

'Mr Mahon?'

'I am not a racist.'

'Just answer the question, Mr Mahon.'

He'd like to push on to something, rip up his own belly, something horrible, irreparable.

The entire room seemed to shrill to the unsaid. He suddenly felt the need to apologize, so when he sat down with Shona he did, he spilled it, and she looked sympathetically at him but said nothing. He was still shaking horribly and when he looked up and saw Julia he knew he should have tried harder. He was an embarrassment, who desperately wanted to leave this room where he'd been royally fucked over, and he eventually asked for the toilet, purple with frustration. No chance. He'd ended up playing the perfect part of a cunt in a smart little sketch written by the prosecution. Without looking up, he knew she was looking at him.

48

Uri stood up, pushed out his chest and looked at Eugene, his face flowering into an overblown 'I love you', but then, after a signal, was quickly told to sit down by an usher, as the prosecution and the judge continued in controlled whispers. Eugene glanced at Shona but her eyes were on the front of the court, her mouth open. Goose-pimples crept up Eugene as he looked to Lee, who was smiling, studying his nails. The judge spoke.

'A recess has been called. We will reconvene in ten minutes. Ms McArdle, could you approach the bench?'

Shona flustered her way to the judge. Eugene and Uri were led by an usher into the oak-panelled waiting room.

Uri was sweating through his suit. 'What's the fuck?'

'I don't know, Uri. Let's just wait and see, eh?'

A second later and Lee appeared at the doorway, waving a piece of paper into the waiting room. It looked to Eugene like a computer printout.

'What does it mean?' Uri barked at Eugene.

'1992? Resisting arrest?'

'It is not on record!'

'Ah, but I'm afraid it is on record for Crown Court, and so,' said Lee, waving the paper, 'you have no witnesses, Mr Mahon.'

At that moment, Shona pushed past Lee into the room. 'There's been an oversight. I can't believe it, but that's what's happened.'

Lee still slouched in the doorway. Eugene was confused at what Shona was saying but he stood up and asked Lee, 'Can you leave us alone, please?'

'What is oversign?' Uri was standing again. Lee stayed in the doorway.

Shona encouraged Uri and Eugene to sit down. She looked at Eugene's face, then swivelled sharply to confront Lee. 'Please!' She lowered her voice. 'Uri, calm down. You can't testify. You cannot be a witness. Your record stands. The judge won't move on it.'

Eugene wanted to drop through the floor. Uri spewed Russian expletives and punched the wall. He screamed that he should go back to being *gaishnik*, fucking policeman who checks cars! Shona kept calm. Eugene grabbed Uri, sat him down.

'We're going to have to adjourn – have to sort this mess out. Cornelius is going to get a rocket,' Shona said.

49

Court was adjourned and Eugene had no choice but to go to work, and the work on site was wretched. Smashing up the unwieldy concrete was bad enough but what he hated was Buck speaking to him through the other men. Without Babe as a node in their network they seemed to be short-circuiting. No one could get in touch with Babe, and things seemed to have shifted just enough to make them awkward: nothing fitted properly any more for Eugene. Buck wouldn't speak to him, hadn't even asked how the trial had been going. Worst of all, Noble had started sitting at their table, trying to get in on *durak* hands. All wrong.

It was the Friday after the trial stalled that things felt most clumsy. Eugene was wrecked, completely exhausted and out of sorts. He was kicking himself for not just pleading guilty in the first place. It would have been so simple. He was trying to play cards with Uri and Horace when Noble dragged a clattering chair over to join them. He sat down, rubbing his hands.

'This time tomorrow, eh?'

Horace looked up and smiled meaninglessly.

'I'll be up to the nuts in dago pussy.'

Eugene kept his eyes on his cards. Noble wasn't getting the attention he wanted, so he dug and sniffed, sensed frailty and nosed on, then paused. ''S up with you, Genie?' He had waited for Buck to be in earshot. 'You haven't been on the old rustle dust, 'ave you?'

Eugene now looked up from his cards.

'Shouldn't alter the mind,' Noble tapped at his temple, straight-faced in front of Buck, 'not when you're at work, mate.'

Eugene stared at Buck's face and saw that it looked suspicious.

Eugene distinctly felt that he was watching himself as he gripped the table and heaved it – and the cards, and the cups, and the plates and ashtrays – over on to Noble. He did not look at Buck again, only at Noble. From behind, Uri laced his arms through Eugene's and held him back, afraid for everyone involved. Ash hung in the air. Eugene couldn't move in Uri's iron grip so he spat at Noble. It landed in his hair. Buck came and stood between them, his feet planted on the upturned table, his arms out, the table rocking unsteadily under his feet.

'Dad! Will you listen to me now?'

'Quiet.'

'He's a fucking lunatic!'

Eugene had never heard Noble call Buck 'Dad' before. It made him spit again, this time at the upturned table. Uri held him firmly.

Buck quietly said, 'Go home,' to Eugene.

'You!' he said to Noble, lifting him by his collar. 'You come with me.'

At the end of the day, Buck was packing up. He had sent Noble home to his mother. Thank fuck, thought Buck, that they're going away. Awful as it was, he had already planned to stay late in the office, knowing that the taxi for the airport would have collected them by the time he got home. Let Noble tell Deirdre what he wanted. He'd had enough.

He was about to leave the office when the hospital called.

'Mr O'Halloran?'

'Yes?'

'This is Sister Carmichael at the Royal London Hospital. You gave us your contact number.'

Buck's heartbeat slowed as he realized what this was about. 'Has he gone?'

'I'm afraid he has, yes. I'm very sorry.'

'That's OK. Thanks for letting me know.'

'Who'll be looking after the funeral?'

'I will.'

Buck hung up. He couldn't tell anyone yet, not with everything else. He got out the Milk of Magnesia and swigged half of it. His head was in his hands when Uri knocked at the open door. He looked up. Uri always had to turn to the side a little to get through the office door. He sat down on Buck's desk.

'Buck, there is something I am not telling you.'

'Spit it out.'

Uri looked confused.

'Tell me.'

'OK . . . but first is that you promise something. Do not explode like bomb, but be quiet like landmine, OK?'

It was Buck's turn to be confused.

When Buck got there, he was glad of the empty house but disappointed when he saw what a mess they'd left between them. Noble's work boots and trousers were strewn across the landing, and when Buck got into the bathroom, Noble had used his razor and left it in the water with the blond whiskers and the foamy scum. Buck reached in and pulled out the plug and used his hand to rinse what clung to the basin. Downstairs, the sink heaved with dishes and the answer-machine flashed. The butter was out on the table, black flecks of burned toast stranded in it.

He left the kitchen and sat in the chair in the living room with the remote in his hand, but he didn't turn on the TV. He hitched his chair forward so that he couldn't see the wink of the answer-machine.

Uri had begun by telling Buck that Noble was trying to blackmail him. That he was threatening to shop Matilda because she was in England illegally. Because of this he could tell no one the truth. Here Uri paused. Buck had never seen him afraid.

'Carry on. What truth?' urged Buck.

'If Noble finds out . . .'

'Get on with it, Uri.'

'First you promise.'

Buck hesitated before he agreed. 'All right, I promise.'

'Eugene is arrested for Noble.'

'What?' Buck screwed up his face.

'That night it was Noble who started trouble with policeman.'

Buck blew his breath out slowly, processing the information. His face, with its wrinkled brow, seemed beaten, made pliant by pounding and ready to be pounded again by news like this.

'Eugene, he does not know this because I gave him cocaine, blew up his memories. I am very sad for this part.'

'And Babe, did he know?'

'Ah . . . it is very sad for Babe also. He doesn't know of this.' Uri was on a roll now that he trusted Buck's silence. 'He only selling drugs for his little *kabuni*. He sell drugs for Noble. Your Noble.'

'You'd better leave me alone, Uri. Thanks for letting me know.'

'You won't tell Noble?'

'I won't tell Noble. Now go on, get home.'

The house phone rang and it shocked Buck. He didn't move, just listened with everything he had. It made the ringing painful: each peal electrified the air and his stomach was flushed with a new burn. A click let him know that the machine had picked it up. Apart from the fire in his stomach, Buck felt heavy and dead; glassy. At the same time, he was overactive, alive with his own mechanics, his organs finally ending their silence, confessing their drudgery. He was always resourceful, but now his motivation lay inside him, maimed. He poked it, cajoled; there were important things that only he could do now, stuff to set straight again, and it was the weight of these chores that was squeezing the breath out of him.

He must have thought about it for an hour before he got up and went to the phone. First, he forced himself to listen to the messages. They were both from Deirdre. Her credit card wouldn't work in the airport. He imagined her picking up books, reading the back of them and and putting them down out of order, wrong way round, as if they had insulted her by not being about her, trying on glasses that didn't suit the square forehead – Buck knew that in the white light she didn't see the face at all. Only the glasses. 'I'm getting them.' The message told him he must ring the bank and sort it out.

She wasn't having this all holiday. End of message. He put down the phone.

He opened the address book and looked for Gerry's card. There it was, sticking out of R. The primary colours of the R and the C of Reilly and Corrigan stared from the corner of the business card, blue and red for straight talk and integrity. The derivatives of due process. He tried Gerry's number. When it went to answer-machine, Buck left a simple message.

'Gerry, sir, I need your help. Again.'

50

Buck stood in the yard at the Beacon and felt the shutter click of *déjà vu* as he shouted up to the window in the End. He almost imagined that Seamus's head was going to appear at the scruffy glass. Buck wanted to get across London before the worst traffic so he'd called to collect Eugene, unannounced and early. He stood in the yard and threw a bottle-top at the window, then another, and Eugene's face appeared, alarmed and sleep-addled. He was down in a minute and got into Buck's car without a question. On the drive, Buck only explained that they were going to see a lawyer. Eugene was confused, claiming that he had one. He sat low in the passenger seat and the silence was thought-thick and ominous.

Buck started speaking: 'Jack died a couple of days ago.'

All Eugene could think was that this was the first time Buck had spoken to him of his own accord since his arrest. He rubbed the pad of his thumb across his palm, tried to make himself listen instead of crying.

When they got to Gerry Reilly's in Holborn, the office was lit with soft apricot-coloured lamps and comfortable uplights. The flowers were artfully natural. Dramatic photos of the sea made Eugene desperate for home. There was something about Buck, about how he'd put his hand on Eugene's arm on the way in, something about the lawyer's easy manner, such a straight and decent bloke, and the clean lines and air in the office that made him tell the whole truth for the first time. He admitted the cocaine that Uri had given to him before the incident, and the lawyer dismissed it as if he'd said his shoelace was untied. He said it had nothing to do with the charges that were being brought against him.

At Eugene's confession, Buck didn't flinch either – he took it in his stride. When they left Gerry's office Buck squeezed him round the shoulders and told him he'd done well to tell the truth. Eugene bit the inside of his lip.

The next day, a letter arrived, registered, at the site office. Buck read it and was pleased, and when Eugene turned up, he pulled him out of the cabin and handed it to him. 'I have instructed the solicitors at Reilly and Corrigan to consider my future civil action against the police . . . if all these charges are immediately dropped against me and an appropriately drafted letter of apology is received from the police force, I will not need to pursue my civil law claim against the police officers and the police force.' He blushed to read, 'I have never sought out violence or held racist beliefs.' One paragraph was starred: 'My enquiries to date, not surprisingly, indicate that the police officer in question has a history of being involved in such situations.' Simple points of logic pierced the exaggerated parts of the police statements, and Reilly had widened the obvious holes in their stories, allowing the foolishness of their claims to whistle through them: 'The police officers' excuse as to why they stopped and approached me is as untrue as it is absurd.' Eugene felt as proud as if he'd written it himself.

When he looked up at Buck this weak vanity led him to smile but Buck remained worried-looking and said, 'We'll have to wait and see. Here is where you've to send it.'

Eugene was thinking, He said 'we', when he realized that, faintly, a future for himself was glimmering – uneasy, yes, but a future, like a star that glowers and fidgets under steady scrutiny. He delivered the letter to the court by hand.

Jack's funeral was a small affair. A toy funeral. Buck had to go, as much as he didn't want to, and Eugene had agreed to go with him. On his way to the crematorium Buck had an overwhelming urge to turn around and go back to work, but he didn't: he drove to the funeral worrying about how few people there would be to pay last respects to a man like Jack, concerned that he'd be scalded with pity and that he would have to work hard to avoid the memory of it for the rest of his life. He was worrying for himself.

On the drive, he'd replayed the conversation between himself and Uri. He was going to have to find Babe, that much was certain, and he tried not to think what he was going to say to Noble.

Eugene met him, smoking outside the small chapel. They went in together, almost cowering. There was Bart, a JCB driver, from ten years ago, Eugene and Buck. Some stragglers that Buck didn't recognize. Della stayed at the back. Buck noticed that nobody cried. He felt more pity for his own situation than he did for Jack's as the curtains slid round the coffin. No more failure, lucky bastard, was what he was thinking.

In silence they all thought about their own part of Jack, and a few of them mourned the bits of themselves that had been tied up with him, but Buck couldn't help noticing a hurry to leave and a shaking off, a scraping, as if Jack had been a mess that they had all stood in.

51

Courtland House was an unambitious, six-storey dunce of a block. Buck looked at the address again and then at the building. Uri had said that Babe lived in 103, on the top floor.

At the edge of the housing estate, Buck smelt sulphur and saw the rubbish chute smoking. He wondered how it must be to live so close to strangers, to have to rely on others' good nature. There was a concrete walkway that ran past the hutchy-eyed kitchen windows of the flats, and the landing was open to the air on one side, but still had an indoors smell of melted margarine and some sweet, synthetic sauce that Buck couldn't name.

He knocked. After a short time, a little girl answered the door, leaving Buck in no doubt that he'd got the right flat. She didn't say anything, just looked at him with eyes borrowed from her father and waited for instruction. She flattened herself to the hall wall, going up on tiptoe, placing her heels above the skirting-board. A smell wafted over her from the interior of the flat. This time, it was from real food, not thin and quick-fired, but thick lamb juices, slow released. The fading light picked out Babe's astonished face.

Buck said, 'I've come about the wages.' Babe's frightened face relaxed as he leaned against the door jamb and he spread his hand over his chest in thanks as a woman looked over his shoulder.

'This is my real boss, Fatima. That is my *kabuni*, Maryam! Come in and eat.'

'No, no,' said Buck. 'You're grand.'

Babe pulled him in and shot out an instruction in Arabic – Buck heard the rasps from the throat mixing with the little waves that came to the front of it.

Sitting in the living room, Babe looked at Buck, his face alive with an energy that had built up around the need to explain. Fatima placed a heavy plate of food over an almond-eyed warrior inlaid into the table, then stood back, sweetly oblivious to Buck's worry as to the ingredients. She pointed proudly with the fork. 'This heart . . . heart.' She touched her own.

'Right so.'

'And eggs, eggs.' She prodded a white lump with his fork.

He tasted some and tried not to let the novelty get the better of him. The little girl sat quietly eating her own dinner, the same thick stew as Buck but she also had baked beans in a glass cup and scooped them out with flat bread. She kept flicking looks at Buck that were pointed, full of quick assessment rather than just curiosity. Like Babe, he thought.

Fatima nodded encouragement to Buck whenever he looked up and eventually he finished the meal. Then Babe brought out a urine-coloured drink that he hailed as Albanian brandy. Buck looked above the gas fire at a picture that had suffered from being enlarged – the pixels were bloated and bled into each other. It gave the portrait a martyred look.

'Family?' asked Buck.

'My brother Ordil.'

'He lives on holiday,' peeped Maryam, through beans and bread.

'We have no idea where he is,' Babe said quietly.

Fatima entered, beckoned her husband and whispered something to him, her hand resting on the child's head.

'*Haya*, Fatima! *Haya!*' Babe snapped. Being stern was an effort. He turned to Buck. 'Sometimes she forgets about *haya*.'

'*Haya?*'

'For Muslim, is modesty.'

The girl was scurrying to her mother, who had retreated to the kitchen, when Babe cried, 'Maryam!'

She ran in and hopped on one leg to stagger her stop. Her body sloped away in a cartoon brake. She knew her daddy very well. Her face was bursting to smile but she didn't: she stood to attention, a candle desperate to be lit.

'Get your wiolin!'

A single clap came from Fatima in the kitchen; the crack of victory.

Maryam wore her Irish dancing costume. Fatima waved some newly washed socks at her daughter through the serving hatch but the child shook her head. Babe stood up and gently but firmly pulled the black bunch of plastic curls away, saying, in Arabic, what Buck could only imagine was 'Would ye gimme that?'

After a few screeches of the bow, Buck just recognized 'Pease Pudding Hot', and as he looked briefly at Babe on the settee and Fatima through the hatch, he saw a clear but momentary lapse in their modesty that gave him a rare twinge of jealousy. He could see in that second just how far they had come. All the way from nowhere. All the way together. And here, in front of the three of them, murdering a tune, was the brown-eyed fruit of their endurance.

Buck clapped his bear's hands and swallowed hard before saying, 'Aye, very good.'

Maryam bowed, and Babe once more straightened his face. 'Now get changed.'

Finally they could talk. Buck drained his glass first and began, 'Uri told me everything. I want you back on site.'

'Buck, as Allah is my witness, I did it for her . . .'

'I know.'

After all this time, with such a longing for absolution, Babe was surprised that he had found relief in these few words. 'And Noble? What will you do?'

'He's nearly cost me the business.'

'But he did what he thought was right.'

'Would you have signed off concrete like that?'

The truth stuck out too far. Neither of them could get round it. Babe shook his head.

'If that eejit Eugene had been there . . .'

Babe frowned, cocking his head to one side. 'He was there.'

'No, when the concrete fucked up. Eugene. Swinging the lead.'

Babe screwed up his nose.

'Missing from work,' Buck explained. 'Pissed!' He was surprised that Babe didn't understand.

'Oh, no, Buck. No, no. Eugene wasn't drunk. He was there. Waiting to do his job.'

'And what stopped him?' But the answer was dawning on Buck. Babe nodded, and Buck rubbed his face.

'And the fool never said a word.'

52

Roll-ups wouldn't do when your hands were sweating and shaking, so for the final day, Eugene'd bought straights. Not just any fags, he'd bought the thin, dense, cocktail cigarettes that Uri smoked. Noble called them bitch sticks, so if Eugene's reasons for buying them were laid bare, they would include one in the eye for Noble. Last night, after court, he'd gone especially for them to the tobacconist's in Spitalfields. Inside the door of the shop it had smelt like his father's work coat. Even as a kid Eugene knew it was odd that a man's work coat smelt exactly like the pub.

The room was inlaid with dark wood, and blond-wood tobacco pipes floated like museum pieces in illuminated niches. He didn't trust that he could say the name of the cigarettes so he described them at length to the tobacconist. The shelves behind the counter were softly lit and Eugene eventually spotted what he wanted and pointed instead. A sleek black box of thirty cost ten pounds, but as the tobacconist handed them over Eugene realized they might be his last fags outside a nick. The thought made the gold tips and fondant-coloured bodies of the cigarettes seem a religious artefact.

The next morning, in his cold hand, the cigarettes looked like flares; something to be used in desperation. He lit one off another outside the court, and a new memory jabbed at him from an age ago. It pinned him outside Kenny's shop where Vincent had got a kick in the arse for trying to pay with a handful of screws. Eugene laughed at the rudeness of the memory, of the improper timing of it, but then it scolded him. Wait, it said, and drew him to the forecourt of the shop before it wafted off, with Vincent running like a girl down Crawshaw Street. The memory said, Wait. See what I got for you. So he did wait, looking at the forecourt. What was it but a puzzle of tarmac and concrete? And then the feeling lifted out of the patched floor and hovered at the feet of the man looking out of the door, a childless Scrooge shaking his fist at Vincent, after making him crawl into the window like that. The feeling floated and left the shopkeeper behind, then fixed on little Eugene waiting outside Kenny's on the patchy forecourt because it was there where he would wait for his father. Eugene felt a wakening because a memory should not come from so far away: a memory was there to be used, thumbed over and over. This one hadn't been touched.

In this memory, Seamus suddenly takes his place and they find themselves where they used to wait for the bus, on either side of the plate glass of the shopfront, and Eugene knows that he cannot be more than five years old but also that there is no need to be any closer to his father. He is a good boy and is learning to live with the space between them.

It is the only time that Seamus beckons him over. When Eugene doesn't move, Seamus draws out his comb and beckons with that. Eugene walks over slowly, the comb somehow making the passage safe. Sensing a reluctance, Seamus spits on his comb and Eugene stops in front of his father and closes his eyes, ready for a scraping. When he doesn't feel one, he opens his eyes too late and Seamus is planting a fat kiss on him. Seamus puts his finger to his lips. 'No one saw,' he whispers, and makes the space between them again.

Such a little thing. No wonder he hadn't remembered it before.

He was wiping the snot from his nose when Shona appeared beside him.

'The letter could work, eh?'

'Please, Eugene. Forget the letter, will you?'

'It might make all the difference.'

'It's too late. They won't turn round now.'

'Gerry Reilly's got clout.'

'Not as much clout as a police force.' She wanted to say, 'You idiot.' She shocked herself. She was annoyed because he just didn't trust her any more, not since Uri had been pulled. She stared hard at him, shivering and smoking, hoping she could pull him back round to the choices they had left for the cross-examination.

'And you're positive you can't say anything about him doing this kind of thing before?'

'Eugene!' She clasped his shoulder, but in his eyes she saw damage that she wasn't going to be able to repair so she let go of him in disgust, as if he were an insect she had unintentionally injured. 'Trust me, OK?'

He threw a half-smoked cigarette to the floor and crushed it; tight rust strands burst through the Della Robbia blue belly of the cigarette. He pulled her hands down and went to pass her, but she blocked his way, grabbing his shoulders.

'We can do this.'

Eugene looked away from her face and above her head to the lugubrious entrance to the court. 'We'. Get to feck. The gold cigarette tip luxuriated on the grey slab and, without looking back at her, he wrestled himself gently from her hands thinking, *We* could be in Pentonville by tonight.

'So you are now telling me,' she flashed an arch look to the jury, 'that you don't remember an Irish accent?'

'I remember an accent. I can't be sure it was Irish.' There was a bored or lobotomized quality to Lee's delivery.

'And you agree with PC Darren Morton that you may not have announced your status as a police constable as soon as you got out of the car?'

'It was very confusing. There were lots of people.'

Eugene watched as Lee looked to the gallery and he quickly swivelled to see an older police officer sitting stone-faced. Julia was on the same row. A bubble of hope popped in his chest. He turned back, glued himself to Shona.

'You were confused?'

'I was.'

It was all Eugene could do to keep his mouth closed, and although he knew he shouldn't, he couldn't help but sing for Gerry Reilly in the back of his mind. He flipped back to Shona, who was now working this for all she was worth. Eugene almost believed it was her skill that sucked these fresh admissions out of Lee.

'You agree with your partner's testimony on that night that the word "Chinky" may not have been used?'

'I agree, yes.'

'Please, PC Lee, speak up.' She spread her arm over the jury: her new friends. 'I want the jury to hear everything you have to say.'

Shona had put down her notes.

Outside the court, it was raining on Eugene. He'd broken one cigarette in half from flicking it so hard. The next had been soaked by the rain. He had had to come into the doorway of the court so that he and his third cigarette would stay dry while he could still hear the Tannoy announcement, but he had not expected it so soon. 'Court One, to resume in five minutes.'

He gagged and threw the half-smoked peach-coloured grenade into a grating before he hurried back through the corridors. He looked at his watch. His heart was a rock. Not even thirty minutes: the jury were sure of something. His rubber soles chirped against the polished floor. Shit. Shit. Shit. Shit. It seemed miles.

The jury came back into the courtroom, heads up, filing to their seats. Eugene hardly dared to lift his own head. Half an hour! That couldn't be good, could it? It wasn't even time enough for a feed of fags. The jury: heads up? Defiance? Support? Disgust? His eyes swam. Distaste? Pity. It was pity.

'All rise.' Eugene shook from head to toe as he stood for the verdict. He put his hands out to rest them on the desk before him, but they shook uncontrollably and he drew them back to his sides.

The judge's words seemed to last a long time, hang in the air, lethal with meaning, before plunging to earth. Even then, he felt he was left to listen to the echo of them and couldn't quite react. During the final pronouncement, one of the jurors let out a very loud YES! And Eugene turned, shocked to see that the jury were clapping, some with their hands above their heads. That was for him. He wasn't guilty. They knew it. Eugene didn't even begin to try to stop his tears.

A middle-aged juror laced his way through those leaving court to shake Eugene's hand, but was quickly pushed to one side by the old lady, whose hair had given up trying and lay in snowy licks around her face: she pumped Eugene's hand up and down and gave him her handkerchief. Someone else pulled her away. Eugene looked to the gallery to see Julia laughing through her own tears. The whole court was standing. Somebody cheered through the door at the back.

Not guilty! The words could melt bone and seemed to as, finally, Eugene slumped to sitting. He stood again as the older copper, who introduced himself as the DC, came over and shook his hand.

'I'm sorry . . . we're sorry you had to go through this.'

'Thank you.'

'Get on with the rest of your life.'

Life. The rest of it, thought Eugene. He smiled. 'I will surely.'

'Good luck.' The DC shook his hand again and Eugene nodded graciously. He looked behind the DC to see only half of Lee's wan face, and in this one eye of his, he thought he saw fear. Lee pulled back his head and Eugene said quietly, 'I'd get out of here, if I were you.'

53

Eugene appeared, expressionless, at the doors to the court-house. The men from work were there and they turned to him slowly like stone flowers. No hope. Then he flipped, gave the thumbs-up and they cheered like madmen, some of them shouting, 'The Galway one, he is free!' Eugene laughed at them, overwhelmed, and, sniffing through his tears, he walked down the steps clutching Shona and slapping his workmates' hands.

Julia looked up at him and he thought he saw a squint of jealousy at his arm around the tiny barrister. She knew that Eugene didn't grab a woman easily.

'I told you we'd do it, didn't I?' Shona was saying.

'You did indeed,' he said, and with that he kissed her. When he looked up, Julia had turned away.

She waited outside the nimbus of those people who had been involved with this from the start: the circus of friends from God knew where felt magical to him. Uri put Eugene up on his shoulders and tried to crouch and do some kind of Cossack dance but he couldn't get back up and they laughed as Eugene hopped the couple of inches from his seat at Uri's neck to the ground. Finally, he swivelled and saw Julia wanting to speak to him. He walked up to her and left the others jumping on Uri.

'I'm glad you came.'

'Me too.' She hugged him.

'It's definitely been quiet without you and Rod.'

'He's gone.'

'For good?'

'I'd say so.'

'Della'll be glad.'

Julia paused. 'She knows now that nothing happened.' She was blushing.

'Good.'

'Friends, then?'

'Friends.'

They had ended up where they should be, and it showed in the way they looked at each other. He squeezed her hand and suddenly Shona was under his arm again. Eugene put his free arm around Julia.

After a few moments more of handshakes, punches and hair ruffling, Eugene turned on his phone. It had been off for days. He called Buck immediately, his arm now around Uri. Buck answered the site phone.

'We must have done something right!'

'Tell me.'

'Not guilty!'

'Thank God for that!' Buck said, his voice thick with emotion. 'A party, then?'

'That'd be grand.'

There was a message from Vincent. He listened to it and had to sit on the court steps. He called him back.

'At fucking last!' bellowed Vincent.

'How are you, sir?'

'Grand. What's up with you? Got a cold?'

'Something like that.'

'So, have you room in the bed?'

'Plenty – what the fuck's going on? I thought you were . . .'

'Not me, sir.'

'Where are you now?'

'Getting off the ferry. I'll be there in a few hours. I'll meet you at the Beacon.'

'Do you know how to get there?'

'I'll jump on the tube.'

'Get you and your tube, big man!'

'Shut up to fuck!'

'Good luck.'

'Hey!'

'What?'

'You on your own?'

'Who'd be with me?'

'You know . . .'

'With the heart that she has still bleeding for you? Good luck!'

Eugene picked up Julia, put her over his shoulder and, as he spun her, he stopped suddenly to see PC Lee. Eugene stared at his face until he realized that he was enjoying Lee's misery and so, after a couple more seconds, he turned away. He didn't want poisoning. The last Eugene saw of him were his bony little shoulders hunched in the back of a patrol car.

'Come on,' he said, to Shona and Julia, 'let's get a drink into us.'

54

A few of them turned up at the Beacon well before seven and waited for Eugene, with the lights off and the curtains closed. Behind the bar, they squashed into a cramped queue, looking towards the door in the blackness. Horace had dressed up as Tina Turner – it was a special occasion.

'Uri, man!' Horace hissed. 'You some kind of harse-bandit?'

'Where you would like me to go?'

'On a diet,' Babe sniped. Silence for a second then: 'Uri, you scarecrow, what are you smiling at?'

'How do you know I am smiling?' said Uri.

'I can feel the windows opening in your head.'

Horace sucked his teeth. 'It mean 'im 'avin' a good idea.'

'Is it a crime to be happy? I am happy for Evgenie. That is all.'

Despite their suspicions, they were all smiling now, to themselves, in the dark. They listened to each other breathing and Babe said, 'He will have that face.'

THE CURE

'W-w-we can't see you,' Ravi said, from behind.

'But you know it, that face. What have I done?'

'An 'im won't say a word. Mute as a tombstone.'

'And everyone will be waiting for him to s-s-s-say something.'

'And so he won't.'

The thought of Eugene spread down the line, up in the mind of each, joined by the smiling and the quiet.

'I have a present for him,' whispered Uri.

'Allah protect us.'

'Cha! What me tell you?'

Uri plonked something on the bar and sparked up his lighter. The light settled into a halo around what looked like jelly cubes shining at the bottom of a plastic bag. Uri picked one up and held it to the flame where it shone blue. Then he sucked it into his mouth. Horace craned, then tottered in his heels, his wig coming dangerously close to the flame.

'What is it?' said Ravi, as Uri pushed one into his hand.

'Only for Vikings,' Uri purred, looking at Horace, and he snapped the lighter closed.

'What's in dem?'

'Vodka, Viagra and jelly.'

'Gimme two.'

Uri placed a couple in Horace's hand, then found Babe by feel, pulling him gently by his good shirt and pawing around his mouth until he managed to push one between the tight little lips, saying, 'The most beautiful mess a man can make of himself.'

They heard heels at the door to the bar. Della put down a tray to turn on the light. The brightness set them still: Uri had his thumb in Babe's mouth and Horace, in his wig and a sequined frock, looked better than your woman herself.

283

'Turn it off. He'll be here any minute,' Babe whispered loudly.

'Are you telling me what to do?' Della snapped, but she turned off the light. 'What a set of fucking queers I've let over my step tonight.' She clipped, quick-march, through to the back room, the light wasted on her.

The next time the light went on Ravi started to cheer, but stopped short as Vincent blinked in the doorway.

'Brother of Eugene!' called Uri, arms in the air.

Vincent dropped his bag and held out his hand. 'Rambo! Gimme some hoof! Where's Eugene?'

'On his way.'

'Still at work?'

'Turn off the light!' Babe hissed.

Vincent did as he was told, but barrelled on loudly as he crossed the room: 'That useless eejit never finishes work on time.' He rounded the bar. 'You can tell that boss of yours that I'm twice the worker that dunkey is!' He tapped loudly on the bar. 'Come on, you set of fecks!' He felt for the opening. 'Hoick up your bollocks and let me in!'

'Here,' said Uri, catching him by the wrist. 'Open your mouth.'

55

Buck had let the men go early. Sitting in the cabin he squeezed his knees because he could feel the flutter in his chest, the right thing threatening to escape him. He was irritated because he'd had to wait, but money was no use to anyone in prison. It should be done quickly now. There would be no need for announcements.

It was the silence in Eugene that Buck had recognized as his own from the very first day he'd met him. They both had the damage: the holes pulled in them from keeping quiet. Deirdre had become his wife precisely because she could fill a gap in the talk with no effort. Talking takes away the room for thought, and thinking had never got Buck anywhere except back down into himself. He could never have made it alone.

His thoughts turned to Della, forever shouting or sighing behind the bar. She had managed to pull herself through life with a fatherless child to bring up. Of course, he had never let on that he was sorry for her, but after all that had happened, it struck him now that Della could never have been lonelier than himself.

He got up and stalled for a second, knowing that this money saved for Noble would be a fat deposit for a house. He made to move but the floor around him was treacherous with the ground glass of his guilt. Practice meant that, soon enough, he was walking around the cabin steadily again, checking drawers were locked and chairs pushed under – because this crunch underfoot? It couldn't stop you. You kicked hard and you cleared a path. When things got tough, you had a word with yourself: Look forward and should anything obscure your duty, a speck or a splinter, blink it away and blink hard. Keep blinking and you'll hardly see the yearning, the desperate need for a nod in the right place and a hate of the silence you became expert at. He picked up his keys. Close those eyes tight and you never need to fathom how to soothe, to smooth over.

The keys felt heavy in his hand. There were some things they'd never let him forget. Like the time he had dragged Noble out of a playground for making an unholy mess of another boy. Noble had squirmed and wailed through Clapton, and the attention it drew became too much for Buck, who shook his hand out of his son's, leaving the boy a street away from home. Deirdre had not forgiven Buck – moreover, she had seemed glad of the punctuation it allowed in their relationship.

He let go of the keys a little. You wouldn't have to drag a kid like Eugene: he'd be pulling and turning his hand in yours as he footered and skipped along a path – the only fuss would be from the boy's legs. Eugene'd have been a scrawny kid. Buck would have fattened him up with a fry, given him a cat's lick with the flannel and they'd have stepped out together into the secret of a Sunday morning, saying nothing. Home again and at the back door, just up, Deirdre might have smiled at them.

Buck looked out on to the deserted site and straightened himself because today was not about Buck O'Halloran. He crossed to the filing cabinet and took Eugene's details from the finances folder. He shut down the computer and closed himself up again, good and tight. 'Seamus and Jack? Only for me is this money here at all.'

He walked off the site, glad for once to turn his back on work because he had something to look forward to and it beckoned him, all the way out to the high street. In the pale sun of a Shoreditch Friday afternoon he felt good for something and he played through his mind what he might say to Eugene. 'The Lotto,' he'd say. 'Would you believe it?'

'What Lotto?' he'd say, a crooked smile, a shoulder up, hair in his eyes.

Buck blushed thinking about it, knowing full well he should keep his hole shut.

The girls were already outside pubs in their belts and straps, smoking and owning the street, and Buck admired them. They were brave with their bare arms. Walking up Hackney Road, the idea came to him again: he could renege on himself, after all, and tell everybody but, once more, he felt foolish when he imagined the many ways he could say it. The pain of it was sweet, alluring, like pressing a near-healed wound. He must leave it alone.

He veered right up Columbia Road, a shy street on every day but Sunday. At the bottom, he was hit full in the face by the volume from the kids in the school playground. It was a racket all right, but it made him smile for the rude joy in it, and as he passed he wanted to whisper up through the shrieks, 'Never let the quiet take you over.' Crossing the dog-leg of Hackney Road again, he followed the cycle path, glancing through the hedge at the families eating together outside the city farm, where the fathers with soft hands had time to talk about comics.

He put his head down and quickened his step up Broadway Market, following the path across the road and through the dwarfish park to the back door of the pub overlooking London Fields.

When he saw the crowd on the deck, he was anxious that there might be someone there he knew, but inside, the pub was deserted. He ordered quietly. Through the back door he could hear the outsiders humming with the steady start-up of a weekend. His pint arrived and he lifted it automatically. Even in his imagination he was reluctant to chink glasses with men like Seamus and Jack, but he did so for the sake of the boy. A handover. *Sláinte!* To Eugene! He must be quick about it now. With his half-sunk pint, he hung over the bar, staring for the last time at what he should do.

They knew Buck at his own branch down on Mare Street.

'I'd like to transfer some funds.'

'Into another of your accounts?'

'No. Here.' He handed her a paying-in slip that had already been filled out. 'From this account,' he pointed, Noble O'Halloran, 'to this one,' Eugene Seamus Mahon.

He looked down at the names: two birds and one heavy stone. There would be damage. The traffic out of the window seemed to stop moving altogether. In the few seconds it took him to decide, he imagined Eugene and that look of his, the one from under the eyebrows. Frightened. Grateful.

56

She'd cut her hair to her shoulders and he felt betrayed for an instant. He'd say she was definitely thinner than when he last saw her, but it could be the clothes she was wearing. Navy tights – fit for autumn but not for her, he thought. Eugene had always loved her legs bare. The grass was slightly wet under him, but a small price to pay for this first extended look.

Reapy's was heaving as usual. It seemed foolish now that he had been wary of its noise and ambition not so long ago. He watched her put her glass on the outside table and wished that she knew he was there because that would mean she'd chosen the outfit for him. She could always take the tights off, he reasoned, and smirked to himself at the secret distance between them. She was talking to a couple of her friends and the late-September sun made good long shadows in front of the bar. She was doing some sort of gag for them, her face twisted into an impression, and they were repaying her with the laughter that was demanded.

Turn around and look, he willed, but only half-heartedly. He rubbed his thumb over the illustration on the front of the book. A fern. Frail and prehistoric. Contradictions, he thought. He'd earned his badge. Poems, words, he could use them now.

He pushed himself up from the grass and walked to the pavement that edged the little park across from the pub, but his eyes never left her. Her hair seemed redder and her legs more coltish, but he thought that was probably his eyes being greedy for what he loved most about her. She was teetering, had a hand on her friend's shoulder, altering the strap on her shoe. He felt jealous and imagined her touching him. His hand gripped the book tighter.

Standing now, he brushed himself down, then walked slowly to the middle of the road and, waiting for a car to pass, he stood still. In an instant, he'd turned swiftly and retraced his steps to the grass of the miniature park. He moved towards a bin and, with only the slightest hesitation, he hoyed the book in with the the ice-cream wrappers and the little bags of dog-shite, then went and sat up on a swing. His legs dangled awkwardly but he was smiling. He had time.

He'd look a bit longer yet.

Acknowledgements

Thanks and love go to Declan, who stays cool whatever we weather together; to Jane Rogers for her wisdom and friendship; to Mary V. Peace for understanding.

Listening to tales from my brothers and Declan gave me some golden threads for the rope of this story – thank you. Along the way there have been many generous readers of drafts and givers of perspicacious comments. I especially thank Toby Finlay, Susan Elliot-Wright, and the writing group in Sheffield.

There is no knowing the size of the debt to my 'husband' Victor Zimmerman. The Sandburg poem was a pretty generous gift. *(How much? 55?)* To Lisa Baker I owe a bucketful for her guidance, and to Conor O'Callaghan just as much for help on the road in. I am much obliged to Hannah Westland and Jennifer Hewson at RCW for faith in tough times, James Gurbutt at Constable & Robinson for providing the chance, and Hazel Orme for logic. I am grateful to Professor Richard Peace for Turgenev nicknames; to the Russian Criminal Tattoo Encyclopedia (Danzig Baldayev, Ed., Steidl/Fuel, 2003) for a dirty peek through barred windows and to Yana Rodgers and friends for help with prisoners Russian.

Special thanks to Noble Moore for allowing me to abuse his name; Stella McKinney for giving me space; the Siddalls for hospitality and tolerance, especially my hero, Tina. The Canadians for long-distance love; A.J. and U.D. for earnings and learnings.

For worldly sustenance I am indebted to Graham Siddall, Matteo Bragazzi and crew, and Trudi and Justine at Homemade.

Final thanks go to my daughters, Esther and Ingrid, for making me sit still and listen.